STORM

GURPREET KAUR SIDHU

It was lovely meeting you, Carol!
I hope you enjoy reading
Storm!

Best,

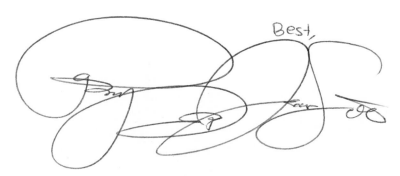

Printed in the United States of America
Edited by Kristen Corrects, Inc.
Formatted, interior and cover art design by
Vanessa Maynard

First edition published 2018
10 9 8 7 6 5 4 3 2 1

Sidhu., Gurpreet Kaur
STORM / Gurpreet Kaur Sidhu
p. cm.
ISBN-13: 978-1-7322344-0-6
ISBN-10: 1-7322344-0-X

FAMILY TREE

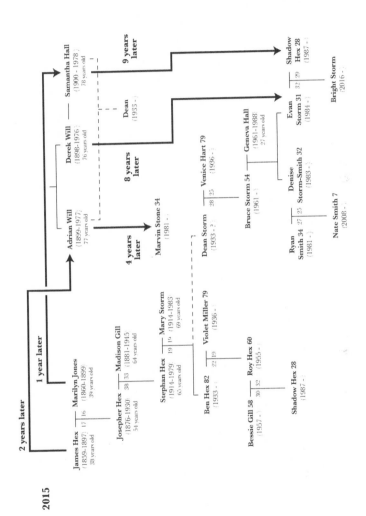

TABLE OF CONTENTS

CHAPTER 1

Their fairytale all started with one look. Derek Will fell in love with Samantha Moore. Everyone envied their love story. He was the perfect gentleman and she was the beauty with class.

Six months after dating, Derek proposed on one knee with a 5.36-carat yellow cushion cut micropavé halo diamond. It was stunning to the eyes and left Samantha in awe. But that was far from important.

After the honeymoon phase ended, things started to settle in—and that's when Samantha realized who Derek really was.

The night took a sickening twist in the home of Derek and Samantha Will.

Derek came home, aggravated about something unclear to Samantha. It's not like Derek arrived home, had dinner, sat down, and exchanged the traditional preliminaries—he had changed slowly after marriage. There were no more late-night conversations or handholding. Derek expected Samantha to clean, cook, and keep the house well-maintained without any kind of help. It was unusual to find a housewife who lived in Pool View *not* to have a maid. With the kind of money Derek brought home, there was no question as to why they couldn't afford a maid, a butler, *and* a gardener. Derek's intentions were to keep Samantha locked in the house as long as he could and it was exactly how it panned out. He went to work and was successful at his job, while Samantha stayed at home and made sure the house was tidy and in order before Derek came home. But today, it wasn't the diurnal routine Samantha was prepared for.

Samantha had been throwing up all morning, so as like any other human being, she rested. Samantha slept all through the afternoon, only waking half an hour before Derek's arrival. She started on dinner, hoping Derek wouldn't arrive earlier than usual, but it seemed that the universe was not on her side.

Derek arrived home, pissed about something—it had to be something work related, she figured, but it wasn't Samantha's place to ask. According to Derek, it was none of her business.

Derek walked into the kitchen only to find dinner wasn't set on the kitchen table like it had been every day for the past five years. He glared at Samantha, assuming she was out in the city having a good time, or having an affair. Even if she attempted to explain herself, he wouldn't believe her. Instead he'd believe whatever he made up in his mind because that was what *he* believed to be true.

The silence frightened Samantha. She had no idea what to expect.

Derek took the pot of boiling pasta and watched the water drain in the sink, then threw the pasta all over the kitchen floor. Samantha backed away slowly, not wanting him anywhere near her. The farther she was, the better. But where could she possibly go? She watched his every move. Her heartbeat rang in her ears.

He stood still for a moment, looking around. Samantha eyed the knife that lay on the counter, which she had been using to cut the lettuce. She sensed Derek knew what she was thinking. His eyes followed hers, but once again Samantha quickly became his center of attention. He inched forward, looking at her. She saw the anger, rage, and frustration in his eyes and knew in her gut he was going to take it out on her. But it was just a matter of how.

"I thought I made it clear. Dinner should have been on the table by the time I walked in through that door," he growled. His voice rose. "You take me as an idiot, don't you?"

Samantha shook her head. "No," she quickly answered.

"I work my ass off every single day to make a life for us," he continued. "All I ask from you is to clean this house, and put food on the damn table! But you can't even manage to do that, can you?!"

The corner of his mouth lifted as he unbuckled his belt and admired its thickness.

"Oh god," she whispered under her breath.

Her eyes filled with fear as Derek took a step in her direction. Samantha moved but not quickly enough. She knew all of it would be over sooner if she just took the beating. If she tried to escape, it would only anger him more. Derek came at her and whipped her across the back and then across her chest.

His wife's loud crying pleas didn't stop Derek. He continued to slash her with his belt until he felt satisfied, but the beating didn't end there either. He gripped his hands tight around her neck until her face turned pale, then shoved her to the ground. A mischievous grin crept across his face as he stared at Samantha struggling. She lay there coughing, uttering the words "I'm sorry." But Derek didn't care if she was sorry or if she was sick. He was going to make her miserable until she bled.

Derek continued to whip Samantha across her back, only to turn her over and continue the lashing across her chest and stomach. Her wails became louder.

"Derek!" she cried out. "Please!"

He grabbed her by the hair and dragged her across the kitchen, into the living room where he continued to severely lash Samantha on the face. She covered her face in agony.

"Derek! Please stop. I-I-I'm sorry, I'm sorry!"

He forced her hands away from her face, then slapped her once, twice then a third time before he brought the brutal beating to an end. He stood baring over her as she lay on the floor.

Samantha's eyes, red, began to swell. By the end of the night, her eyes would be swollen shut. Her lips were cracked. Her teeth were covered in blood. Her back and chest ached. She could see the blood on the white carpet, through her blurry vision. Her mind slowly began to shut down.

Derek turned her face over with his foot so he could see the pain in her eyes. He looked at her and shook his head in disgust.

His voice was calmer now. "None of this would've happened if you made dinner. When will you learn?" He scoffed. "I'm tired, so don't waste your time in the kitchen...but I do want this mess cleaned up before you go to bed," he said, fanning his index finger over the blood on the carpet. "This all better be spotless by the time I wake up tomorrow morning, do you understand?"

Samantha gave no response. She merely couldn't. It hurt to move her lips, and had no energy to speak.

"I didn't hear you. What did you say?" he said, expecting a response he knew he wasn't going to get, but he was going to force it out of her anyway. "I can't hear you, Samantha. It's not that hard to say yes."

Samantha used all her strength to nod, agreeing to do what he asked her.

"I need to *hear* you say it. Say the word, Samantha. I know you can do it. I need a verbal agreement." He crouched near her.

She could hear Derek breathing over her. Again, with all her strength she had left in her, through her swollen and bleeding lips, between sobs, Samantha uttered the word "Yes."

Satisfied, Derek went upstairs, leaving Samantha on the living room floor.

There was really nothing she could do. She had no money. She didn't have a way of making her own living. Derek, the clever man he was, gave her the option of leaving. But where would she go? To her family? She was too ashamed to ask them to take her in. They warned her for marrying Derek in the first place. Did she listen? No. She dropped out of college and gave up everything to be with this man and...now he'd taken her life. It came as a shock to Samantha that after all this, he still continued to let her breathe. Why not end her life instead?

And then...

CHAPTER 2

E van Storm woke up panting and sweaty. He looked
around and realized where he was. He was in his home
in Lake View. He was sitting up in his bed, his hair and
back drenched in sweat. He reached for the hand towel he'd
set on the nightstand the night before.

He glanced over at his alarm clock. It was 3:30 in the
morning. This memory of his past life had been haunting
him for months and every night he woke up at the same time,
terrorized. He wiped his face, trying to remember everything
he could. Evan had questions that no one could answer. Why
was he remembering his past? What was the meaning behind
all of this? Why was this happening to him? And why all of
the sudden?

Evan crawled out of bed, steadily walking to the bathroom.
He flipped the switch as he stepped on to the warm tiles.
Even though it didn't snow in Lake View, winters had become
more cold in the recent years, but bearable. Thankfully, Evan
had renovated the floors of the house, having heated floors
installed. "The beauty of technology makes life a lot simpler,"
he said to the installer. He stood with his hands resting on both

sides of the sink, looking into the mirror before him. He looked a lot like Derek Will. His blue eyes twinkled as he raised his chin upward. Evan traced his finger across his jawline, feeling the growing fuzz.

He didn't know much about himself in his previous life. Whether or not he had children, he wasn't sure. There were a lot of things that were unclear. However, he was aware of how cruel Derek was to Samantha. It made Evan's body cringe as the image of Samantha laying on the floor, bloody, crept up on him.

He turned the faucet, letting the cold water run for a moment, wondering how inhuman a person could be. He took another look at himself before splashing his face with the water. As Evan raised his head, he looked into the mirror and behind him stood Derek, with a grim face and a smile that made the tiny hairs on his back stand up. Evan felt his soul slip away from his body for a moment before jumping back in. Time stood still. The only thing that Evan could hear was his loud thumping heartbeat.

"He's not real," he repeated to himself, "he's *not* real. *You're...not...real!*" Evan grasped the sink with both hands and shut his eyes. His body shivered with terror. Evan knew this was imaginary, but seeing Derek made him feel like death was waiting to take him. He let out a grunt in agony. He felt his soul was being grasped by Derek's presence. He took a deep breath and counted to three. When he opened his eyes, Derek was gone. "It's just your mind playing tricks," he told himself after gaining composure.

Very rarely Evan would see Derek after he'd wake up from the night terrors. The first time he'd seen Derek was during the first week the nightmares began. Evan had punched the bathroom mirror out of horror and shock. Now, he was still trying to figure out why Derek would appear out of the blue.

What role did Derek play in his life with the current situation he was dealing with? Evan knew Derek's appearances served some type of purpose but he couldn't pin the exact reason just yet.

He wiped his face with the towel and hung it behind him next to the shower.

On his way out, Evan switched off the light, and slowly got under the covers. The bed sheet was a little damp from his sweat, but he'd gotten used to it.

Evan lay in the dark as the moon illuminated his room, making the painting on the wall visible. Evan studied the painting, remembering how he had purchased it. It brought some sense of peace when he couldn't fall back asleep.

The painting, called *The Twister*, was a mixture of bold colors swirled together. It was created by a local artist in Pool View—it was the first painting that caught Evan's eye when he stepped into the art gallery, on the day of its grand opening a year ago. It was the same day he met Harmony. He thought that there was certainly no one as beautiful as she was. After standing and stalling for fifteen minutes, he finally worked up the courage to ask Harmony out on a date.

It had been two months since Harmony broke up with Evan. All of her belongings had been moved out and the painting was the only reminder of Harmony that was left in the house, along with the memories they created together.

When his mind wandered back to Samantha, Evan mentally replayed what he remembered from his dream. This helped him recall the memory more vividly in the morning so he could write it down in the journal he kept.

* * *

At the crack of dawn, Evan went downstairs and made himself a hot cup of espresso. It was the right way to start off the day. It was a peaceful sunny Saturday. He went about pouring in a small amount of milk and sugar, stirring it around with a spoon, and tossing the spoon into the sink afterward.

Evan sat at the kitchen table in his pajamas with his journal and pen sitting in front of him—replaying the entire dream in his mind.

He picked up his pen and began to write.

December 12, 2015:

Woke up at 3:30 again, remembering Samantha throwing up. She laid there on the bathroom floor, with her hand over her stomach. When Derek came home, he beat her with his belt over and over because dinner wasn't ready. It all started from the kitchen and then the beating moved to the living room. He hit her in the face. She was crying and kept asking him to stop but he wouldn't. After I washed my face, I looked in the mirror and saw Derek standing behind me. It made me cringe. It's been two weeks since the last time I saw him.

He put the pen down beside his journal, staring at the words that quickly dried on the paper. Evan ran his fingers through his short chestnut brown hair, trying to make sense of the memory he was haunted by. There had to be a reason for Evan to remember his past life, but whether Evan's past life had anything to do with him now, he was unsure. He took a sip of his coffee as his eyes lingered over the other entries.

The creak in the hallway disrupted Evan in his thoughts. He turned to the living room to see his grandma, Venice Storm, looking over the coffee table. She was a tiny old woman, with the softest voice that coincidently matched her kind soul. She almost looked like Mrs. Claus, with her rosy cheeks, her sparkling blue eyes and her face almost wrinkle free. Her glowing skin truly disguised her age well. She was a year shy from turning eighty, but didn't look a day over sixty.

Evan gradually walked into the living room with his coffee mug in one hand.

"Darling, what happened here last night?" Venice asked, looking over at Evan, even though she already knew.

She was a psychic.

Evan looked at the mess he had left on the coffee table last night before heading to bed. Since it was winter vacation, his teaching duties as a psychology teacher at Walsh Pierce High School were currently on hold. Evan, partially drunk, had unloaded a box of old family photos all over the table to put in to a family album. But instead, his productive evening ended up reminiscing about all the things that had gone awry.

"The goal was to get all these pictures in to an album," Evan said, pushing the photos toward the middle of the table, making room for his mug.

"Yeah, I can see that, darling," she said, scanning the table.

He picked up a photo with his parents and his sister, Denise, at the beach. Evan was four years old and vividly remembered chasing Denise around with a dead crab. It was the last photo taken before his parents' death.

"Unfortunately that didn't happen," he said, setting the picture back on the coffee table with the rest.

"Put these pictures back in the box," Venice ordered. "I don't want you spilling coffee all over them. I'm not even sure if I have the negatives for these pictures."

"I'm sure Dad put them somewhere." Evan paused, wondering what Venice was doing here on a Saturday morning. "Aren't you supposed to be at work?"

"I had thirty minutes to spare, so I thought, why don't I go visit my little darling and see what he's been up to lately?"

Venice worked as a therapist in her private clinic located in the central business district, where she used her psychic abilities to her advantage. She hid the fact she was able to predict what was going to happen in the future from her patients for many reasons.

Many years ago, when she tried to prevent her husband's death, Grandpa Dean, she learned what the consequences were for trying to change his fate. The universe was not too pleased with Venice trying to prevent what was meant to happen. The only way Venice *could* use her psychic abilities was to answer questions, favorably yes and no questions. It kept her out of trouble from the universe, since there was a *very* thin line that was easy to cross.

Venice's soft bouncy gray hair brushed against his cheek as she planted a kiss on his forehead. She headed into the kitchen with her purse hanging off of one shoulder.

"There's coffee if you want some," Evan said, carefully stacking the photos in a pile and putting them back in the box. "It was nice of you to drop by," he said as he put the lid back. "Unannounced," he added.

Ignoring his last comment, she replied, "I think I'll just have orange juice."

Venice retrieved the juice from the refrigerator. She poured herself a full glass before putting the carton back in the refrigerator. Venice sat at the kitchen table with her fingers wrapped around her glass. She noticed the ungraded papers in his office.

"I know what you're going to say," he interrupted, pulling out the chair in front of her and taking a seat.

"I wasn't going to say anything," she said as her eyes flicked away. "You're still in your pajamas," Venice pointed out. "What's going on, darling?"

Evan looked genuinely confused. "What are you talking about?"

It was a Saturday and being in pajamas was comfy.

"You're not the kind of person who leaves things unfinished," she said, subtly eyeing the stack of papers. "You haven't been the same ever since you started remembering your past life, and I know this breakup wasn't easy either."

Evan wasn't much the feelings kind of guy. He wasn't comfortable talking about a situation unless he felt the *need* to. With Venice being a professional therapist, Evan never felt comfortable letting her in, but somehow she always managed to lure Evan in and just as he started to express his thoughts, coincidentally she had to be "somewhere" or was "going to be late for a session with a patient." It was almost as if she wanted him to explore his feelings on his own, and the only way to achieve that goal was by her poking her way in.

He analyzed his blue mug all around, finding it to be flawless. "So much has happened in the last couple of months. I'm trying to figure out where to go from here."

She nodded. "I know it's hard when people walk out of your life. I understand that, but you can't keep moping around here and feeling sorry for yourself."

"I'm not doing that," he quickly answered. His eyes met hers for a moment before they traveled back to his mug. "I've been doing some productive research," he added.

"Oh darlin', are you still trying to figure out what your past life memories mean?"

"The Sikhs believe that you're reincarnated over and over because of your previous life's wrongdoings. Reincarnation ends when you live a rightful life and that's when you get to become one with God."

"Will you stop with that nonsense? You're not even a Sikh!"

Evan nodded. "True. But it's one reasonable explanation. There are some people out there who remember their past life but it's just something they remember. Unlike them, I'm taunted by these memories, over and over. It's not normal Grandma. There's a meaning behind it. There has to be."

"You're being ridiculous. You're wasting your time with this, Evan. I know you don't like to hear it but I have to be honest here."

"Let me ask you this then. Why is it that when I wake up, I feel like I've done something wrong? I feel guilty for something I did in another lifetime, another place. That feeling lingers throughout the day." He looked at her sternly. "Something's telling me that there's a bigger picture here. I'm not gonna stop until I figure it out."

Venice sighed, not knowing what else she could say or do that would convince Evan to give up chasing a memory that meant nothing. To Venice, Evan was chasing a ghost. She wasn't sure how long it would be before Evan realized he was wasting his time and put it all behind him.

As long as he was on winter vacation, he had every minute to spend analyzing, researching about this phenomenon that he couldn't explain.

"Have you met your next-door neighbor yet? It's been a while since they moved in, haven't they?" Venice asked, changing the touchy subject.

"No," he said pausing for a moment, wondering how long it had been since the house was sold. "I've seen their car parked out in front when I go for a run, but that's about it."

"Is dinner at Denise's this time?" she asked, taking another sip.

"Yeah. She's going to the hospital afterward to see Ryan. So I'll be babysitting Nate."

There was dead silence in the room. Venice never discussed what happened the night Ryan was sent to the hospital. In the past, when Evan or Denise asked whether or not Ryan would make it through, or why Venice never warned Denise, she would change the subject. Neither of them knew whether or not Venice hiding Ryan's accident was a good or bad thing.

"How is she?" she said, taking a deep breath.

Evan broke eye contact. "Not much has changed, Grandma."

"She's not still upset with me, is she? I want to give her some space but she needs to understand I was doing the right thing. I'm always trying to protect this family and…"

"I know, Grandma but that's not how Denise sees it. It's going to take her some time to come around. Give it some time."

Venice let out an anxious sigh.

"She's been short with me ever since."

"I know," he said softly.

It pained Venice to know that Denise indirectly blamed her for Ryan's accident.

He retrieved Venice's glass once she was finished and placed it in the sink. He looked out the kitchen window and saw the unfinished garden that he had planned to finish during the break. Mud was all around the garden and holes all around the fence. It seemed as if a gopher had made its way around the premise, trying to make itself at home.

Every morning while drinking coffee, he stood in front of the kitchen in his pajamas looking out the window and thinking about getting to work—perhaps doing some landscaping, changing the atmosphere of the garden his mother once planted. He had a lot in mind with what he wanted to do with the garden. Evan envisioned a long pathway that separated a Japanese garden on the left-hand side with a koi fishpond. He'd planned on building a bridge that would cross over the pond. He wanted to work in a waterfall, loud enough to drown away surrounding noise. On the opposite side of the pathway there would be grass where Nate could play soccer, and someday he would kick the ball around with his own children. There would be simplicity and tranquility once he stepped into his backyard, something that he longed for. At the end of the pathway, he pictured a gazebo where he could sit back and relax and let the worries of the day slip away. He imagined Harmony sitting beside him, his arm wrapped around her. They were supposed to grow old together with the changing world, but the one thing that wouldn't change would be the two of them sitting together and simply enjoying each other's company.

"This is another one of your projects that are yet to be completed, I see."

Evan chuckled.

"Harmony and I were supposed to finish the garden, but things don't always pan out the way you'd hope," he said with a forced smile. Life had a funny way of proving how plans were ultimately a human's way of trying to control life. "I bought a gardening magazine from the nursery downtown. I'll finish it."

Venice raised an eyebrow, not completely sure if Evan had this gardening project under control, or his life under control for that matter. The unfinished family album said so otherwise.

"I hope so," she said, planting a kiss on Evan's forehead. "Take care of yourself, sweetie," she said before making her way to the front door.

Evan stood in the doorway and watched as Venice got behind the wheel. Moments later he heard the engine come to life.

Before she pulled out of the driveway, Venice looked back at Evan and waved goodbye. All she managed to think about was what was going to happen in the next week. As always, she was guilty for keeping this secret to herself for all these years but never found the right time to come out and tell Denise and Evan something that they should've known years ago. She felt burdened with this secret. Venice would go over the scene of how she would tell them the truth, but the fear kept her from coming to terms with what she hid from them. Her grandchildren may hate her for the rest of their lives.

The truth was going to come out soon, but how prepared was she?

And like before, she was stuck right in the middle.

But as always, the universe always managed to throw a curveball at her.

CHAPTER 3

Venice sat in her office with her worn out diary resting on her lap. Some pages were loose and the writing from the beginning of the diary was now faded. She had her diary ever since she made her first prediction. Everything that she had predicted was noted and every prediction that occurred was written to the exact detail from memory—the time, date, place, people who were involved.

Venice's mind was fixated on Evan and Denise. The future was heartbreaking. It made Venice lose all interest in helping her own patients. She was furious, sad, and angry at what was going to happen. There was nothing that she could do to stop any of it from happening either. Even if she did take action, consequences would soon follow. This gift at times seemed like a curse.

Venice closed her diary and shut her eyes. She needed to take a mental break before her next patient.

Just as she started to drift off, the unexpected knock on the door startled her.

"Venice, there's someone here to see you," said Candice Bridge, Venice's secretary. Candice quietly slipped into the room, closing the door behind her.

Candice was a tall brunette, who liked to dress in floral and silhouettes regardless of what the weather was like. She loved wearing bright lipsticks and heavy mascara.

"Who is it?"

"He wouldn't say, but he claims he knows you very well."

"He refused to give you his name?"

"I told him you wouldn't see him unless he had an appointment."

"And?"

"He sent me in here," she said, flustered.

Venice thought about it for a moment. The light bulb went off in her mind. It wasn't often that she had unexpected visitors but she knew exactly who it was.

"Okay, send him in."

The old woman leaned over and pulled open the bottom drawer of the rectangular table next to the chair where she placed her diary.

Even though she knew who he was, it took her back a bit when Bruce walked into her room. She could see Bruce was aging well. His hair had started to gray. He was a lot thinner than the last time she saw him. Candice closed the door behind him.

"I wasn't expecting to see you so soon."

"Not all your predictions are on point, from what I recall," Bruce said. He made himself comfortable on the sofa across from Venice, with the coffee table separating them. He unbuttoned his blazer, crossing one leg over the other. "So how've you been? What's new around here?"

"Bruce, it's really nice seeing you, but you're here for one of two things. Which one is it?"

"I can't come and see how you're doing once in a while? Do I need a reason to be here?" He chuckled.

Venice sighed, knowing with Bruce there was always a reason. "What do you want?"

Bruce kept steady eye contact with her before breaking the tension. "I think it's time to tell them the truth. They deserve to know what happened, what *really* happened that day, and I think you would want the same for them."

"I agree, but I don't think *you're* ready. I see you once in a blue moon. You don't even make appointments anymore, which is a risk on your end," she said, aggravated. "You can't show up whenever you please then disappear until who knows when. They lost their mother and then their father. I can't have you breaking their hearts again."

"I didn't come here to get your permission."

"I know you didn't come here to get my permission. You're a grown man. You just want someone to tell you *not* to go forward with it. See, you're still a little skeptical about telling them the truth because then it's out there in the open. What if they don't want you in their life? I bet that thought ran through your mind a hundred times, didn't it?"

Venice was boiling with anger inside. She knew this moment was a long time coming but still, she felt the emotions, which were out of her hands. She was only human for heaven's sake.

"If you really wanted to tell them, you would have told them a long time ago, regardless of what was going on in your life at the time."

"You know exactly why I chose to do what I did!" Bruce shouted.

While Candice was supposed to be busy answering phone calls, making appointments for Venice, instead, she found herself listening to Venice and Bruce's conversation through the wall. Candice had never seen or heard of Bruce the entire time she'd been working for Venice, which was almost three years now. But she knew one thing: there was a long history between the two of them. And who was "them" they kept referring to? She continued to listen as she pretended to appear busy.

"I left because I couldn't handle it," Bruce said, raising his voice. His veins bulged from underneath his skin as he defended himself. "My life was a wreck. Do I have to remind you what happened? I couldn't tell them because I couldn't handle the thought of them rejecting me or looking at me just like the way they looked at me when their mother died. But I'm at a place in my life where I'm ready."

"You have no idea what's going on in their lives right now," she objected.

"If you let me be a part of their lives, maybe I would know something. You're the one who told me to leave, remember? And that's what I did. Look where it got me."

"I never said not to come back! You made that call. I waited for you to show up. I waited for a phone call, but you never called." Venice held back the tears that had crept up on her as her voice rose. "I did what I had to do. So *don't* pin this on me. I wasn't the one who walked out on their family. You had every breathing second to come back home…but you didn't. It wasn't easy on me either, Bruce."

"You think *I* had it easy? For the past twenty-seven years, I wasn't living the life. I wasn't taking it easy if that's what you think happened. You knew Geneva was having an affair and you kept that from me. Do you have any idea how I felt when I found out you *knew* about the affair the entire time? It made me question my entire childhood. It made me wonder what else you hid from me."

"I didn't have a choice," Venice hissed.

"I was the reason why Geneva was unhappy. *I'm* the reason

why she killed herself. I couldn't look at Denise and Evan because *I* was the reason why they lost their mother." His lips quivered. The day Bruce discovered Geneva's limp body came rushing back. Bruce took a long deep breath and composed himself before continuing. "Evan and Denise need to know their mother wasn't killed in a car accident. They deserve to know what really happened. I can't have them questioning their childhood like I did. They need to know the truth, Mom, and I'm going to be the one to tell them."

Venice sat in her chair, going back and forth in her mind about what the right thing was to do. She knew Evan and Denise deserved to know the truth about what happened that day. They needed to know why she told them the horrible lie about their father having a heart attack while driving, leading to a fatal car crash that took his life and their mother's. All the lies she told Evan and Denise were catching up to her now. She knew one day the lies would haunt her. However, her predictions were off. Venice predicated she would be dead by the time Bruce came around to telling Evan and Denise the truth. The ambiguity in her predictions made her question herself.

"Are you working right now?" she asked, switching the subject.

Bruce looked a little confused. "What's that got to do with anything we're talking about?"

"I'm asking you a simple question. Either answer it or see yourself out."

Bruce stared at her for a second before responding. She was firmer since the last time he'd seen her. "I'm a contract worker. People hire me to fix things for them."

Judging by Bruce's fancy sleek gray suit, Venice sensed Bruce wasn't telling her the entire truth.

She pursed her lips. "How long have you been a contract worker?"

"Ever since I left. Why does this matter?"

Venice looked down at her watch.

"Bruce, we're going to have to discuss this another time. I'm expecting a patient in just a little bit and I don't like to keep any of my patients waiting."

"What's there to discuss?" Bruce said. He rose from the couch and fixed his cufflinks. "I said what I needed to say. I wasn't asking you for your blessing."

Venice remained seated in her chair. She wasn't at all pleased with Bruce or the way he was going to handle this delicate situation. Ever since Bruce learned the truth about Geneva, there had been friction between the two of them. Although Venice knew Bruce resented her for it, which she accepted, she didn't want the same outcome for Denise and Evan. Bruce was too stubborn to understand that timing did in fact play a huge role in coming clean.

When the time was right, Bruce wasn't ready. Now that Bruce was ready, Denise and Evan were not prepared, given with everything that was going on in their lives.

"Like I said, Evan and Denise have the right to know what happened, but not right now," she said, slipping back on her glasses.

"Who are you protecting anyway?" Bruce asked, raising his voice once again. "I don't think it's about Evan and Denise anymore. You're just trying to protect yourself."

Venice was taken aback by his comment. "I've been protecting this whole family from the moment you were born," she said calmly. She looked deep into Bruce's eyes and saw the little boy he once was, following her around the house as soon as she got home from work. She remembered the tears Bruce had in his eyes when he held Denise for the first time. Now, Venice didn't recognize who was standing before her.

"Close the door on your way out and never raise your voice with me again."

Bruce stood still for a good moment before walking out of the room.

Once the door closed behind him, Venice began to weep. She felt the world turning against her. She knew Evan and Denise would be furious with her for keeping this secret from them for so long. The thought of losing Evan and Denise made her heart ache. Every choice she made was to protect her family, and some of the choices she made in the past were coming to haunt her now. She knew if she had told Bruce that Geneva was having an affair, in time Bruce would've killed himself. On some level, she knew she was being selfish for keeping the secret from him, but it came down to losing either Geneva or Bruce. Not all of Venice's predictions were correct, but she didn't want to risk losing her only son. So, Venice did what any mother would've done in her position given the circumstances.

Venice grabbed a tissue from the coffee table and wiped the tears away at the sound of the knock on the door.

"Come in," she said, taking a deep breath and wiping her nose.

Candice peered in, not expecting to see Venice in a fragile state.

"Hey," Candice said with concern. "Is everything okay?" She hadn't heard the entire conversation. A missing sentence here and there threw her off entirely but something told her the meeting between the two of them did not end on a good note.

She met her eyes. "Yeah…everything's fine," Venice said, clenching the tissue in her hand.

"Okay," Candice replied with a smile. "Mrs. Kingston called and rescheduled for next week Tuesday."

Venice nodded. "Thank you for letting me know."

Candice smiled as she closed the door.

The old woman opened the bottom drawer, pulled out the journal, and began to write.

CHAPTER 4

Evan stood in front of the house patiently on Kentwood Drive in Dusk View, a city half an hour away from Lake View passing through the central business district and MidView. He held a chocolate cake topped off with chocolate-covered strawberries bought from Bernie's, his favorite bakery. He peered into the window looking for Denise. He could see her pacing back and forth in the kitchen. She was wearing a pink apron that hung off her neck. Denise never really bothered tying her apron around her waist. "I'm going to take it off anyway," Evan remembered Denise saying on multiple occasions.

Evan pushed the doorbell button once again, hoping someone would come to his rescue. It was freezing. Dusk View was closer to the ocean than Lake View. The temperatures dropped lower and a lot faster than they did in Lake View but like Lake View, it never snowed. The homes were bigger and newer with very limited space in the front and backyard compared to the homes in Lake View. When he caught a glimpse of Denise as she turned away from the oven, he motioned her to come open the door for him.

Denise hurried over to the door. Her apron swung behind her from side to side like Batman coming to his rescue. The dramatic effect of gravity came to a halt as she stood still, unlocking the door.

"Oh, thank god you brought dessert," Denise said, noticing the brown box with Bernie's stamped across it in Evan's hands.

Denise Storm-Smith held the door as Evan entered the house. It was nice and warm.

"I was going to bring ice cream but then I remembered how much Nate hates ice cream in the winter," Evan said, walking into the kitchen with Denise only a few feet behind him. "He's a weird kid. I loved ice cream in the winter when I was younger. You remember that? Getting brain freezes and then Grandma giving us that look that said it all."

"Tell me about it. I could hear her *I told you so*'s in my head when she gave us that look. I think it rubbed off on me. I do that with Nate sometimes," she chuckled.

"Sometimes? You've given me that look more than Grandma ever has."

Denise rolled her eyes and scoffed. "Stop exaggerating."

"You know I'm right."

"You should call her some time this week. She's worried about you."

Denise turned back with a blank stare. This was the third time he'd mentioned this to her and even though she knew Evan was right, she didn't like hearing it.

Evan set the cake in the refrigerator and looked around the kitchen island. Denise had cooked up a storm today.

"Were you on some crazy diet this past week?" Evan asked, eyeing everything in front of him.

There was cheese lasagna in the oven, garlic bread, Caesar salad, green beans, and the last dish he assumed was a bowl of potato salad. Denise never cooked like this; only during the holidays and special occasions.

She looked over her shoulder as she opened the oven door to check on the lasagna. "What?"

"Holy, that smells good," Evan said. He closed his eyes and sniffed the air as the aroma filled the kitchen. "Why did you make so much food?"

Denise sighed. "I wasn't sure if salad and lasagna was going to be enough and plus, leftovers are always good. You want some wine?" She turned to the wine cooler and pulled out a bottle.

"Sure, why not. Where's Nate, by the way? He's usually in the kitchen trying to help."

Denise frowned as she set the wine glasses on the counter and began to pour. "He's out on the porch. When he woke up in the morning to feed Firefins…"

Her frown finished the end of her sentence.

"Oh, that's horrible. Ryan bought that fish for him, didn't he?"

"Yeah," Denise said, pushing the cork back in the wine bottle. She handed Evan his wine glass and took a seat beside him.

"He came downstairs in the morning with tears in his eyes. His eyes were puffy, like super puffy…it was really heartbreaking. I remember him asking Ryan over and over again if he could get a pet. After all the begging, Nate finally got his fish." Denise's eyes traveled to the screen door where she could see Nate sitting on the porch, with his arms folded on his knees and head lowered. What really pained Denise was Ryan wasn't there to console Nate. Lost in thought, she began to daydream. Her mind jumped from one scenario to another, each worse than the last.

Evan's multiple elbow nudges didn't help Denise out of her trance.

"Denise."

"Huh?" Her pupils, dilated, slowly went back to normal when she met Evan's eyes. She gradually took another sip as she came back to reality.

"You okay?"

"To be honest, I don't know. Ever since the accident, it's just been a nightmare. With running a company, raising Nate... sometimes I just feel like I can't even breathe. I feel like my brain is going to explode."

Evan put down his wine glass and wrapped his arm around Denise. "I'm sorry Denise. I really am."

"I know," she replied as she took a sip.

Ryan's car accident had taken place in October, which put him in a coma for a month and a half. It had been a month since Ryan awoke, remembering everything but not recalling Denise ever being pregnant with Nate.

"Is he showing any improvements?"

"No," Denise said, turning to Evan, "I mean, he's walking and talking. He's getting his physical therapy and the doctor said that he'll be discharged from the hospital in the next few days. That's really good news, but—"

"You haven't told Nate huh?"

"No, I haven't. I don't know how," she shrugged, not wanting to go into detail about how Ryan was handling it, which certainly didn't help Denise.

Evan and Denise sat in silence. When the kitchen timer went off, Denise quickly scooted off her chair. She grabbed the oven mitt off the counter, as she made her way to the oven and pulled out the sizzling hot lasagna.

"Holy, that smells so damn good," Evan said again, eyeing the tray as Denise brought it over to the counter.

The cheese bubbled while the oil rested on top.

"I just hope it tastes as good as it looks," Denise mumbled, as she examined all sides of the lasagna dish. The confidence started to kick in once Denise cut into the lasagna, seeing that it had been cooked thoroughly. "Can you go and get Nate for me please?"

"Yeah, sure thing," Evan said, rising from his seat. He walked to the screen door, peering through quietly before stepping out onto the porch. Evan joined Nate Smith on the steps, who was layered with a gray coat and a red scarf around his neck. Evan looked at Nate, who didn't bother to turn around.

"Hey, buddy," Evan finally said. He waited for a response from Nate, but got nothing. Evan playfully nudged Nate, hoping to get his attention.

Slowly, Nate lifted his head from his knees, craning his neck sideways, meeting Evan's eyes. "Hi, Uncle Evan," he said in a somber voice.

Evan could see the sadness through his big brown eyes.

"How's it going?" Evan asked, trying to make the conversation upbeat.

"Firefins died today."

Evan never had the experience of talking to a child about death. What was the right thing to say? Nate was only seven years old. Evan was pretty sure the topic itself was too much for a seven-year-old to comprehend.

"I'm sorry buddy." Evan paused for a moment, trying to think of something comforting to say that would put Nate in a better mood. "You can always get another fish…"

"I can't replace Firefins," Nate sighed. "It won't be the same."

Evan was surprised by the response Nate gave. He had no idea how well Nate comprehended death. Nate was much wiser at his age than Evan was when he was seven years old.

"That's very true," Evan agreed. "Hey, you lost your toof," he added, noticing the gap between his front teeth.

Nate ran his finger across the gap. "Yeah," he giggled.

"What's so funny?"

Nate's teeth gleamed as he roared with laughter remembering the funny incident.

"Last week when my tooth was really loose, I pulled it out right in front of my mom. She made a disgusting face, Uncle Evan. It was so funny! And she almost threw up." Nate held his stomach as he laughed.

Evan remembered the pranks Ryan pulled in the early years of their marriage before Nate was born. In a lot of ways, Nate definitely took after his father.

"Are you hungry? Dinner's ready."

"Yeah, I kinda am," Nate said, getting up from the porch.

Evan stood tall beside Nate. He followed his uncle back into the house, where Denise had already set the dinner table. She smiled at Evan, feeling a bit relieved after she witnessed the change in Nate's mood.

They sat around the kitchen table, passing the garlic bread, taking one piece each; each dish going around the table once.

"So what have you been up to lately?" Denise asked Evan.

Her eyes flicked over to her right. Nate had just put in a steaming hot piece of lasagna into his mouth. Within a split second, Nate spit it out onto his plate, waving his hand back and forth in front of his face and panting. He scrunched his face while his tongue stuck out like a puppy on a hot summer day.

"Oh sweetie. Here," she said, picking up his glass and handing it to him. "Drink some soda. It'll help cool off the burn. You gotta be careful, hun."

She watched Nate as he took a couple of sips before putting his glass down on the table. On another note, she realized how long Nate's hair had grown in the last couple of weeks, brown and curled at the ends. Just like Ryan's. Even though Ryan wasn't here with them, just looking at Nate made her feel Ryan's presence.

Denise turned to Evan and asked, "Are you almost finished with the garden?"

Evan grinned in embarrassment. "No, not really," he said, locking eyes with Denise, knowing what she'd say next.

She shook her head in disappointment. "You're so consumed in this belief that these episodes you're having mean something," she said, biting into some lasagna before continuing. "You're letting your life pass you by. I mean, what if you figure out—which shouldn't take long—that these dreams or memories, whatever they are, really don't mean anything? You're going to look back and regret not taking that time and doing something that mattered. Something more productive, like, I don't know...*dating*."

"You're really not going to let this go, are you? And I'm not ready to date just yet, either."

Denise put her fork down. "No, I'm not. I understand you want to know why you're having these episodes, but I just think that they're taking control of your life."

"They have, Denise," Evan said, wishing Denise wasn't right. "You don't know what it's like to wake up feeling like you're living a double life. It feels like my past is controlling me. There are times when I dread going to sleep. I don't want to wake up in the middle of the night, screaming, and drenched in sweat. My life is a nightmare, Denise. I want it to end and the only way that's gonna happen is to figure out why I'm remembering these parts of my life."

Denise looked at her brother with concern. She was starting to realize it was more serious than she thought.

"Okay," she said, picking up her fork again. "Just don't lose focus on the things that matter in your life now. Like your career and family."

"Don't worry, I've got it handled."

She gave him that look—the one arched eyebrow, pursed lips, and a glare.

"I know what I'm doing," Evan reassured her.

"Okay," she said, quietly collecting some green beans with her fork. "So, there's this new girl who moved from Pool View. She's one of the interior designers. Real pretty. I was thinking what a cute couple you two would make."

"No, Denise. You're not going to set me up. You do a horrible, *horrible* job setting people up."

Denise gasped in shock. "What are you talking about?"

Evan looked over at Nate, who was quite enjoying the conversation between his mother and uncle. "Your mother," he began, "she thinks she's cupid."

Nate giggled at Evan's comment. "Cupids aren't real."

"Exactly," Evan responded. He turned to Denise. "Nate knows what he's talking about."

Denise stabbed some bits of lettuce and a crouton with her fork and said, "But love exists and you need to go out there and find it, then get married, and if you're not going to look," she said as her voice started to rise, "then let me help you." She gazed at Evan as she chewed, eyes widened in curiosity.

"I don't disagree that love exists, but I don't think I'm ready to give it my all. I did that with Harmony and look where it got me. One amazing year down the drain."

"You're being so cynical. Just because it didn't work out with one person doesn't mean the next one is going to be the same," she said, raising her eyebrow as she continued to chew. "You always had a problem opening up with women—"

"Wait, wait, wait," he said, holding up his hand in defense, "that's not true."

Denise exclaimed, "That's *totally* true! After you go through a break-up, it's like you never want to date again. You're so scared of getting hurt again that you just push the idea of being in love and being happy aside all for a fifty percent chance of getting your heart broken."

Evan scoffed, not wanting to admit Denise was partially true. "I don't want to bring someone in my life if I'm not ready, and I certainly don't want *you* setting me up with anyone. I'll find someone."

"How?" Denise asked, expecting an on-the-spot answer. "You're an introvert. You rarely ever go out." She turned to Nate and noticed three-fourths of his plate empty. "Here you go, baby," she said sweetly. She leaned over, picked up a piece of lasagna with a spatula, and slid it onto Nate's plate.

Nate's eyebrows furrowed and whined, "But I'm not hungry."

"C'mon, you didn't have a good breakfast today. That's a very small piece, sweetie. You need to bulk up. Don't you want to be big and strong when you get older?" she asked, meeting his eyes.

Nate looked down at his plate, not too happy. "Okay," he said in a glum voice.

"Denise, he's only seven. What's he bulking up for?"

Denise turned to Evan, disregarding his comment. "Oh, don't swerve your way around this. Where are you going to find someone, huh?"

Evan shrugged. "A dating website? The library?" He saw the horrified expression on Denise's face and quickly said, "Those are *some* of the ways of meeting people. Plus, why are you so worried about me finding someone?"

Her eyes flicked to the garden. She used her knife and fork to cut a piece of the lasagna. "I don't want you to be alone," she said with a sigh. "Take Mr. Brar, for example. He and his wife loved each other more than anyone I know and after Mrs. Brar passed away, he said something to me that I'll never forget."

"What did he say?"

"He said a life partner makes life a hundred times better. I want the same for you. I mean everyone deserves someone, especially you."

Denise knew the kind of guy her brother was. He was a gentleman with a soft, kind heart. He was the type of guy who would open the car door, cook dinner, buy cute little presents, and ultimately make the woman feel like a princess. Denise knew her brother would make a great husband and father one day and she knew deep down, that's what Evan wanted too.

Evan smiled and reached over, softly squeezing her hand. "Stop worrying. It'll happen when it's supposed to." He sighed, knowing Denise's concern was coming from a good hearted place. "I envied Mr. and Mrs. Brar's relationship, though. They were the neighborhood lovebirds."

"It's hard to be a cynic when you see a couple like that."

Later that evening, Denise drove down to Lake View Hospital where Ryan was admitted while Evan stayed home with Nate. The big plans Evan had for the two of them was to sit in front of the television, watch movies, and eat some of the delicious cake he'd bought from Bernie's Bakery.

As Denise pulled into the parking lot, it started to feel a lot like home. Sometimes Denise would come and visit Ryan during lunch and after work before she picked up Nate from the recreation program she'd enrolled him in. Or she wouldn't go at all. Those were the days where she would cry to herself after the day at the office was over. She tried her best to keep herself from falling apart but life got the best of her at times.

She got out of the car and felt the cold winter breeze against her face. Denise walked through the parking lot in her long beige coat, looking at the surrounding cars. There were families who were sitting in the hospital waiting room hoping for good news, or sitting by the bedside of their loved ones, hoping to take them home. For the longest time Denise felt alone in her situation. But as her visits became more frequent, she realized she wasn't the only one going through a rough time. Other people were walking in the same shoes as her. She shivered, feeling the warmth take over as she entered through the automatic doors. The lights were bright and sharp, causing Denise to squint.

As she waited for the elevator, Denise heard a woman sobbing. She looked down the hall and saw a middle-aged woman standing outside one of the rooms, wiping away tears. Denise's heart sank. The woman looked helpless as she stood there, trying to pull herself together.

Death.

Denise was constantly reminded of death when she went to see Ryan. She didn't see this building as a place where people came to be cured. To Denise, this was a place where people came to die. Lives ended here. Her perception of hospitals was molded by the tragic accidents her mother and father had been in when she was just a child. And now, it was Ryan.

Denise stepped onto the elevator, feeling oddly nervous. The day of the accident came rushing back in bits and pieces. The arguments they had leading up to the accident were all too vivid. Everything flashed before her eyes, putting her back two months ago when she didn't think Ryan was going to make it out alive.

Exiting the elevator, she shook the thoughts away and took a deep breath. When she reached the doorway to his room, the sound of her heels caught Ryan's attention.

"Hey," he said, pointing the remote control in the TV's direction and pressing the green button. The screen went blank.

Ryan's deep-set hazel eyes gazed over at Denise. For the past few days, Ryan started growing a scruff. He ran his hand through his hair and sat up straighter.

"Hey," Denise replied softly, pulling the chair in the corner closer to his bedside. "How are you doing?"

They looked at each other knowing very well how Ryan was doing.

"I'm good. How about you?"

"I'm..." She thought for a moment, not knowing how to answer the question. "Doing good," she finally replied. "I brought some more pictures for you."

Denise unzipped her purse and pulled out a brown envelope containing a couple dozen photos of them in various locations and events. "These are the ones from when Nate was just born," she said as she handed Ryan the envelope.

Although a little irritated, Ryan remained calm and opened the flap, pulling out the pictures Denise had gathered. He flipped through them, analyzing each one carefully, moving onto the next with the hope it would trigger a memory that would help him recall his son. And just like the day before and the day before that, nothing. He shook his head as he put the pictures back into the envelope, handing it back to Denise. Ryan knew Denise was trying to help but it felt like a smack in the face every time he looked through the photos Denise brought along, not being able to recall that specific memory.

She looked at Ryan with disappointment. Not that it was his fault, but because just like every day, she'd hoped today was the day Ryan remembered just a tiny piece of his life that he'd forgotten after the accident.

Denise put the envelope back into her purse, and set it aside.

"It's okay, babe," she said, reaching for his hand. She held on tight. "We can try again tomorrow. The doctor said it was going to take time. We just have to be patient."

"Yeah…"

Denise gave his hand a squeeze. "What's wrong? C'mon, talk to me."

He ran his fingers through his hair, thinking about Nate.

"How the hell am I supposed to do this…?" he said, his words trailing off.

"You're not in this alone."

He turned to Denise, meeting her eyes. "I *am* alone in this," he said agitated. "I don't remember anything about my own son. *My own son, Denise.* How am I supposed to act around him? How do I treat him? What kind of relationship do we have? I don't feel like a father, so how am I supposed to *act* like a father to a child that I don't even know?"

Denise's heart sank. "I don't know the answers to those questions, babe, but we're going to get through this. We'll get all the help we need. We'll do whatever it takes to get your memory back. I promise."

He sighed. "It feels like empty hope. What if I don't regain my memory? Then what?"

Denise gripped tighter to Ryan's hand with her own. She looked at him, sadness filling her eyes because she too feared life would never go back to normal. "The doctor said we should keep a positive attitude. We *are* going to get through this." They had to.

She kissed the top of his hand, staring off into the distance, reminiscing the night of the accident. Denise remembered that night with Ryan vividly as if it happened yesterday. It was an odd windy and rainy October Saturday night. Nate was upstairs in his room while she and Ryan were downstairs, cleaning up in the kitchen.

"Do you want to watch some TV with me, like when we used to…maybe open a bottle of wine?" he had asked, putting the last dish in the dishwasher.

"No. I've got some work I need to finish that I didn't get around to back at the office."

Denise wanted to be alone that night. She knew Ryan would want to talk about having another baby because that was something he had been bringing up lately. Denise was not in the mood to have that conversation with her husband tonight.

"You can do that later. We can watch Late Night with Jimmy Fallon," he convinced. "You need to take some time out to relax." He was leaning against the kitchen counter hoping for a "yes."

Denise started to walk away, and that's when everything spiraled out of control.

"So that's it? This is what it's come to?"

"Ryan, I really don't have the time for this right now," she said, looking over her shoulder. "I've got a big project I need to finish."

"You never have time for anything these days. What's *really* going on, Denise?"

Denise turned around with rage in her eyes. "I don't want to talk about having a baby. I'm sick and tired of having that conversation!"

He looked at her funny. "Are you sleeping with someone else?"

Her jaws clenched. "What?"

"Are you having an affair?"

"You're insane!"

"You've been ignoring me. You don't make time to hang out. Every time I suggest we go do something, all you ever say is that you don't have time. What the hell am I supposed to think? Yeah, *of course* I'm going to think you're screwing someone else! Do you even love me anymore?" he asked.

Denise could see the hurt and anger in his eyes but it had already gone too far before she could cool off and have a civil conversation. "Just shut the hell up! Shut the hell up!"

"Why? Is it because I'm right? Is that why?"

"Listen to yourself, Ryan. Do you even hear what's coming out of your mouth right now?" Denise was still yelling at the top of her lungs. Her face, bright red, was filled with fury and her eyes stone cold. "You're fucking insane. I don't want to be anywhere near you."

"Oh that's soo wonderful of you, cursing, with Nate in the house," Ryan said with his temper now flaring. "You think being an anesthesiologist, working twelve, sixteen-hour shifts is easy? But—"

"You think running a business is easy?! Are you kidding—"

"Let me finish!" He shouted. "As husband and wife, we're supposed to make time for each other. I've been trying for weeks just to get you to myself. You don't even give a crap about me anymore." Ryan looked at Denise in disgust and hurt.

They stood in the kitchen, giving one another cold-hearted stares.

"I'm so tired of being treated this way," Ryan said coldly.

Denise felt her throat closing. This was the first time in their marriage they'd argued like this. The stress Denise was carrying had taken a toll on the both of them and it was too late until she realized it.

Ryan walked past her, looking at Denise dead in the eyes as he stomped through the front door. She felt paralyzed yet she could feel her body shaking. She wanted to move, but couldn't. It felt as if her feet were glued to the ground. She stood there, trying to keep calm and together, but as her emotions amplified, the harder it became to control the tears and the cry she held in.

She slowly took steps toward the table. She pulled up a chair and sulked. She cried and whimpered. She placed her hand over her stomach where she had carried Ryan's baby for ten weeks. She knew how much Ryan wanted to have another baby and all she wanted was to surprise him. She wanted to break the news in the most romantic way she could think of.

They were supposed to have a candle-lit dinner and she was going to make his favorite meal. It was going to be perfect. Time, however, was not in her favor.

CHAPTER 5

After a forty-five minute drive, being stuck in slight traffic due to an accident, Evan finally pulled into Knight's Drive. By the looks of it, everyone was asleep and the only lights that were still on were the streetlights. As Evan pulled up into the driveway, he spotted Mr. Brar, his next-door neighbor, sitting in his wheelchair out on the porch. He put the car in park, turned off the ignition, and opened the door.

"Hey Mr. Brar," Evan called to his neighbor, "you're up pretty late." He walked toward Mr. Brar's house.

The homes in Lake View were much more spaced out compared to the other neighboring cities. Lake View itself was a much older town. Most of the homes had been fully remodeled, inside and out. Some of the homeowners had installed pools in their backyards, perfect for the summer. The downside of living in Lake View was that it had become an expensive town. Few young couples had moved into Lake View in the past five years. Most of the families that lived here had bought the homes years ago when the market had been down.

Mr. Brar was a Sikh who wore a black turban as a symbol of his faith. He never ate meat or drank alcohol. His beard was short and silver. And every time he smiled or laughed, crow's feet appeared. He dragged his oxygen tank closer to his chair, making room for Evan to sit.

"I couldn't sleep," he replied in his raspy voice. "You're coming home so late. You had a date tonight? Or was there a new club opening in downtown? I don't know what you kids do these days to be honest."

"No, I wasn't on a date or at a club," Evan said, chuckling. "It was Denise's turn to host brunch. I was there most of the day. Then she went to the hospital afterward to visit Ryan. I was on babysitting duty," he said, with a partial smile.

"How is my little girl doing? How's Ryan?"

Evan hesitated. "She's doing the best she can. She's a strong woman. Ryan's getting better over the days, but he still doesn't remember Nate." He sighed. "You can only hope for the best at this point."

"I can't imagine. Are the doctors doing everything they can to help him?"

"Yeah, they are."

"And how's the little one doing?"

"He misses his dad," he said, gazing out into the brightly lit street. "Denise still hasn't told him that Ryan lost some of his memory."

"When is she planning on telling him?"

He shrugged, not knowing exactly what Denise's plans were. "She's hoping that Ryan starts to remember so she *won't* have to explain all that other stuff to Nate. It reminds me of when we lost our parents," he said, gathering his thoughts. "I don't think she wants Nate to go through what we went through, I guess, in a way."

Memories flashed in Evan's mind of his parents. He

remembered bits and pieces. His father always wore a suit to work. The first thing Evan would do when his dad came home from work was run into his arms. He remembered his mother working around the house, singing to herself every now and then.

"Our loved ones will always be missed. Everything they leave behind is associated with some kind of memory. I can't even look at a book without remembering Ekam. She knew how much I loved it when she read out loud and sometimes I'd fall asleep," he said, laughing. "Some books I didn't find interesting," he said, quickly defending himself. He chuckled under his breath.

Evan witnessed on many occasions Mr. Brar and his wife enjoying lunch on the porch, laughing as if they were on their first date. She would wipe his mouth with her napkin and plant a kiss on his cheek. Sometimes they would sit together, silently, just enjoying each other's company. Evan witnessed true love. It had been almost two years since Mrs. Brar had passed away.

"I miss Ekam so much," he said, looking up at the stars, "but they're always here with us in spirit," he added, breaking into a smile.

The moon's glow shined across Mr. Brar's olive skin, making the sadness visible in his eyes.

"It gets easier, Mr. Brar," Evan offered.

"Sometimes I think she's gone on vacation. I wait for her every day knowing she's not going to come back but yet I hope." He paused for a moment, wiping away a tear. "A little part of me doesn't believe Ekam's really gone, but she really is gone."

Evan reached for Mr. Brar's hand and held it. "I'm sorry," he whispered. It was all he could say.

There was nothing anyone could say or do that would heal a broken heart. It had to happen on its own pace.

As midnight approached, Evan looked over at Mr. Brar.

"Mr. Brar," Evan said, yawning, "I'm gonna head home."

Evan rose from the porch, brushing his backside off of dust.

"All right son, rest well."

"Aren't you going to sleep?" Evan asked, stepping down.

"In a bit," Mr. Brar said with a smile. "Did you know a moving van came today?"

"Oh yeah?" Evan's eyes flicked to his neighbor's house.

"I saw them hauling in more furniture, but I didn't get the chance to see who the new movers were," Mr. Brar said, a little disappointed.

He yawned. "I should go say hi sometime," he said, walking off the porch. Evan waved goodbye, leaving Mr. Brar on the porch.

As Evan walked into his home, Mr. Brar looked out into the corner of the street, away from the streetlight's reach. A black sedan had been parked there earlier in the afternoon. Until now, there hadn't been any movement all day. The headlights switched on and the vehicle slowly drove down Knight's Drive. Mr. Brar watched as the sedan passed by his house, realizing what was going on.

After the sedan was in the distance, Mr. Brar wheeled his way back into the kitchen, where the phone lay on the table. He picked it up and pressed the speed dial.

Mr. Brar held the phone close to his ear as it rang, feeling intense and anxious. After six rings, he heard breathing on the other end.

"It's only me, Bhuhadar."

"Hi, Mr. Brar," Bruce replied on the other end of the line.

Mr. Brar faced the window from the living room, just in case the black sedan decided to make another trip. "It's been a while since the last time we talked, huh. How've you been, Bruce?"

"There have been better days." There was silence for a moment. "I'm sensing there is something urgent…"

"I think someone from the agency has Evan under their radar."

"Are you sure?"

"A young girl, probably around the same age as Evan, moved in next door to him about a month ago. Around the same time, I noticed the black sedan here and there. I've been keeping an eye out, making sure nothing's out of the ordinary. But I have a feeling his neighbor isn't the only one that's on their radar."

"I can't start a personal assignment unless you're a hundred percent sure. It's going to raise questions, Mr. Brar. Evan can't be on *anyone's* assignment."

"I know, I know, but I don't have a good feeling about this, Bruce. The timing of it all…I know he's on their radar. I can just feel it."

There was a long sigh from the other end of the line.

"I've looked out for Evan like my own son," Mr. Brar said. "Once the agents from the Secret Eye Agency get involved, you know there's nothing much I can do to help him."

"Yeah, I know." He paused for a moment, knowing that interfering with another agent's assignment was never allowed before getting an approval. "Look, I'm going to search up the ongoing assignments in the system and if I come across Evan's name, then we'll know for sure."

Bruce entered his access key and pin enabling him to log into the system to access all the missions and assignments the agents were currently working on.

"I'll wait on the line as you do that."

Bruce entered Evan's name into the database to find any assignment associated with his name. Only one popped up. Bruce eyes' scanned over to the right, looking at the location and to Bruce's dismay, Knight's Drive was listed as the address.

"You're right," he said, feeling faint. "Evan's on their radar but I don't know why." He looked under Evan's name to find what stage the assignment was on. "He's under stage one right now." Bruce slammed his fist on his desk.

Mr. Brar sat in his wheelchair. His heart sank. Flashbacks of his time at the agency brutally reminded Mr. Brar of what agents were capable of.

"This is only stage one, so they're just checking him out right now. But you have to put an end to this, Bruce. The longer this assignment stays open, there's a higher chance of it moving up to stage two."

There was a long pause on Bruce's end as he sat there, in front of his computer. His eyes were fixated on the purple dot next to Evan's name.

"I gotta see what the hell is going on. Just look out for Evan for me, Mr. Brar. I'll keep you updated." Bruce hung up, putting his cell phone back into his pocket.

This wasn't good. *Not at all.*

CHAPTER 6

Bruce sat at his desk, looking out of his office. The Secret Eye Agency ran a twenty-four-hour, seven-days-a-week operation. People came in and out for a hundred different reasons. One was to retrieve the special gadgets the Secret Eye Agency made available to the agents. Every gadget had special and multiple functions. The watches recorded conversations that took place within a hundred-foot radius. The navigation system in the black sedans converted into surveillance cameras. The pens recorded conversations only in confined areas. The pitch black glasses agents wore in the day had the capability to take pictures and be the eyes for agents who were positioned for backup. For every scenario, there was a gadget.

Any work done in the field was sent back to the headquarters. Since every gadget was connected to the server, all the information was automatically downloaded. The agency was the only place where an agent could go to retrieve the information. There was no way to get rid of evidence, as long as it was on the server.

Before Bruce could take any action, he had to figure out

who ordered the investigation and why. Once he understood those two crucial pieces of information, he would have to file to nullify the assignment. Given that the grounds to nullify would pass with the board of directors, it would take a couple of days to put a stop on the investigation. That was one of the options Bruce had. The other option was to go off the record and sort it out on his own without involving a third party. But that had consequences.

Either way, the clock was ticking and Evan's life was on the line.

CHAPTER 7

It was a calm, sunny Monday morning. Shadow Hex stood in her bedroom wearing a sheer black lacy undergarment. Ever since she'd moved to Lake View, life felt less stressful. There were some things she simply couldn't ignore, like the distance between she and her parents. It wasn't the six-hour drive from Pool View. It was how she left things with her parents.

She stared at the photo frame that sat on her nightstand. Her parents hugged her as she held her high school diploma across her chest. It was the last family picture they took. Her lips began to quiver and eyes welled up. It made her heart hurt seeing how happy her parents were back then before everything changed. What tugged at her heart the most was that she knew nothing was going to be the same again.

They had picked their side, which made Shadow question how much of a parent's love was really unconditional.

Shadow moved to Lake View for one reason and that was to start over. To start her life the way she wanted to live, no control or say by anyone else. She had escaped from all of that. She wanted to leave her past behind her, but Shadow knew she would always look over her shoulder. No matter how hard she tried, or where she went, there was no escape. Shadow didn't want to believe she *couldn't* live a normal life. But for the time being, she felt she was safe. There was hope. She believed one day her past would fade away and she would finally be able to live in the present. But as long as *he* was out there, she would always be looking over her shoulder.

Mr. Jingles, Shadow's furry gray cat, pounced on top of the bed. He looked at her with his big yellow eyes, his tail swaying. He was happy too.

"Good morning, Mr. Jingles," Shadow said. "Had a good night's sleep?"

Sometimes Shadow talked to Mr. Jingles like he was a human. Mr. Jingles gave his undivided attention as his tail swayed from left to right and then right to left, like he understood the conversation.

"I know *I* did. You look hungry." She paused. "I'm sorry for pointing out the obvious."

She stepped into her spacious walk in closet, looking for a gray pencil skirt she recently bought. Shadow shuffled through her neatly hung clothes before coming across the skirt. She walked back out and put together her outfit. She wasn't quite in the mood to wear blue today. Shadow rested a finger on her chin, thinking of different blouses she had that would go better with the new skirt she was excited about. After much contemplation, she slipped into her skirt and buttoned her blue blouse.

She examined herself in the tall mirror, wondering if she'd gained weight. Her eyes traveled to Mr. Jingles who was silently sitting on her bed. Her attention went back to the image of herself. Her short wavy hair, the color of a walnut, had given her trouble the last couple of days. She figured trying out a new look for a new start wouldn't hurt. She walked into the bathroom and as she began to straighten her hair, Mr. Jingles watched carefully.

Shadow sighed, knowing he was hungry and the longer Shadow kept Mr. Jingles waiting, the grumpier he would get. He was an expert at giving her the silent treatment.

"Okay, I'm almost done. Just one more minute," she said, pulling the straightener to the end of her hair.

She stared at herself in the mirror and noticed how closely her blouse matched the color of her eyes. Her attention flicked back to her lips. They needed more color.

Scattered in the bathroom were the products she wore on her face. She picked out a shade of red lipstick, softly applying it on her bottom lip, followed with the upper lip.

She pressed her lips together, then viewed herself one more time before heading back into the bedroom closet and pulling out a black coat.

Shadow headed downstairs, carrying the coat over her arm and placing it on the sofa as she walked into the kitchen.

When Mr. Jingles heard the food hit his bowl, he jumped off Shadow's bed and trotted downstairs into the kitchen. Shadow checked the time on her watch; if she didn't head out for work in the next couple of minutes, she would definitely be late.

Shadow sped across town, racing the clock. As soon as she arrived to work, Shadow parked her car in the nearest spot she could find. She stepped out in her heels, slammed the car door shut, and strutted across the parking lot to the entrance of Storm, Inc. When she stepped inside, Shadow noticed the receptionist, Zoe Davenport, at her desk.

Zoe was fresh out of high school, tall and slender, and sported a bob, which she dyed ink black. Zoe preferred minimal human interaction. When applying for the job, she was only interested in the salary and not what the job entailed.

"You're late," Zoe said, obnoxiously chewing her visibly pink bubblegum.

"Yeah, I know. Twenty minutes."

"That's like...so unacceptable. Denise is going to be like... super pissed with you."

"Wait, what?" Shadow said, catching her breath. "Denise?"

She pointed at her computer screen, which Shadow couldn't see. "You had like...a 9:00 with Denise."

Shadow's hands rested on her hips and her eyebrows furrowed. "Seriously? No one told me about this meeting."

"Is that supposed to be like...my problem?" Zoe responded.

Her eyes traveled over to the clock on her desk. Zoe stared at Shadow and blew a bubble. When it popped, Zoe smiled, which quickly faded.

"What are you still standing here for?"

Shadow, in a confused state, took a couple of steps forward, only to realize she didn't know where she was supposed to go. She turned back, not wanting to face Zoe again. "Where is the meeting?" Shadow asked.

"See that hallway?" Zoe said, pointing behind her.

"Yeah."

"Her office is like...down that hallway. Take your first left and it's the second door. I shouldn't have to remind you that you're already late, hunnay," she said, fluttering her eyelashes.

"Okay. Thank you."

Shadow was a little afraid of walking in the room, knowing Denise was waiting for her. On top of that, this was going to be the first time she was meeting Denise. She had no clue what Denise was like. She prayed Denise was not like the horrible bosses people talked about as they stood in line to get coffee in the mornings. When she approached the office, she took notice of the nametag on the front door. It read: *Denise Storm-*

Smith, CEO. Her nerves began to kick in. She had no idea she was having a meeting with the company's CEO.

Shadow knocked on the door and waited for Denise to respond. A moment later, Shadow was opening the door to Denise's office.

In the corner, she saw the woman sitting at a round table with a manila folder in hand. "I'm so sorry—" she began.

"It's okay. Don't let it become a habit," Denise said with a warm smile.

Shadow was struck by how young Denise was. She had long brown hair pulled into a ponytail that framed her slightly pale oval face. Her almond-shaped eyes matched the color of her hair and her pink full lips made her look more of a model rather than a businesswoman.

"Why don't you take a seat?" Denise suggested, glancing at the vacant chair in front of her.

Shadow smiled as she sat. She placed her purse on the floor and straightened her back, making sure she was giving the right first impression. In her mind, she knew being punctual was already counting against her.

"How do you like Lake View so far?" Denise asked Shadow.

Shadow was taken aback by Denise's kindness. CEOs back in Pool View were never this kind from what she'd heard.

"It's...nice—it's different. I'm still getting settled in, but it's good." Shadow crossed her legs, becoming a little more comfortable.

"Oh, it's *very* different compared to Pool View," Denise said, propping up her elbow and resting her chin on her fist.

Denise very well knew the difference between the people of Lake View and Pool View. Quite a few of Denise's clients were in fact from Pool View, where the houses and lawns were much bigger than homes in Lake View. No woman cooked or cleaned because everyone hired help to do all that work.

Every client she worked with believed they were better than everyone in Lake View. Living in Pool View was like living like a royal. Appearances were everything and being judged by material things was a hobby. It wasn't about *who* you were, but *what* you had.

"I believe it's…either a hit or miss, if you're going to live in Pool View," Shadow said. "Either you fit in with the rest of the crowd, or you're an outcast. I grew up in Pool View, but…" she said, pausing and raising her eyebrows. "As I grew up, I realized I didn't fit in. I wouldn't survive in that kind of environment."

Denise let out a burst of stifled laughter. "I'm glad we agree on something." After clearing her throat, Denise didn't waste any time getting down to business.

Denise opened the folder and handed Shadow a sheet of paper, which was an overview of the new client Shadow would be working for.

"All right," she said, folding her hands together in front of her and getting ready to give Shadow the rundown. "You'll be working with Mr. and Mrs. Pence for their nursery. They're expecting their first child together. They've been married for two years. They decided that they were going to keep the sex of the baby a mystery. They took a look at your portfolio and wanted to work with you on their nursery. How do you feel about that?"

Her heart sank into the pit of her stomach but she didn't let that stop her feeling excited for her new client. Shadow raised her eyebrows in excitement. "I love it."

Denise nodded and continued with her rundown while Shadow gave her undivided attention.

"The colors they chose are gold and pearl white. And those are the *only* colors they're going to work with. They want everything—large moldings, curtains, blinds, a chandelier—

everything that's going to make the room look elegant and classy. Currently it's an empty room so I think it'll make it easier on you to visualize where the furniture will go along with all the other stuff." Denise closed her eyes for a moment. She was forgetting something that was vital for this assignment. Denise pressed her fingers against her temples, as if she had a migraine.

A minute later she brought the most important aspect of this nursery to Shadow's attention.

"I can't believe I forgot about this. The closet is a walk-in. They're getting the doors removed and want to install shelves and cabinets. They want the walk-in closet to be efficient. Anything and everything is accessible, easy to find... no shuffling around. The closet is their biggest concern, so I advise you to be creative, really creative. They are expecting a talented interior designer today at 1:00. So you have until then to come up with sketches of your vision for their nursery. Don't let me down." She grinned.

"When do they want to start on the project?" Shadow asked, referring to the paper Denise handed out earlier, since Denise hadn't mentioned it during the rundown. Starting the project was just as important as knowing when the clients wanted the job to be done.

"Darn it. I forgot to ask them that question." Denise rubbed her forehead and scrunched her eyes.

Shadow sensed Denise wasn't herself. Even though it was only an assumption, it was apparent Denise had other things on her mind that were distracting her. "It's okay. I'll ask them when they want to start." She pulled out a pen from her purse and took note.

"I usually don't forget to ask my clients important questions like that," Denise stated, thinking back to the day when she met with the Pences. It was the day after Ryan's accident.

Denise worked half a day just to keep herself calm and then the Pences walked in, ready for a consultation.

"We all forget sometimes. Don't worry about it," Shadow replied, breaking into a soft, sympathetic smile.

"It's not a good sign when a person in their prime starts to forget things," Denise said, chuckling. "I'm getting old."

"Maybe you should take a couple of days off," Shadow suggested, peering over as she put her pen back in its designated pocket.

Denise leaned back in her chair, her arms stretched out beside her. She looked up at the ceiling, looking for some sort of sign to Shadow's suggestion.

"I *could* use some time off." Denise chuckled. "But clients come first and some of them are very demanding."

Shadow nodded, understanding there was more to the story than Denise was providing. After all, she was from Pool View. There was *always* a story.

Denise got up from her seat and walked to her desk. "You should get started on those sketches and I'll send you an email with the address."

"Okay, sounds good," Shadow said, rising from her chair. "I won't let you down." She flashed her straight white teeth.

"I'll hold you to that. Please don't be late," Denise said, pulling out her big brown leather chair.

Shadow left with more confidence than she did when she entered. She liked Denise. It came as a surprise how friendly she was, but then again, this was Lake View. Majority of the people who lived in Lake View were nice and kind.

Winter had been sweet. People of Lake View were enjoying this particular winter since it hardly rained. The gust of winds that would usually whip off the hats of the elders during this time of year were calmer, but a long coat and a scarf was still needed.

Snow was never an issue because Lake View didn't have the

climate for such weather. Pool View, on the other hand, would be covered in three inches of snow this time.

* * *

Marvin Stone stood outside of the forest overlooking the lake, looking very dapper in a dark gray pantsuit. He took out his red handkerchief and wiped his nose. He was more sensitive to the cold than the average person. If Marvin didn't have business to attend to, he would be in his home with the heat cranked up at eighty-five degrees in a tank top and shorts.

Marvin slipped his handkerchief back into his pocket as he admired the lake that extended beyond view. The aroma of the towering pine trees behind him reminded him of his home back in Pool View. His parents had planted a couple of pine trees in the backyard when Marvin was just a child. As the pine trees reached their peak, it had become a great hiding place for him. For years, it had been his safe spot. His parents had become verbally abusive as Marvin got older and the only place that made him feel safe was between the trees.

His childhood made him grow up into a controlling, spiteful, and deceiving man. Only those close to him would come to find out underneath the sea blue eyes and short brown hair combed over, there was the other side to Marvin Stone. A side no one could escape.

Marvin turned and faced the trees. The dirt beneath his feet left a little dust on the tip of his shiny black shoes as he walked into the woods. He kept his hands inside his pockets for warmth. Marvin could see the trail of his breath as he exhaled. During these days, there were no signs of birds or any other creatures. It was quite peaceful. He grinned.

Marvin stopped as he came to an intercom that stood in the middle of a circle of pine trees. It was the size of a football field. The sky was rarely visible from where Marvin stood.

Other than minor cracks from the branches of the trees, here, there was only darkness.

He pressed the button and waited for an answer. Marvin stood looking up, outlining what was created here decades ago. A regular person would not be able to see what Marvin knew existed before his eyes. However, a few steps past the intercom was a brick wall. The only thing visible to the naked eye was the trunk of the pine tree yards away from where he stood.

"Please give me your full name, your birthdate, your agent number, and your ID please," answered a woman's voice.

"The name is Marvin Stone. Birthdate is 12/6/1981. Agent number is 212 and my ID is 212-412-061-980."

"Please hold."

Marvin waited patiently as the woman on the other end confirmed his authentication. Moments later the woman thanked Marvin as the door opened. Marvin walked inside the building, locking the door behind him.

This was the Secret Eye Agency known as the SEA.

The SEA was a five-story building. Every floor had agents with a certain amount of experience. The first floor only consisted of the newly hired agents who answered calls by potential clients and drafted up paperwork that was requested by other agents from upper levels. The responsibilities, experience, and security clearance increased on each level. Once becoming a fourth floor agent, which would take years of experience, agents had the opportunity to apply for vacant positions on the fifth floor.

Every year the SEA held a meet and greet event where only the fourth and fifth floor agents were invited to join in. The event consisted of the chief of staff, the chief, defense team, the head of the departments, managers from every floor, retired agents, and of course, the head of the agency.

The event allowed the fourth floor agents to ask questions and have one-on-one conversations with the higher levels, who would fill the empty positions on the fifth floor as they saw fit. However, the turnover rates weren't very high. For a fourth floor agent to land a spot on the fifth floor was therefore very limited and competitive.

Marvin examined the floor, seeing first floor agents drowned in their work. Some were on the phone screening potential clients for upper level agents and others were looking at data and gathered evidence given by the upper level. Each agent worked closely with their client, making sure the two parties were satisfied at the end of the mission.

Marvin pressed for the elevator. Within seconds the doors opened. He stepped in, thankful there was no one else accompanying him up to the fourth floor. Marvin despised small talk. If he didn't have any interest, there was no point for any sort of conversation. He rarely uttered hellos and goodbyes to anyone, unless it was a client or someone higher up the chain. Other than that, Marvin kept to himself when at work.

As he stepped off onto his floor, he could see straight ahead a man in his fifties, judging by the gray hair, sitting in his office. He walked with stride, unsure whether this person would give him good news about the assignment he'd taken on or trouble that he wasn't quite ready to handle yet.

As he pulled the door toward him, the man rose from his seat.

"Agent 513, Bruce Storm, chief of staff," he said, extending his hand for a handshake.

Marvin, a little curious as to what brought one of the highest respected agents down to his floor, cautiously shook his hand.

"I'm well aware of your work, sir," Marvin said, slowly pulling out his chair from underneath his desk. "What can I do for you?" Marvin made himself comfortable as he awaited an answer.

"Can you explain to me about the assignment you're on? Assignment 01-02."

Marvin was stunned. This wasn't Bruce's area of interest or expertise. This had nothing to do with Bruce.

"My personal assignment?" he asked.

"I looked into your file and you've put in this assignment once before but it was terminated."

"No disrespect to you sir, but this assignment was already approved by the board of directors. I'm sure you know how it works around here," he said, leaning back in his chair. Something didn't quite add up to Marvin as he studied Bruce. "You don't have the authority to come in here and question why I do what I do."

"I'm well aware of my duties and boundaries," he said slyly. Bruce unbuttoned his blazer and pulled out a folded piece of paper from the inside pocket. He placed it on his desk, with confidence. "That's why I had this document drawn up and signed for approval."

Marvin was overcome with a deep, bubbling anger. He loathed being questioned about his work. Marvin snatched the document from his desk. He read in detail about Bruce's concern for this specific assignment Marvin was going to carry out. It gave Bruce permission to take whatever files he felt necessary in order to review them.

Taking another agent's file with documentation only meant one thing: It would slow down the process to have the assignment completed. Assignments took more time to get approved than the missions agents carried out for their clients.

Marvin looked at Bruce with a smile, but his eyes twinkled with rage.

"You took the time to have one of the rookies write up this

bullshit?" He was still smiling as he spoke, making sure not to let any sign of discontent appear.

"Drawing up documents for assignments is not something listed under my job description."

Marvin knew something. Even though he was just a fourth-floor agent with no authority, he knew how people worked. He could tell when someone was lying. He knew when someone was hiding something, which Bruce clearly was. This had just made his assignment more interesting. His curiosity about Bruce rose.

"That's true," he replied, folding the paper back into its original form, "but why would you take out the time to have this document written up, signed, and then hand deliver it? There is a level of concern for you, which raises questions in my mind. People only go out of their way if something matters. You care about something or someone," he said, pointing at Bruce. Marvin grinned, knowing he was on to something here.

"I'm here to take files associated with this assignment. That's all."

Marvin, completely ignoring Bruce, had his own questions he wanted to ask. "You could have just left this document on my desk. Why did you wait for me? I'm sure you have other important things to do. Why is this more important?"

"I wanted to get a sense of the kind of person you were. The profiles on the database only do so much justice. It's different when you meet the person and get a feeling firsthand."

"What kind of person am I?" he asked with a mischievous smile across his face.

Marvin smiled as he leaned forward, folding his hands together. He was intrigued by Bruce.

"What kind of person am I, Bruce?" he repeated.

Without any hesitation, Bruce replied, "I think you're a paranoid psychopath."

Marvin snorted. "You think I'm a psychopath? What makes you think that?" He chuckled, trying to contain his laugh, but it was the only way Marvin knew how to contain the real beast that lay hidden. He rested his elbow on the armrest of his chair, his chin on his fist while he gazed at Bruce.

Marvin was going to figure out what it was that Bruce cared so much about. He had all the information he needed. It was just a matter of cross-referencing his current assignment with the previous one. Something was different in this assignment and Marvin was sure going to catch whatever it was. He was going to create hell on earth just for Bruce.

No one got in the way of Marvin. *No one.*

"I've heard worse," he said. "Here, let me give you what you're looking for. I don't want to take up too much of your time, *sir.*"

Marvin unlocked the desk drawer that contained the last few missions he was working on and pulled out the assignment Bruce requested.

"Here you go, sir," Marvin said, rising from his chair. He held out the black folder in front of Bruce.

As Bruce rose, there was a difference of height. Marvin happened to be slightly taller than Bruce. But that wasn't the intimidating part. Bruce had no idea what scheme Marvin was working up in his mind at this very moment. If he knew any better, staying out of Marvin's business would have been the *best* option. It wasn't until *now* that Evan's life was in danger.

Bruce buttoned his blazer as he took the folder Marvin held out for him. "Thank you."

Marvin looked deep into his soul and said, "No, thank *you.*"

Marvin was still smiling as Bruce left his office. When Bruce was off in the distance, Marvin sat back in his chair and went to work. He pulled up the agency's database, knowing everything he needed to know about Bruce was available.

"Agent 513, I will destroy you," Marvin said under his breath.

Marvin typed in Bruce's agent number in the database. Every piece of information on Bruce pulled up in front of him. He carefully looked into Bruce's profile with great thirst to find what it was that he cared so much. Marvin pulled up his personal files from his database and crosschecked the two files to find what was different from the last time he started his assignment. Who was involved this time around? The change of place? Something was definitely different. He couldn't put a finger on it.

He scrolled further and further as he crosschecked everything that had been the same. After a couple of more scrolls down the pages, he noticed one thing different. And this was going to give him the answer he was looking for. It would unlock the history of Bruce's past, which Bruce kept secret.

Marvin grinned. Today Bruce stepped into his territory, and now, Marvin was going to destroy his.

CHAPTER 8

Shadow stood patiently in front of the door to Mr. and Mrs. Pence's home. She held a blue folder in her arm, ready to present the various designs she'd been working on all morning. As seconds passed, the more anxious she became. This was the first time she worked on a nursery. Shadow's portfolio consisted of mainly bedrooms and bathrooms, sometimes kitchens. Her designs were purely meeting the Pence's requirements intertwined with how she would have designed her own nursery.

As she waited, Shadow studied her surroundings. The homes in MidView were more close together in proximity compared to Lake View. It was a cozy town to say the least. Medium sized front lawns and picket fences seemed like the trend. Some homeowners had put in obvious effort. Shadow noticed a home across had Spanish garage doors and a driveway made of bricks. Some lawns had more landscaping done than others. The Pences' home was traditional from the outside. It had the white picket fence that surrounded the Egyptian blue-colored two-story house.

Before Shadow could ponder any longer, the front door

gradually opened and Mrs. Pence, whose dark skin glowed, peeked behind the door.

"You must be Shadow," she said with a smile.

Shadow nodded, feeling a little relaxed.

"Please come in. It's freezing out!"

Shadow stepped inside, feeling the warm air hugging her body.

"Thank you. This weather is kind of lovely, to be honest."

Mrs. Pence shot a confused look. "It's below thirty degrees out there. How on earth is that weather lovely?! And you're wearing a skirt?"

Shadow chuckled. "I'm originally from Pool View. The temperatures drop close to twenty degrees, even more sometimes and it snows on top of that. So I'm used to it."

"Ah, okay, that makes sense," Mrs. Pence said as she rubbed her stomach. "Let me show you the nursery."

* * *

Denise walked through the front door, followed by Ryan. After Ryan closed the door behind him, he stood still for a moment. A part of him hoped that coming back home would ignite a sensor in his brain that would cause a domino effect of regaining lost memories. Nothing. Ryan walked into the kitchen where he found Denise pouring a glass of wine.

"Wine in the afternoon?"

She smirked. "Do you want me to pour you a glass?"

"No, but do we have beer?"

The corners of her eyes crinkled. "I'm sorry," she said, plugging the cork back into the top. "We have Coke...and some lemonade left."

"Lemonade it is," he said as he moved to the refrigerator. He came to a halt as he reached for the handle. There was a picture of him and Nate at Nate's kindergarten graduation.

It was a day filled with joy and excitement but Ryan didn't remember it. He didn't remember his eyes welled up out of happiness as Nate walked across the stage to get his certificate. He didn't remember his heart flooding with joy, seeing his little boy growing up so quickly.

Denise took a sip before setting her glass down. She wrinkled her forehead, wondering what was going on in Ryan's mind at the very moment. For the past month, whenever she showed him pictures of him and Nate or just family pictures in general, he wanted the reminiscing part of it to be over. She knew Ryan didn't like being reminded that he had lost his memory.

"Does that picture remind you of something?"

There was silence.

"Babe…"

Ryan's eyes flooded with tears. "I want to remember," he cried. "Why don't I remember him? Why?" He looked over his shoulder and gazed at Denise helplessly. "I'm his father. I'm *supposed* to remember."

Denise dashed to Ryan's side, accidently knocking her wine glass over with her elbow. Her heart sank hearing him cry. She wrapped her arms around Ryan, feeling helpless herself.

The red wine spilled over to the edge of the counter, dripping onto the floor, one droplet at a time.

"I know, honey," she managed to say, sobbing.

Denise still felt the guilt from that night. She couldn't help but feel it was all her fault.

CHAPTER 9

Shadow stood in the vacant room, jotting down ideas on her notepad as Mrs. Pence stood leaning on one leg scanning through the sketches.

"See, for this one," she said holding up the second sketch, "I really like the ceiling but I don't like the layout of the closet or the moldings. I like the closet in the first design, especially the built-in changing table."

"I liked that one too. Don't worry, I'm going to make sure you get the perfect nursery for your baby. When is your due date?"

Mrs. Pence looked at her stomach and rubbed it in parallel. "One month from today."

"Oh wow. Kinda cutting it close, huh?"

"Tell me about it. My husband, bless his heart…I love him, but sometimes he just doesn't listen! We were supposed to already have the nursery ready by now."

"Do men *ever* listen?" she offered.

Shadow and Mrs. Pence shared a good laugh together. For the next half an hour Shadow went over the changes and other items on the list that the Pence's had under their requirements.

* * *

Bruce sat across from Venice in her office. He looked down at his laps for a brief second before meeting her eyes. They hadn't said a word to one another after Candice had let Bruce in.

"How are you?" Bruce asked, breaking the silence.

Venice nodded. "Times have been better, but that's life."

Bruce let out a sigh, feeling there was still some resentment and tension toward him.

"Why are you here?" she asked.

"I need to talk to you about Evan," he began. "He may be in danger but I'm not a hundred percent sure yet."

The unsettling feeling Venice had tried to avoid for the past month was now making its way to her gut.

"What's going on?" she asked.

Bruce shifted in his seat.

Venice stood up and walked over to the corner where she had her cappuccino machine set up. It was a gift given by Denise three Christmases ago. Never did she believe she needed such a materialistic product that complicated the beauty of simple coffee. But after she made her first cup, she felt rather differently about her miracle machine.

"Would you like some?" she asked, turning on the machine.

"I'm good, thanks though," Bruce said, craning his neck in her direction.

"Okay, suit yourself."

"Do you know anything about this?" he asked, referring to Evan. "If you do, you need to let me know, so I can do what I need to do on my end."

"No."

"You sure? 'Cause you tend to hide these kinda things away from your family."

Venice pursed her lips. "You know exactly why I keep my mouth shut about these things."

Bruce scoffed.

The room fell in awkward silence, neither of them knowing what to say next.

She peered over at Bruce. "Don't beat around the bush. Say what you want to say."

Bruce scratched his jaw as he raised an eyebrow. Venice walked back to the couch with her mug in hand.

"You could have saved her, you know? Evan and Denise would still have their mother today."

"She was a drug addict, Bruce," she said in a stern voice. "You knew that going in and I know you believed she changed because I did too. But sometimes people's addictions are so powerful, there's really nothing you can do. Even after getting help, which you did, people relapse. That's what happened with Geneva. She slipped and her addiction to cocaine and meth was powerful enough to make her think there was nothing left for her to live for. You don't want to believe it and I don't blame you. She was the love of your life." Venice took a sip from her mug. "What really locked Geneva in that path were the people she started spending time with—her old buddies. They didn't care about her well-being or her family," she said, pausing for a moment. "That's around the time she started having the affair."

"If I had known, I could've saved her."

Venice saw the sorrow in Bruce's eyes. "Oh darlin', there was absolutely nothing you could have done. She was going through stuff of her own before you even met her. There's nothing you could have done to save her."

She took another steaming sip.

Bruce frowned. "Life really screws with you sometimes, doesn't it?"

"When you truly love someone, then yeah, it does," she replied.

The moment of silence between Bruce and Venice that felt comfortable. Bruce scanned the beige walls and then the rest of the room. A plant was placed near the window and the curtains had been draped. A painting hung in front of him of a cabin in the woods, with a river flowing in front of it. He remembered when Venice first bought this space. It stayed the same ever since.

"I thought a lot about seeing Denise and Evan."

"Yeah?" Venice leaned forward to place her mug on the table. "And?"

"The timing isn't right," he confessed.

Evan's life was in jeopardy. Before Bruce created more chaos, he wanted to make sure whatever Marvin was up to would be put to an end.

Venice was relieved. "I'm really glad to hear that."

"I'm going to head out. I've got a lot of things that I need to do," he said, rising from the couch.

"You don't visit often," she said abruptly.

Bruce cleared his throat. "It's safer that way."

"Oh, is it really?" she asked sarcastically with a hint of seriousness.

Even though Bruce sensed the sarcasm, he was in no mood to talk about the last twenty-seven years. He knew Venice wanted answers. As much as she had the right to know why he left for a longer period than they initially agreed on and why he never phoned his mother to make sure she was doing all right, this was not the time for that talk.

"I'll try to come by more often," he said as he opened the door. "Just promise me that you'll keep an eye on Evan."

As he turned to look at Venice to say goodbye, he remembered the day he'd left Evan and Denise with her. It was the only day he clearly remembered as the other ones had become a blur. He'd hugged Venice tightly and kissed Evan and Denise goodbye. Venice waved goodbye with a faded smile across her face, knowing that having Bruce leave was the best thing for her grandchildren. She knew it was only a matter of time before she saw Bruce again.

Deep down, Venice knew the choices Bruce made weren't easy and she would never know the burden those choices carried on his shoulders until she walked in his shoes. She never held it against Bruce. However, she wasn't going to let him off the hook so easily either.

***

Shadow was sitting in her office, working on the nursery. It was far from perfect but perfect was what her client was looking for. It was what *every* person was looking for even though there was no such thing as "perfect." It was a standard that people had made up in their minds. Every person's definition of "perfect" varied.

A long time ago, Shadow had a picture perfect life set up in her mind. Shadow knew it was impossible to have the perfect life, but regardless of the obstacles that were thrown her way, she knew she would manage to have the life she imagined growing up. She would have three kids, an amazing husband, and a cat and a black Labrador. They would live in the suburbs, in a peaceful town—but her life had been far from perfect. She sighed as she looked at her sketches of the nursery. More than anything, Shadow wanted a family. She wanted to be pregnant and carry a child. She wanted to be a mother and she knew in her gut, it was going to be the most fulfilling job she would ever do in her entire life, but the chance was taken away from her. Now, even thinking about having a family seemed close to impossible. To bear another child would be much harder the second time around.

Second chances were rare.

A few hours later, Shadow was packing up, getting ready to head home. The parking lot was still fairly full, aside from the fact that it was half past five. Usually now, everyone would be scattering around the parking lot to their cars. But it wasn't like that, here at least. In Pool View, the town of the very rich, every working man and some women would have been turning on their ignitions right about now.

She searched for her keys in her purse as she stood by the car door. *Why do I always have trouble finding the darn keys?* It was one of those annoying perks of having a purse. And it was always the case with the bigger sized purses. With the small ones, just the bare minimum would fit, and that was only if Shadow squished everything in herself. On the other hand, the bigger bag, she was able to fit everything she needed but there was no organization. It was apparent she would have to sit down and organize her purse.

After finally pulling out her keys, she unlocked the doors to her C-Class Mercedes—a gift from her generous father. She knew driving a Mercedes didn't mean anything, but to her father, it meant there was newfound respect. He had this idea that driving luxurious cars automatically made you worthy of respect. But in Shadow's world, it simply didn't work that way.

Once she was behind the wheel, she leaned over to place her purse on the passenger seat. That's when she noticed a black envelope. Within a few seconds, Shadow's heart started to race. She felt her heart pounding through her ears. Thoughts ran across her mind at the speed of a hummingbird's heartbeat. What was this?

And then, everything hit her at once.

It was him.

He was the only one capable of pulling a stunt like this.

It couldn't be anyone else. It had to be *him*. Shadow looked around the parking lot. Gradually, everything around her became a blur. Her hearing was limited to only the sound of her heartbeat.

This was not good. She wondered what he wanted and how he managed to track her down. Shadow was sure she had been discreet about her move and whereabouts.

Shadow frantically opened the envelope and out she pulled a piece of paper. Etched on the paper was:

Peek a boo, I see you.

Slowly, she started to lose feeling in her legs. Her hands started to shake. Her lungs started to close up, but as her body was put into such shock, everything she felt was amplified. *This is how I'm going to die*, she thought. *At work, in my car, this is how they're going to find me.* She was panicking out of control.

It took Shadow a couple of minutes to calm down by taking deep breaths, like the pregnant women in Lamaze class. Not that she ever went to one of those classes, but she'd seen it on TV shows.

After a few minutes regaining her composure, she looked down at her lap, where the piece of paper lay. Right now she worried for her life as she was in danger.

She took another quick glance around the parking lot. No one was watching her, not that she was aware of, but still, it was clear. She shoved in her key and turned the ignition, shifted the gear into reverse, making sure not to hit any car in a panic, shifted back into drive, and peeled out of the parking lot. It was going to take her forty minutes to get back home with traffic. Within that time, anything was possible. She had to be extra cautious as she drove. Every time she came to a stoplight, she looked both to her left and right. He could be anywhere. She feared to look in her rear view mirror to find him staring back with that smile.

Mr. Jingles! He was in danger too.

Her hands gripped the steering wheel. She desperately needed to get home to make sure Mr. Jingles was all right.

Shadow was on his radar, after she barely managed to escape the first time around.

***

Venice sat in her living room, in peace as she sipped on her favorite tea, Earl Gray. Usually after a long day at work, Venice would curl up on the couch and read a good book. It was a great distraction from the reality she faced every day. Lying to her grandchildren, keeping secrets from them, trying to protect them from the horrific events that would take place in their lives—it was mentally draining at times.

After Bruce made his appearance earlier, Venice hoped she would get some kind of vision that would shed light about Evan's potential risk. There was always the chance Venice's predictions were wrong. She liked being wrong, especially if something terrible was about to occur in her loved ones' lives. Sometimes living in constant fear was the price she had to pay for her psychic abilities. This gift she was given served as a purpose to remind her, at the end of the day, she wasn't their protector.

After she finished her tea, she got up from the couch to start dinner.

Just as Venice moved into the kitchen, her head began to throb, the pain increasing every minute. The kitchen lights seemed to have brightened on their own, stinging her eyes. She leaned against the countertop to keep from falling. Her jaws clenched with pain. The room started to look distorted. Everything was becoming a blur. The floor felt as if it were melting away. Her body, not as strong as it used to be, started to give up on her. She sluggishly crouched to the floor for support. She grunted and moaned as the pain became too much for her to handle. She was moments away from having a vision.

Minutes passed by in agony. Venice sat on the kitchen floor, with her knees up to her chest and held tilted back. Her hands pressed hard against the tile floor. She shut her eyes. Her forehead creased from the pain. In any given minute, this would all be over and she would know what the future held.

Evan sat on a bench at Cherry Park.

It was cool and calm outside, more than the usual. He was in his workout gear, feeling spent. He looked around and saw families with their kids. A little boy learning how to ride his bike for the first time. Parents hung around as their children played with the other kids on the jungle gym. He saw a little girl in a pink dress with a jacket over it, feeding the ducks in the lake, as her father stood right beside her. Ducklings followed their mother around the edge of the pond as she waddled her way to the nearest bush as their nesting ground. On the far right, a boy around Nate's age was having a birthday party with his friends. They all wore party hats and some were blowing whistles in each other's ears. There were presents surrounding the table with a double-layered cake. Oh, how Evan loved cake. Bakery Village, one of the most popular bakeries in Lake View, made Evan's favorite: Chocolate fudge with hazelnut whipped frosting. It was rich in texture, which complemented the luscious icing. Thinking about it made Evan's mouth salivate.

As he looked around, Evan was reminded of the times he missed out with his parents. When he saw children with their parents, he saw the smiles on their faces. Through strangers, he felt the happiness he didn't get a chance to experience as a child. There were only a few memories he had of his parents. But there wasn't something he could hold on to or learn from.

Oftentimes Evan would look through pictures of his parents to remind himself what they looked like.

When Evan looked down at his watch, he realized it was time to head back. Evan took in the scenery once again. It was one of those peaceful places where all worries were lost. Coming to Cherry Park put his mind at ease. Especially after those long teacher meetings at Lake View District High School after school was out. Sometimes during teacher conferences, he would find himself wondering why they even held them in the first place. Most of the time it was the vice principal, Mr. Stow, who would make the final decision, which had no input whatsoever from anyone present in the meeting. And there were those times where he questioned his line of work. He could have gotten his PhD, opened his own clinic and treated patients. Instead he was treating sophomores and juniors for their heartbreaks, which they were convinced they'd die from.

Evan jogged his way back as the cold winter breeze brushed against his face. Home was only fifteen minutes away. His cheeks flushed, exposing the pink tones underneath his light skin.

He passed through the neighborhoods. Inhaling and exhaling. Cars passed by, pulling into driveways. Three kids jumped out of a gray minivan just as their mother pulled into the driveway. Evan could hear her yelling but the gust of wind drowned her voice, making her words unclear. But it definitely wasn't something pleasant. She looked like the typical Lake View housewife. Hair pulled back into a ponytail, fashioning a long blue cardigan and faded blue boyfriend jeans.

Evan continued to jog as he observed his neighborhood. It was a nice place to raise a family. The homes had more than enough room for children to play in the front yard since the houses were set apart from each other. The floor plans were cozy and family friendly. Houses were well kept from the outside. Even though they were more than one hundred years old, they still looked fairly new from the outside as well from the inside. And the schools were high in ranking compared to some of the other towns.

* * *

Shadow pulled up in the driveway, with her heartbeat in control. The only thing on her mind was Mr. Jingles. A frantic look stretched across her face as she stepped out of her car. Her purse hung over her shoulder as she walked to the front door, keys in hand. Shadow walked in a steady pace, making sure she didn't trip and fall. Her heart pounded in her chest.

Her knees started to become weak just as her hands started to tremble with fear again. She felt an odd presence behind her. Shadow slowly tilted her neck to the left, with eyes focused on the ground. There was no one there. She glanced all around to double check. No one was there.

She struggled to insert the key into the lock. It was as if she had lost mobility in her fingers. Her keys slipped and landed on the cold concrete. For a second, she stood paralyzed in fear. She looked down at the ground, knowing very well she needed to pick up her keys. She took a couple of deep breaths to keep herself calm then sluggishly crouched down to grab the keys. Her hands trembled as she carefully inserted the key into the lock. She turned the knob, entering her home. Then shut and locked the door behind her. Shadow calmly slipped out of her high heels before doing anything else.

Mr. Jingles stood in front of her and looked up at her as if he'd been waiting for all day. *Oh, am I glad to see you.* Shadow picked up the furball and kissed him in between his ears before putting him down. She felt calmness for a brief second before she remembered she needed to check the rest of the house. He was capable of anything.

Several different scenarios crossed her mind. He could be

waiting in her room with his most sincere yet serial killer-like smile. The thought of him gave Shadow the creeps.

She crept into the kitchen. Nothing looked out of the ordinary. Not yet anyway.

She walked back to the front of the staircase and looked up the stairs. Her heart started to pound louder. She looked at Mr. Jingles, who clearly had no idea what was going on. He was clueless. He brushed against her legs, only to then stand on her feet.

You're no help, she thought.

She picked up Mr. Jingles and carried him up the stairs, as slowly as possible. While he was purring, she was in complete panic mode. Shadow held on to him tightly, preparing herself for the worst.

There were three bedrooms: the master bedroom, her office—which she had yet to set up—and a guest bedroom.

She looked down the hall. There was no movement but that didn't always mean someone wasn't there. She walked by the bathroom down the hall, peeking through the doorway, making sure it was empty. Next door, the room was still vacant.

Shadow walked into her office, peering around. Her desk facing the window was empty. A sense of relief overcame her but withered away in the blink of an eye. Now, the only room remaining was hers. Her own home was beginning to feel like a trap.

She held her breath, and held tighter to Mr. Jingles, who was getting a little antsy. He didn't like being carried for too long. He peered up at Shadow with his big yellow eyes. *What are you doing? It's supposed to be my dinnertime right now. Can't this wait?*

Shadow ignored the thoughtful look he gave her. *Just hold on, you'll get your dinner.*

She stepped into her bedroom, standing in the doorway,

afraid to go any farther. Her eyes widened, feeling someone's presence around her. Cautiously, she turned around. No one was there. She could feel her back and armpits beginning to sweat. After taking a couple of deep breaths, she crept forward, looking into the bathroom.

Empty.

She sighed in relief. Shadow let down Mr. Jingles.

Just as the sense of relief started to overcome her, the doorbell rang. Her heart dropped. She wasn't expecting anyone. All of a sudden, she was instilled with fear once again. It was going to be him. *This was wonderfully planned*, she thought. He was a master at playing mind games. She tried to prepare herself to see him standing on the other side of the door but couldn't. Once again, she would come face to face with her obsessive ex-fiancé.

She wasn't ready for this.

Shadow made her way down the stairs, walking over the heels she left in the middle of the doorway. She looked in the peephole. To her dismay, there was a handsome man standing in front of her door. She turned the knob, pulling the door toward her.

He smiled, but suddenly his smile faded.

Shadow was intrigued by the stranger who stood before her.

Evan wore a confused look. Samantha? *No.* There was *no way* it could be her. But how? Her brown hair flowed down the sides of her face, making her features stand out. There was a part of him that wanted to reach out and trace her Roman nose with his index finger to see if she was real. He was in awe. She stared at him with heavy blue eyes. Her lips were as rosy and full as those models in the Victoria's Secret catalog.

This couldn't be.

"Hi," she said, extending her hand.

Evan, still taken aback, shook her hand, unable to

comprehend what was going on. He cleared his throat, knowing he should say something right about now.

In a previous life, she was once his wife. Not that *she* was aware of that fact. Mentioning that would end with the door slamming shut in his face; definitely a bad idea. But this was her.

He cleared his throat again. "Hi." Still, he was taken aback by her beauty and at a loss of words. "I'm Evan. I live…next door," he said.

Shadow broke into a smile.

"I'm Shadow." She smiled.

Evan scratched behind his ear. *What do I do now? Jeez, why is this so hard?*

"So…um…how do you like the neighborhood?" He mentally smacked his forehead as the words slipped out. What kind of question was that?

Shadow leaned against the doorway, finding him cute. She could tell he was nervous. She too was feeling the presence of butterflies in her stomach.

"I'm fairly new to it." She chuckled. "It's nice, though. Really quiet."

"Where are you from?"

"Pool View."

Evan was amused. "Oh, from Pool View," he said. That was interesting. "We don't have many people moving from Pool View to here. You must've done something." Evan, gaining his confidence back, smirked.

Shadow responded with a smile. "You're funny."

Evan watched as she crossed her arms at her chest.

She looked deep into his eyes. His lean figure towered over her, but just enough that it didn't make Shadow feel intimidated.

"It was time for a change, and living in Pool View with everyone's standards, it was hard to keep up. Plus, it's closer to work."

He nodded. "Where do you work?" Evan was still trying to comprehend. He'd never seen someone from his previous life before. And what were the odds for the first person to meet would be his wife from a previous lifetime? Surreal.

Again, Shadow smiled, putting Evan at ease.

"I'm an interior designer at Storm, Inc. I started right when I moved out here. You probably haven't heard of it. It's a small startup."

Evan chuckled. "I think I've heard of it," he said with a beaming smile. He figured Shadow was the new girl Denise was trying to set him up with during their dinner. "How do you like working there so far?"

She thought about it for a moment, recounting her day. Shadow looked out into the street before answering. "I really like it."

"Let me know if anyone gives you a hard time there," he said, looking down at his feet and then meeting her eyes once again. "I know the person who runs the whole show."

"Denise Storm-Smith?" she exclaimed. "How do you know her?"

"She's my older sister."

Her eyes traveled across his face, trying to find a resemblance. She couldn't. "Wow. I would've never guessed."

Evan chuckled, bypassing the comment. "Let me know if you'd like to get a tour of Lake View. There are some pretty good bakeries if you have a sweet tooth. There's a lot to see around here, especially Cherry Park. I just came back from there."

"Yeah," she said as her lips curved up into a smile. "I think I'll take you up on that."

Mr. Jingles paced his way to Shadow, wondering who the new guest was. The cat lingered in the doorway, looking up at Evan.

"I see you have a house mate." Evan grinned as he bent over to scratch Mr. Jingles behind the ear. To Evan's surprise, the feline enjoyed it. He could hear him purr with satisfaction.

With a smile she responded, "Yeah. This is Mr. Jingles. It looks like he's fond of you. That doesn't happen often."

"I love animals. I used to help out at the shelter in downtown, Athens Animal Shelter, but I couldn't really commit to a whole year."

"Oh."

"You have to sign all these papers saying you'll commit to these many hours for an entire year," he said, stroking Mr. Jingles' head before rising to his feet. "I wasn't sure if I could make that big of a commitment. Didn't want to let down the little guys, you know?"

Subconsciously, Shadow put her hand over her heart as if she was about to be proposed to. "I understand." She tried to remain nonchalant but couldn't help but grin.

From having a really long day to fearing for her life, Evan's voice managed to make her smile and feel calmer. There was something about him that made her feel at home. It was like if she'd known him from somewhere but couldn't grasp where.

"It was really nice meeting you, Shadow," Evan concluded. "I gotta get dinner started and work on some stuff." He took a moment to study her face and features. "I'll see you later," he said finally.

"Yeah, sure. No worries."

"Have a good one." Evan waved as he walked across the lawn to his front door.

There was no way he was single. Women would be fawning over him. She was sure every time he stepped into the grocery store, or just into the world in general, ladies and teenage girls would help themselves to a long, exaggerated stare. Who wouldn't?

Shadow stood in the doorway as she watched Evan enter his home. Closing the door behind her, she leaned against the door with her hand planted against her chest. She broke into a smile and covered her eyes. She felt like a giddy schoolgirl with a crush on the quarterback.

* * *

Shadow stood in the kitchen as she poured Mr. Jingles his dinner. She still couldn't manage to wipe away the smile Evan had left her with. It had been a while since she had the butterflies after meeting a cute stranger, who just so happened to be her neighbor. She fantasized about what his body looked like. She rested her elbow against the cold countertop, forgetting about dinner, the nursery she was supposed to work on for the Pences, which wasn't complete. All she wanted to do was fantasize about Evan. The feeling of knowing him some time ago lingered in the back of her mind.

A moment later, she was distracted by the sound of the doorbell. She gradually walked toward the door in hopes of seeing Evan again. Maybe he needed to borrow an ingredient for dinner, she hoped...

She opened the door and to her surprise, *he* was standing there.

"Hello, Shadow," said Marvin. The corners of his mouth lifted, knowing how fast Shadow's heartbeat must have been right now.

Shadow's face grew pale. He looked at her, feeling a sense of satisfaction by Shadow's reaction. She couldn't hide from him forever. Even if she thought she was out of his sight, he would find a way to get back into her life.

Just as everything was registering in her mind, she pushed the door shut but Marvin was quick. With his two hands, he pushed back, throwing Shadow off her feet and let himself in.

Marvin unbuttoned his blazer as he graciously walked in. Shadow looked at Marvin with disgust as she closed the door behind her. There was no way he was going to hurt her, she was guaranteed of that, but still, she feared him. Being around him raised her stress level and gave her anxiety. Much of it she hid pretty well.

"Why are you here?" she said in a stern voice.

Shadow made sure to keep her distance from him.

"Begin dinner preparations and I'll tell you why."

Marvin's pronunciation was clear-cut, which made him sound sophisticated, matching his appearance. His attire always consisted of a pantsuit. It was the only thing he wore once he stepped out of his house; it didn't matter where he was going.

He removed his blazer, placing it on the couch as he made his way into the kitchen.

Shadow, anxious, followed.

CHAPTER 10

This is insane!

Evan was mind blown. Shadow, no, *Samantha* was living right next door. He paced back and forth in his living room, trying to make sense of it all. He rested his arms on his hips, staring down at the floor. He scratched the side of his head, not knowing how to feel, or what to think. It was overwhelming.

This had to be a sign from the universe.

He slumped into the couch. A moment later, after feeling the dampness against his back, he realized he needed a shower.

Evan jogged upstairs to his room as he removed his shirt. He pulled out a clean white T-shirt from his drawer and threw it over to his bed. Then pulled out comfortable pants from the second drawer, also throwing them over to the bed, along with a new pair of underwear.

Right now, all he could think about was Shadow.

He ambled into the bathroom, turning on the shower. He turned to view himself in the mirror. This was surreal. He was a doppelganger of Derek and Shadow was the doppelganger of Samantha. How was this possible? Questions started to pour in and it was up to him to figure it out. There was always a reasonable explanation for things that happened out of the ordinary. There had to be.

Evan threw his damp shirt and Nike pants in the hamper before stepping into the steamy shower. Evan squeezed shower gel onto the loofah and rubbed his entire body. As he scrubbed himself clean, water running down his face, he thought about Samantha. She didn't deserve to be treated the way Derek treated her. Cruel and inhumane were among many words to describe the way Derek treated Samantha. Alongside many other memories he had, the night Derek had a fit because dinner wasn't ready on time was the one that stood out the most, mostly because it had become a repetitive memory. Her lying on the floor, with her lips bleeding from the cracks, made Evan's soul jump out of his body. It was gruesome and heart-wrenching.

He pressed his forehead against the shower wall. Why did Samantha stay? She could have filed for divorce. She could have gone down to the police station and filed a report for domestic abuse. She could have run away. Why didn't she do that? What made her stay? What made her want to continue her life with Derek?

Why? Why? Why? The question would linger in his mind until he found the answer.

* * *

Shadow worked quickly in the kitchen. The quicker she had dinner ready, the faster she'd have Marvin out of her hair.

Asparagus marinated in olive oil and seasoned, was ready to be pulled out of the oven. The pot boiled with penne. She poured basil pesto into a big glass bowl and scurried her way to the refrigerator, where she pulled out the fresh mozzarella.

She gracefully made dinner for two.

He looked pensive as he peered out the window.

This reminded Shadow of the days when they lived together and were set to get married. She didn't receive any help in the kitchen from Marvin other than his company and prude comments about the people he worked with.

"You are very good at hiding things from me," he said, turning back to Shadow, who was cutting cubes of mozzarella.

You found out where I moved, so not really, she thought. Shadow continued to dice, feeling uncomfortable in his presence.

"Sometimes I don't understand what I did wrong. I don't know what I did to lose you."

Shadow shot back a glance. *Really? You don't know what you did? Are you that delusional?* This, she answered herself. He was more than delusional. He was a flippant human being who worked for a secret agency, high on marijuana.

She continued to dice mozzarella while Marvin continued to spill his unanswered questions.

"You took away everything I wanted, Shadow, but I still love—"

"Listen to yourself!" Shadow blurted as she slammed the knife on the wooden cutting board. "Do you have any idea what *you* took from me?"

"Shadow, my darling, I did not take *anything* from you. You made all those decisions on your own. *You* aborted our baby, without telling me. *You* moved here, without telling me." He looked at her forcefully. "I deserved to know, did I not?"

Marvin was exceptional at keeping a cool, calm composure when it came to Shadow. Rarely did he lash out, but his gentleman-like aura made up for the threats and blackmail. Yes, he represented himself as a gentleman and spoke like one, but he was far from it. Pushing the right buttons would reveal what Marvin was really like.

"I had a reason for all those things. Having an abortion was my only option. It was the best thing I could do for that baby," she said, pausing for a moment. "Maybe I'll go to hell, I don't know." She shrugged. "But I sure as hell know that I didn't want to raise a baby with you."

"Now you're just making a mockery out of me. We could have had the baby and it would have grown up in a home filled with love. Perhaps it was because you were afraid of becoming a mother?"

Shadow pressed against her temples. "Are you kidding me right now? You really think I was afraid of being a mother? I have *always* wanted a baby, more than anything. But *you* being the father is what I was afraid of. Even if I put the baby up for adoption, you would somehow manage to meddle in the baby's life. Kill the parents and bring the baby home. I know what you're capable of, Marvin." She glared at him for a moment. "You're a *killer*," she whispered.

The word made the hairs on her neck rise.

"I am not a killer," Marvin reassured. "You know exactly what I do for a living."

Shadow shook her head and laughed under her breath.

"You did everything possible to lose me. You're obsessive. A control freak. Manipulative. Scary as hell. Crazy, and not to mention…a murderer!"

Marvin snorted in disbelief. "I am far from those evil labels, dear. I took care of you. I gave you everything you wanted. Is that something you have forgotten?"

"Took care of me, as in make sure to have me followed to and from work? Everything you gave me was not everything I wanted. I wanted someone who I could fully trust, whose soul was genuine and filled with love."

"Was I not genuine, my love? Was my soul not full of love for you?" he asked, confused. They were on two different pages.

Shadow scoffed. "Your soul? It's dark. It's pitch black," she said as she threw in the mozzarella cubes. "There's no love there."

He navigated toward her from the window. "This is coming from the very person who hid her pregnancy from her fiancé?"

"Why do you think I hid it?" she screamed. "You're a menace. You fool people into thinking you're this amazing guy. But you're really not. You're full of corruption. It's disgusting. I can't and will never trust you, knowing what you do for a living."

"I should have never told you." He said softly.

"No, *thank you* for telling me. Otherwise I would have married a monster," she said, turning back to the boiling pasta.

In a couple of minutes the pasta would be ready to drain. Marvin was standing next to the sink. For Shadow, he was too close. She dreaded the walk to the sink.

"I'm not a monster. I care about your safety, Shadow. I care about you." He paused. "I want you to come back home. You do not belong here. You will not fit in here with these peasants."

Shadow scoffed. "I like it here. I fit in just fine."

He looked at her for a moment, feeling as if Shadow had completely changed. Marvin's eyes flicked toward the boiling pasta. "Here, let me help you with that."

Before Shadow could utter a word, with utmost grace, Marvin jolted toward the stove. He placed the colander upside down on top of the pot and made his way back to the sink, where he poured the pasta into the colander. The steam fogged the kitchen window and within seconds, the window was clear again.

Shadow looked over her shoulder as she threw in the rest of the mozzarella pieces. Marvin didn't look frightening at all, but that was all a disguise and for a person meeting him for the first time, they were sure to be deceived.

"Thank you," she forced out.

He brought back the colander, placing it in front of Shadow.

Marvin stood behind her, breathing against her neck. Shadow's heart started to pick up the pace. Before being overwhelmed with fear, she moved away.

Shadow pulled out the asparagus from the oven, keeping her attention focused on everything but Marvin.

"Are you making what I think you're making?"

Her eyebrows furrowed. "I don't know what you're thinking," she seethed. She used tongs to pick up the asparagus, then placed them on the cutting board.

"It looks like you're making pasta Caprese." He grinned. "One of my favorite dishes."

"Oh, I didn't know," she said, sounding the least bit enthusiastic.

Shadow let the asparagus sit and cool as she set the dinner table. She wanted to drink wine with dinner, but given the circumstances, knowing how Marvin was around alcohol, it definitely wasn't the best idea—he would get drunk, and she certainly didn't want a drunk Marvin in her new home. There was no telling what he would do. Thankfully there was a liter of soda in the pantry.

Marvin stood in the kitchen with his hands in his pockets. "Is there anything I can help you with?"

She looked at him, confused. He'd never offered to help ever before. Why now? "Uh," she said, thinking for a moment, "yeah, the soda is in there," she said pointing to her left. "The pantry."

"No Cabernet?" he said, smirking. "It seems you have changed a lot in a short amount of time."

It had been a month since Shadow had broken off their engagement. Within that time frame, Shadow learned a lot about herself. Being engaged to Marvin for a year took away her independency, her sense of control—she was merely a marionette. Now, she was beginning to find who Shadow was as an individual.

"I have changed, but I still drink wine," she said as she walked toward the cutting board. "Just not with you."

Marvin found Shadow's new attitude to be comedic. But he knew over the façade, Shadow was still the same girl he loved. She was going through a phase, which he was sure would pass.

The asparagus cooled down enough to touch. She cut one-inch pieces. Shadow stopped cutting for a moment as soon as she felt Marvin's eyes lingering on her.

"Where do you keep your glasses?" he asked as he held up the liter of Pepsi.

"Umm...just use the wine glasses. They're over there." She pointed to the upper left cabinet.

"Okay."

Marvin snatched two wine glasses off of the shelf, holding the stems between his fingers as he walked to the dinner table. He poured a glass, reminiscing his first date with Shadow. It was similar to today, except she had burned the asparagus and had little experience in the kitchen. She had come from a home where she had her own butler and never had to lift a finger. She could have had her food cut into little pieces if she wanted. Everything was practically done for her, but it was evident that things had improved in the kitchen. There was no smoke coming from the kitchen. The fire alarm hadn't gone off. Things had gone smoothly compared to three years ago.

One thing that didn't change and probably wasn't going to change any time in the future was Shadow's fondness of drinking out of wine glasses, regardless if there was wine or not. There was elegance the way the wine glass looked, tall and slender, a nice round large rim. The way the wine swirled inside the bowl, around and around. Then slowly, it would settle down as the legs appeared. There was a unique chemistry involved in winemaking that intrigued Shadow. She always had the interest in learning more about winemaking and the different types of tastes and fermentation. For now, it was on her bucket list.

Once the asparagus was added into the bowl, Shadow poured in the pasta, mixing it together; making sure each pasta noodle was coated with basil pesto. After seasoning the dish with salt and pepper, it was ready to serve.

Marvin seated himself across from Shadow. Mr. Jingles sat on the living room couch, where he could see Shadow and Marvin having their dinner. The cat didn't like Marvin much. There was always an uncertain vibe Mr. Jingles felt every time he was around Marvin. The man made him cautious. It was the reason why Mr. Jingles kept his distance from Marvin whenever he could.

Marvin, on the other hand, always wondered why the cat never came around to him. He would sometimes catch the cat staring, whether if it was during dinnertime, or out in the backyard sipping on iced tea—he was always staring at him.

"This tastes delicious, Shadow. Even better, if I must say," Marvin said, after taking his first bite. He smiled as he wiped the corners of his mouth.

"Thank you," she said without making eye contact.

She took a sip of soda and her eyes fluttered over to the living room. Mr. Jingles sat like a statue. He hadn't taken his eyes off of Marvin since he'd sat down. Shadow felt Marvin's eyes gaze upon her from his plate, which made her feel uncomfortable.

She continued to eat, pretending not to notice.

"Have you spoken to your parents since you moved here?"

She forked around a piece of penne before responding. "No, I haven't," she said as she looked up.

Why was he asking her this? He knew exactly the kind of relationship she had with them. Her mother was an uptight country club class act and her father was a biological scientist who was barely around.

"You should call them. They're worried about you," he said, pinning down pasta with his fork.

"I wonder why they're so concerned now, since we barely even spoke all last year."

Marvin chewed, knowing why Shadow's parents hadn't kept in touch with her.

Yes, they had a few dinners throughout the year and a phone call here and there when she lived in Pool View, but it was more of a formality than actually wanting to stay in touch. In reality it came down to this: Shadow wasn't the child they'd hoped for. In their eyes, they wanted a scholar, a doctor—a neurosurgeon to be exact—and they weren't too happy when she told them she was not going to marry Marvin. Her father surprisingly was more upset by the news than her mother was, from what Shadow recalled. The Hex family wanted their daughter to be the center of attention in Pool View. They wanted the folks of Pool View to speak highly of Shadow, to keep the legacy going. But, now, it was far from that.

"I miss you, Shadow," Marvin said, changing the subject. "You don't belong here. Pool View…that's where your home is. You are much safer there. That's where you belong."

Shadow looked Marvin dead in the eye, knowing it was far from the truth. "Really?"

Marvin wiped the corners of his mouth, reaching forward to his wine glass. He sensed the dead enthusiasm from the tone of her voice. He took a sip then placed the glass back on the table, keeping his focus on Shadow.

"I love you, Shadow, and I will never stop loving you. You need to come back home," he said pausing for a moment. "We'll have the big wedding we talked about. Kids. We'll have the whole picture perfect family you always wanted."

Shadow's forehead wrinkled at the thought of having a family with him.

"You kill people for a living and on top of that, you've been stalking me." She threw her hands up in the air. "What makes you think I would ever come back to you, or to Pool View?"

Marvin pushed back his chair, setting down his napkin on his plate. He leaned forward, keeping little distance between himself and Shadow. This was the Marvin she knew, the one who was going to make a threat, to make it clear who was in control.

"You're no different from me. You had our baby killed," he said through his gritted teeth. Marvin's veins bulged from his temples. He slammed his hand against the table, trying to control his rage, which had been building up since the moment he stepped through the door. "Either come home, or I'll make your life so miserable, it will be the *only* choice you have. I'm the only one who can save you when everything goes to a shit storm, dear."

Shadow stared right back, not blinking. This was all too familiar to her. She remained calm but her heart thrummed faster and louder in her chest. At a certain point, she was sure Marvin was able to hear her pounding heartbeat. Marvin didn't make empty threats. He would deliver on what he'd say he would do.

Now, her life had just become more dangerous.

Marvin got up and walked toward the door with a slow and steady pace. He glanced at Mr. Jingles out of the corner of his eye, who was ready to pounce if Marvin laid a finger on Shadow. Marvin picked up his blazer off of the couch, peering over his shoulder as he walked out of the door.

As the door slammed shut behind Marvin, Shadow hurriedly got to her feet, trotted to the door and locked it. She gawked up the staircase and listened for a moment to see if there was any sort of movement coming from upstairs. She didn't know every detail of the SEA or how they operated because Marvin shared only so little, but if there was a Secret Eye Agent present, most likely there were more around.

Shadow headed upstairs, aware there was a possibility there was an agent who rummaged through her belongings and laptop. By the time she reached the last step, she was short of breath. She looked through each room. There weren't any obvious signs of someone sneaking in. Everything looked in order. She examined her bedroom, trying to find something out of place; something she would know was out of place, but found nothing. Everything was exactly where she'd left it before she gone to work.

The agents were excellent. If they wanted to be noticed, they would leave a trace. But Shadow found no trace, which meant one of two things: Either she was under their watch every second of the day or she was tricked into thinking she was being watched.

Paranoia. One of the first tactics second floor agents learned to master.

* * *

Venice sat at Bernie's coffee shop, one of her favorite local coffee shops in Lake View. She knew the owner, Willow Marx, since high school. He had the biggest crush on Venice during their sophomore year, but at the time Venice had no interest in Willow, or any boy for that fact. Her parents geared her to focus on her education, knowing boys would come and go.

Her gaze was focused on the brownie and coffee in front of her. The vision she had was still engraved in her mind. The scene kept replying over and over in her mind and every single time, it made her soul cringe. Last night, she tossed and turned, feeling restless in the morning. All she could think of was Evan. She was torn between telling Evan what she saw and keeping it to herself, hoping her vision was far from the truth.

"You haven't touched your brownie, Venice," Willow said with concern, approaching her table.

"I don't really have the appetite for it, to be honest."

He took a seat in front of her. "What's on your mind?"

She noticed his eyes crinkled from the sides when he smiled. It was the first time she noticed it—odd, since she observed everything in sight. But Willow hadn't interested her any more than just a friend. She noticed the laugh lines, which formed over the years, and how his nose curved at the tip. His hair was silver, and thick. All these observations made Venice contemplate whether or not she was starting to develop feelings for Willow if not a crush.

"Nothin'." She smirked.

"Oh come on now, that's what us men say when we don't want to share what's really going on."

Willow was a fine looking gentleman. Venice remembered how the girls at school would chatter about how his sea blue eyes twinkled when he smiled. Willow had charm. His baby face, curved smile, and fair skin made him appear trustworthy, which he was.

"I just worry about Evan and Denise a lot. I know I shouldn't, given that they're all grown up now but I can't help it."

He frowned. "Well, you practically raised them after their parents died. I don't blame ya for worrying so much."

"Yeah," she said, her voice trailing off.

"I assure you everything will be all right, Venice. Think positive."

Venice nodded. "Do you ever do anything else besides babysit your employees?" she asked charmingly.

Willow grinned. "Now, what's that supposed to mean?" He

leaned back, enjoying Venice's beauty.

"You've been here your entire life. You should go out and explore the world. There's so much to see out there."

"You're the one to talk, Venice. *We've* both been here our entire lives and I know you haven't been on expeditions yourself either."

"Well, that's because I had to take care of the kids, remember? I never got the time."

"Yeah, I remember those days. You would bring them in here and they were the most well behaved kids I'd seen."

"It's only because of all the time I spent raising them," she said with a wink.

Willow thought about Venice's suggestion. "I don't know, Venice…" He paused, collecting his thoughts. "I've gotten comfortable where I am and I never really experienced anything out of my comfort zone. It seems tempting, though."

"Well, I think it's time to explore the unknown and before you say anything," she said, chuckling, "I'll also go on an expedition once I get things sorted out with the kids. And if you don't mind, I'm going to need a to-go box a little later," she said, pointing to the brownie.

"Yeah, no worries," Willow said, looking over his shoulder, making sure his customers were being attended to. "Are you waiting for someone?"

"Yeah," she said. "Evan called to meet him here."

"How's he doing, by the way?"

"Kids," she said. "They always have something new going on in their lives. I went by the other day and he had dug up the entire garden. He's landscaping." Venice chuckled. "He says he can do it on his own…I guess he's going to have to prove me wrong."

"Now, I see how much faith you *really* have in me," Evan chimed in, walking in from behind Venice.

Venice looked over her shoulder then peered back to Willow.

"You could have told me he was behind me," she sneered to Willow.

"Don't look at me, Venice, I'm a loyal man." He cackled. "I swear I would have said something if Evan hadn't shushed me."

Evan kissed Venice on the cheek and pulled up a seat beside Willow.

"How's it going, Mr. Marx?" he said, giving a slight pat on the back.

"Always doing good, son," Willow responded. "I'm assuming you're on vacation with all the teens who've been coming in and out of here for the last hour."

Evan snorted. "Yeah, we get a month off for winter vacation," he said, thinking of how ridiculous it was for high school students to be on a one-month vacation. He saw no need for that long of a break when the workload wasn't overwhelming. *Wait until these kids go to college, they'll experience the real stress*, he thought. "It's definitely difficult having nothing to do other than grading papers."

Venice and Willow both chuckled at Evan's response.

"Hey, if you need any help with that backyard of yours, give me a call," Willow said, getting up from his chair. "I gotta take care of that customer," he finished, looking in the direction of the man who'd spilled coffee all over himself.

"Thanks, Mr. Marx," Evan said. "I'll keep that in mind."

"Remind me to get you that to-go box, Venice," Willow reminded, grinning as he made his way toward his customer.

Venice could not help but smile.

"Clearly, he's into you," Evan said, pointing out the obvious after Willow was in the distance, "and has been for a while. I know you know, but you aren't going to admit it."

"I don't really have the time to date anyone."

He let out an exhausted sigh. "That's a load of crap,

Grandma. We both know it's not true."

"Hush," she said, trying to be stern. "You're different today. What's going on?"

"Yeah," Evan responded. "I think I've figured out why I've been having those memories."

She raised an eyebrow in curiosity. "Okay," she said. "Go on."

"You're not going to believe what happened today," he said. "You know, the house that was for sale next door…"

"Yes," she responded, waiting for the big drumroll.

"I met the neighbor and it turns out to be the same woman I married in a previous life."

Taken aback, she said, "Are you pulling my leg, Evan?"

"No, no," he said, leaning in closer, reassuring her he was in fact being serious. "Her name is Shadow. She moved here from Pool View."

She was confused. "Wait, hold on a minute. How do you know it's her?"

"When she looked me in the eye…I connected with her soul. I just knew it was her. She looked soo much like Samantha. I feel that the universe is giving me a chance to make things right."

"Hold on for a second there, hun," she said. Her forehead wrinkled in confusion. "What do you mean by that?"

"You've always said that everything happens for a reason, right?"

Venice agreed.

"I believe the universe is giving me another chance to make up for what I did in my previous life to her. I mean, it makes perfect sense. I've been having these specific memories of my past life for no apparent reason, and then out of all the possibilities, she's my new neighbor. The two and two go together."

"Okay. I can see why you would think that," she said, taking a moment to gather her thoughts. She reflected on the vision she had of Evan and what Bruce had informed her about. Shadow was definitely bad news. Thinking about Denise, she didn't want to see Evan get hurt. "Don't you think that's a little farfetched, though? You don't know what this woman is like, Evan. You don't know her story."

Evan sighed. "For the past couple of months, I felt like death knocked on my door and murdered my soul. I have to live with that pain every single day and even if I wanted to block it out by drinking or whatever, my mind replays that scene over and over again. I'm aware I'm not that same person, but I still feel that pain. As much as I want to block out every memory of my past, I can't." Evan remembered what he had put Samantha through. "Every day I wake up and I'm aware that it's all a dream but even when I've tried to push away that memory of me hurting her, I can't. I don't want to feel that way again. I know in my gut that this is the right thing to do. It's my chance to wipe my slate clean."

Venice looked at Evan, unsure about how to react to all of this. She knew Evan was the sensitive one. He always had been, but he didn't need to get involved with Shadow. Just because he had done something in his previous life didn't mean he was obliged to make up for it, now.

According to Bruce, Evan was a person of interest for some sort of investigation, Venice gathered. It was one thing to have a vision, but having Bruce inform Venice about keeping Evan safe, it concerned her even more. Something was going on. She didn't know exactly what it was but all she knew was Evan could not get involved with Shadow.

"How are you going to make things right? You don't know this woman. Are you going to tell her you were married to her? How would this work?"

"No," he said, leaning back in his chair. "That's a little insane. There's a reason why the universe brought her into my life again. Maybe she needs help?"

Venice shook her head in disagreement. "Don't you think this whole idea is a little insane? There's no need to look back and dwell on what you did. Move forward and do better in this life. That's what we're all doing…"

She took a sip, trying to keep her emotions in check. All she wanted to do was blurt out why he couldn't get involved with Shadow.

Evan observed Venice. She was more reserved than usual and not as talkative or friendly. Something wasn't making sense.

"Is there something you're not telling me, Grandma?"

"No," she lied.

"Then why aren't you being supportive?"

"In order to make up for your past, you have to do good things—make good karma, as some say. Do good in this life. I don't understand why you would want to get involved with someone from your previous life. Wouldn't that be repeating history?"

"I don't expect you to understand it," he said, agitated. "It's obvious the universe is giving me a second chance and I'm going to take it. I don't understand why you can't be happy I got the answer I was looking for. Six months of agony and pain. Maybe this is what I'm supposed to do to put an end to it."

Venice sighed. She could hear the certainty in his tone and knew Evan wasn't going to give up the idea easily. "It's just better to stay away."

"Why?"

She looked around, not wanting to bring attention. "This is not the place to talk about it."

"So, you are keeping something from me. What are you not telling me?"

Venice was stalling. She didn't want to tell Evan the real reason because of the consequences leading afterward, but she had kept so many secrets in the past that at times caused more harm than good. It made her debate what was really good in the long run.

"This is not the place to talk about it and I'm expecting my last patient in about fifteen minutes. I don't want to keep him waiting."

Evan nodded.

Venice got up, wincing at the cramps in her knees. She'd bruised them when she fell in the kitchen before she had the vision. She rubbed them gently, trying to ease the pain. And being as old as she was, didn't help the matter much either.

"You okay, Grandma?" Evan asked noticing.

"Oh yeah," she said brushing it off.

"You can't keep hiding things from us, Grandma. We can handle whatever comes our way. It's all part of life."

She peered into his eyes, knowing he was capable of taking care of himself, being thirty-one years old. It came down to the fact she knew too much. It had become a basic instinct to protect her grandchildren since the day Bruce left.

"I know, honey," she said, smiling and picking up the brownie. "Let me get a box for this."

"All right," he said feeling dissatisfied with how the conversation went. "I'll walk you out."

* * *

Later that evening, Evan sat in his office to grade the final exams and projects of the semester. He told himself the day they were released for winter vacation that he would finish grading everything by the weekend and then enjoy time off. Yet, the exams were still ungraded and all he could manage to think about was Shadow. He fiddled with his pen as he contemplated the questions that arose. He had questions that were beyond his comprehension, only because there were some things in the world that weren't meant to be understood.

Why did the universe bring Shadow to Lake View? What purpose did she serve him? What purpose did he serve her?

Evan shook away the thoughts and forced himself to focus. He went back on grading the essay he'd read over ten times on Antisocial Personality Disorder. Each student was free to choose a topic of their choice. This topic in particular was interesting because had Derek seen a psychologist, Evan was pretty sure Derek would've been diagnosed with ASPD. He showed all the signs for ASPD except for one: irresponsible work behavior. He didn't obey the law but worked above and beyond for his clients. It brought the question of *why*. ASPD as Evan knew was caused by a combination of genetics and environmental influences. Unfortunately for Evan, he didn't remember that far back in order to get the slightest bit of understanding as to why Derek was the way he was.

After staring at the essay, Evan pushed it aside having only read the first page. He leaned back in his chair and closed his eyes for a moment. His mind once again jumped to the one thing that kept it occupied at all times now: Shadow.

He wanted to know what her story was. Having met Shadow with the knowledge of being her husband in a previous life, made him believe they were put on each other's paths for a reason. To Evan, the timing of everything felt more than just a coincidence.

Grandma Venice's voice echoed in his mind as he tried to make sense of the situation. *"How are you going to make things right? You don't know this woman. Are you going to tell her you were married to her? How would this work?"* Venice had some valid points indeed, but still, Evan believed everything happened for a reason. Everything and everyone served a purpose. However it was up to the person to figure out what that purpose was and that irked Evan.

Out of frustration, Evan put the essay back on top of the stack with the rest. When he rose from his chair, he caught a glimpse of a silhouette from his computer screen. He froze. Evan didn't want to turn around knowing who it'd be. The hair on his neck and arms rose with each passing second. Finally, Evan brought himself to face the demon that haunted him.

Derek stood in the doorway, leaning against the doorframe, with that creepy grin Evan remembered from his flashbacks.

"It must be weird seeing Samantha for the first time in this life I bet. She's just as beautiful now as she was back in the olden days, wouldn't you say?"

Evan's heart dropped. He wasn't sure if he was hallucinating but his gut told him what he heard was correct.

"Do you have the urge to beat her the way you used to? Do you want to see her bleed, Evan?"

Evan frantically shook his head.

"We can both indulge in some violent acts. I know I want to. I want to squeeze her throat until her face turns pale. What do you think about that, Evan? Does that interest you?"

Evan's eyes widened with fear. His throat constricted, disabling him from saying anything. He wanted to scream, yell for help. Evan wanted to freak out but he stood in position. Even if he wanted to escape, he felt his legs were locked in place almost by force.

"No? How about…dunking her head in hot water? That seems a bit harsh. It would burn her face and take a lot longer to heal than a bruise. Then everyone would know I did something to my wife. No one would ever harm Samantha. Everyone loves her. Even Adrian. He wouldn't be too happy if you hurt her."

Oddly enough, Evan felt himself becoming claustrophobic. The room seemed to become smaller and Derek's voice rang his ears. Evan's heartbeat began to pace, almost out of control. He needed to get out of his office immediately. Derek wasn't real, not in this reality at least and yet he had some sort of power over Evan to the point where he couldn't handle Derek's presence.

Evan took baby steps toward the door, feeling as if they were made out of stone. The closer he got, Derek began to disappear into thin air. He felt the beads of sweat trickling down the sides of his face. Using the backside of his palm, he wiped them away as he walked down the hallway. As he approached the staircase, he felt the need to sit down for a moment before proceeding up the stairs. Evan slowly sat down on the staircase feeling overwhelmed and sad. He felt his chest was on fire and was on the verge of puking. Derek made him sick. Evan's head sunk to his knees and pressed his palm against his forehead. A part of him wanted to cry because deep down, he felt he was slowly loosing himself to this memory. There were times when he wondered whether he had invested so much time in figuring out what these memories meant that perhaps he convinced himself there was indeed something there. He was afraid of that. Then Venice and Denise would've been right all along and he would have wasted all his time on nothing. That was the reason Evan never shared Derek's visits with Denise or Venice. They would definitely think he had gone insane.

He also was aware of the fact that there was a chance he'd never understand any of it and these memories would continue to haunt him. And that's the way it was supposed to be. Over time, Evan would learn how to deal with the taunting memories. No doubt he would have to see a psychologist in the long run, but in the off chance he did come to understand why he remembered these memories and why Derek showed up randomly, he'd finally be at peace. And that's something he was craving for in the past six months. Peace.

After he took a deep breath, feeling calmer, Evan headed

upstairs to the bedroom, switching off the lights on his way up. He walked by his parents' bedroom where the door always remained open. Sometimes it felt as if one day they would come out walking through that door and surprise him. But that was something he knew never would happen.

It had been twenty-seven years since Denise and Evan's parents had passed away. His father's voice remained distinct. Sometimes he would hear him calling his name, when he was deep in thought. But it was just his mind playing a trick. Other times, when Evan was working in the backyard, he could hear his mother's voice, calling out for him to come inside for dinner. Evan though it was almost three decades ago since his parents' deaths, he still missed them dearly.

Once he brushed his teeth, washed his face, and put on his nightwear, he got into bed and lay there, thinking about his previous life. Who was Adrian? How did he fit into Derek and Samantha's life? After some time, his mind automatically wavered over to Shadow. She endured so much pain in her previous life. It made his heart sink knowing he was the one who caused her the strife.

An hour later, Evan drifted away to sleep.

＊

Marvin sat in his office across from a second floor agent. His eyes were focused on the flat screen that fit in the palm of his hand. He could see Shadow in the kitchen, washing dishes.

"You finished putting the cameras in all the bedrooms upstairs?"

"Yes, sir," answered the agent. "This one is in the backyard and it's angled in the direction of the kitchen. There are two in the front of the house."

Marvin nodded as he switched through the screens with the swipe of a finger.

Marvin could see the front entryway as well as the driveway from where the cameras were located. Now he had a close view of Shadow's life. He smiled as he plugged in the flat screen to his computer. This would come to use soon for Marvin. Timing was crucial. Other than that, he had what he needed. "Thank you for your services. I'll file a report and see how fast we can move you up to the third floor. You have improved in the last year." Marvin stood up, extending his hand. "You're dismissed."

The agent shook his hand. "It was a pleasure working for you, Agent 212."

With nothing more to exchange, the agent quietly walked out of Marvin's office, wearing a blue jumpsuit and a cap.

Marvin watched as the agent headed toward the elevator. The word SECURITY was written across his back. The jumpsuit was a ploy that would have worked on anyone in public. The dress shoes, which were specifically made for each qualified Secret Eye agent, had a tracking device installed inside the soles of the shoes. When on assignment or a mission, one of the job requirements for a first floor agent was to keep track on the assigned agent doing fieldwork. That way, if needed, there was a backup squad ready to move in and handle the situation. These cases hadn't happened in the agency, but were put in place as a precaution.

Marvin pulled up the file containing his execution plan.

Bruce had his hard copies, and was still overlooking his personal assignment. Marvin was going to carry out his assignment regardless and this time, no problem would arise.

He leaned back in his chair with a smirk across his face, knowing Shadow would come running back into his arms.

CHAPTER 11

It was 1932. In the winter, Derek's law firm held an annual charity event at Downtown Izabella, which was in downtown Pool View. It was a fancy, black tie occasion. The hall was decorated in white and gold. Flower vases filled with white tulips sat atop every surface, which was draped in shiny gold cloth that complemented the pearl place settings. In the front, a live orchestra played on the stage while everyone enjoyed themselves as they shared stories and drank champagne.

Samantha and Derek Will arrived hand in hand. Every woman in the room took one look at Samantha's glowing face and assumed the glow was a reflection of her happiness. All they could imagine was the fancy dresses, expensive jewelry, a big house—only because she was married to the richest lawyer in town—but no one knew the truth behind her smile. They didn't know the pain she felt through every bone in her body. No one knew what went on behind the closed doors of their home. But Samantha pretended to be happy…for Derek.

Maybe one day he'd fall in love with her again, just like when they first met. She had hope.

They made their way to their table, smiling and waving at everyone who greeted them. When they reached it, Derek pulled out Samantha's chair like a gentleman. It was crucial for Derek to be seen as a swell guy in the public's eye. It was hard to tear down someone's reputation when everyone saw a consistent side.

Derek whispered into Samantha's ear. "You don't leave this table, do you understand me? If you want a drink, you do not get up, do you understand? If you need to use the ladies room, you can once everyone is having dinner."

And all Samantha did was nod and smile. He treated her like a child. This was typical of Derek. She felt stupid for thinking Derek would actually let her enjoy this night.

Within seconds, Derek was mingling in a crowd of men and women who roared with laughter. She sat in her chair, trying to keep herself from breaking down. She looked around her and saw husbands laughing with their wives, sharing a kiss, holding each other's hands, all while she sat alone. Samantha gulped down her sorrow, fought back the tears, and tried her best not to look so lonely.

Adrian Will, a tall, handsome lawyer with striking good looks and a smile that made women's hearts melt, spotted Samantha sitting by herself. His eyes wandered over to the crowd nearby Samantha's table where he spotted his brother, who stood in the center of attention, telling stories.

Samantha scanned the room looking for no one in particular but felt as if someone was watching her. As her eyes wandered to the corner of the room she spotted Adrian standing with a glass of champagne in his hand, staring at her. He donned a three-piece suit, looking shaper than any of the other lawyers present at the charity event. His brown hair was parted and slightly gelled. Samantha held his gaze for a few seconds before looking away.

Moments later, Adrian stood before her, holding out a glass of champagne for her. His brown eyes twinkled as he peered into her eyes.

Samantha politely declined.

Adrian admired her for a moment before setting the glass on the table. "You look very beautiful tonight," he said, taking Derek's seat. Samantha smiled for a moment, the happiest she'd been since the incident. She looked away from Adrian, not wanting to make eye contact for too long.

Adrian studied her. Something was wrong. He sensed it.

"Hey," he said abruptly. He looked into her eyes, hoping he would see that she was in fact okay and perhaps was just not having a wonderful day. "Let's dance, shall we?"

Samantha shook her head, breaking eye contact just as quickly. Her eyes lingered back to the tables filled with people having a delightful time.

When he saw the sadness in her eyes, his heart sank. He knew something wasn't right. Adrian looked over his shoulder in Derek's direction. He wasn't going to notice Samantha was gone. Well, at least not for a bit before he went out looking for her.

"Come on, let's go," Adrian said.

"What?" she said, looking up at Adrian in confusion.

"You'll see."

"No. I'm not going anywhere."

Adrian raised his eyebrow. He wasn't going to take a no for an answer.

"What is it? Have your feet fallen asleep?" He chuckled.

"No," she said, glancing over in Derek's direction. She looked back at him, expecting him to know the reason.

"Then what is it, Samantha?"

She sighed. "I can't. Derek doesn't want me leaving the table."

Adrian nodded, and continued to nod like a bobble head as he searched around the hall. He looked for an escape route. He had come to Downtown Izabella numerous times for different events and knew every exit, entrance, and corridor. The timing had to be just right.

After scheming an escape plan to get out of the ballroom without attracting attention, he held out his hand, hoping he wouldn't have to convince Samantha once more.

Samantha, looking jittery, sighed as she rolled her eyes. Even though she knew he was persistent, Samantha hoped he would acknowledge the fact she was not in the mood to leave Derek's sight, aware of what he would do to her if she did. Samantha ignored his gesture as she rose up from her chair. Her black silk Chanel dress, with puffy sleeves, that hung halfway down on the shoulders, swept behind her as she walked.

Adrian led the way through the crowds. No one would see the two of them leave. Samantha followed. He grinned as he held the door for Samantha.

A rose bush garden was just outside of the ballroom. Derek's law firm planted rose bushes one spring as a community service event. Samantha remembered that day vividly. She had bought a floral dress to wear. She applied red lipstick as Derek waited for her downstairs, who was in a hurry to leave. Samantha, on the other hand, was in no rush. Excitement to go to another one of Derek's law firm's events was nowhere near as how Derek felt about this event. It was also the day he was going to be named partner. Had she known her husband was going to be celebrating a big accomplishment, Samantha would have not taken her sweet time getting ready.

Without a moment's notice, as Samantha stood in front of her mirror in their walk-in closet, wearing one of her fedora hats, she heard the door open and slam shut. Derek had left without her.

This was her first time seeing the rose garden since then.

"Why are we out here?"

Adrian journeyed on the grass to the middle of the garden, far from any entrance and exit. It was dark out. The streetlights illuminated just enough to make the pathway visible. There was very little chance of someone spotting Adrian and Samantha, let alone recognizing them.

Adrian broke into a smile.

"I wanted to be alone with you. You look so beautiful tonight." He grazed his hand against her cheek.

"Stop," she said, moving away. "I can't be out here with you."

"Why not?"

Samantha, ignoring his question, turned around, but before she could take a step away, Adrian pulled her in. He held her tightly, his hands grazing down her back.

"Adrian," she said, not wanting to leave his arms, "you need to let me go."

"Why, Samantha?"

She looked into his eyes for a moment, knowing how much he loved her.

"Because…" Her voice trailed off.

"Because what, Samantha?"

"I just want to be inside," she lied. "It's warmer in there," she pressed, trying to convince Adrian.

His voice quavered. "Is he hitting you again?"

Samantha didn't quite know what to say.

"Answer me, Samantha. Is he hitting you again?"

"Why would you ask me that?"

Adrian could sense the fear from the tone of her voice. Deep down, he already knew the answer.

"I love you, that's why." He gazed into her eyes slightly confused. "You know I love you, right?"

She sighed. "Yes…I know you love me."

He grazed his hands over her face and held her soft cheeks in his palms. He kissed her neck. Slowly Adrian traced his lips to her earlobe, gently nibbling, sending shivers down her spine. Samantha let out a whispered moan. Samantha held a firm grasp on Adrian's waist, wanting more. She felt they were the only two who existed at this moment. Finally, Adrian kissed her passionately. The kiss couldn't have been more perfect. He pulled back to stare into her eyes before locking lips again.

When he tugged her hips inward, Samantha flinched from the discomfort as he pressed against her spine. As much as she wanted to cry in agony, she couldn't let Adrian see her in pain. He took in this moment before he stepped back, admiring Samantha's beauty.

"I'll have my driver take you back to my home."

"Have you gone mad?"

"You'll be safer there. I need to take care of something."

Samantha was concerned. "What are you going to do?"

"Something I should have done a while ago."

Samantha tugged on his arm. "Are you out of your mind?"

Shocked, Adrian had become anxious about Samantha's decision to stay. Why hadn't she left Derek yet?

"I can ask you the same question! You don't deserve to be treated this way. He doesn't deserve you!" He couldn't begin to imagine the pain Derek had put her through. "I love you and I want to spend every living moment with you. I can't do that if you're still married to him!"

"Do we have to do this right now? I mean—"

"Why do you want to spend another day with him? Please explain that to me because I can't seem to wrap my head around it." She could hear the frustration in his voice.

"I don't want to," she whispered.

"Then let me take care of this. Just wait outside while I have my driver come and pick you up."

Samantha started to panic. She had no idea what Adrian was going to do, yet at the same time didn't really want to know.

"Wait, wait," she said. "Can't we just enjoy tonight? I don't want to ruin everyone's evening."

Adrian gritted his teeth. "You care so much about everyone else, you've forgotten about yourself. Samantha, he's taken everything away from you!" He paused for a moment, looking out into the field. "I want to wake up next to you for the rest of my life. I want you. I *need* you. I cannot have any of that if you're still with my brother." He sighed. He ran his fingers through his hair. "Do you still love me? Are you *in* love with me?"

Adrian fell in love the day Derek introduced Samantha to the family. She was off limits ever since. It was only until a year ago when he confessed his feelings for Samantha, when he couldn't keep them hidden any longer. To his surprise, she had felt the same way all this time. She was sure after she married Derek, her feelings would have gone away. But they didn't. They only grew over time.

Samantha took Adrian's hand in hers and responded, "Yes, I'm still in love with you. But please don't do anything tonight." She desperately needed Adrian to stay away from any trouble. She couldn't bear the thought of seeing Adrian hurt in any way.

Adrian was aggravated. "I have waited a year, Samantha, and every time, you say it's not the right time. It's always a different story. Are you even willing to leave him? What has he promised you that it is making it hard for you to leave?"

"You don't understand how dangerous he is. What if something happened to you?"

"Stop living in fear, Sam. Nothing is going to happen to me. Trust me, will you?"

"I can't bear to lose you," Samantha choked. "Adrian, I'm begging you not to do anything."

Adrian sighed. As much as he wanted to destroy and humiliate Derek in front of his friends and clients, he didn't want to upset Samantha any more than she already had been.

His eyebrows furrowed. "Fine," he uttered.

There was silence for a beat.

"Thank you," she said, fanning away the tears. There was silence between them. "Are you going to go back inside?"

"In a bit."

She studied his demeanor. Samantha knew Adrian wasn't too pleased with her but Adrian's safety was more important to her. She looked deeply into his eyes and kissed him on the top of his forehead. "I love you. Please don't stay out here too long." she said before heading toward the entrance. She lifted her dress as she walked, not wanting to get any grass stains.

Once she entered the ballroom, from a distance, she met Derek's gaze. He stood with a champagne glass in hand, watching her. His attention was focused on Samantha and no one else. A million things ran through his mind.

Samantha felt a knot form in her throat as she approached her table, knowing Derek's eyes lingered over her. She felt she had been caught red-handed. Was he on to her? Adrian and Samantha kept their affair under wraps—as to their knowledge. Now Samantha wondered if Derek knew of anything. He needed just a little bit of suspicion in order to track down a trail back to Adrian and Samantha's affair.

For the rest of the night, Samantha made small talk with the wives of wealthy and corrupt lawyers who came around to her table. She smiled and acted as if everything was picture perfect. Below the surface, she feared what was going to happen on the ride back home.

That night, Samantha stood in the bathroom, removing her earrings, carefully laying them down in the box. To her surprise, Derek hadn't said a word on the ride back home. She leaned forward, examining her face. The bruises were slowly fading, but she still needed extra cover up for some of the heavy wounds. It had taken a couple of days for the swelling to go down. Marks from the belt Derek whipped her with were still very present as she unzipped her dress. The redness had decreased in size, but the pain still stung.

She looked in the mirror to find Derek standing in the doorway, watching her as she examined herself. He was still dressed in his pantsuit.

"I'm sorry," he said, as he approached her.

When he neared Samantha, she became tense and stepped back as a precaution.

"Please don't come any closer," she begged.

"I'm sorry, Samantha. I don't understand what overcame me."

He continued to inch forward, in hopes of potentially rebuilding the trust with his wife.

"Please," she said. She shivered from the thought of Derek's hands on her body.

Derek's voice started to quaver. "I'm sorry, Samantha. I don't know what's happened to me. This is not like me. You know that, do you not?"

Samantha looked into his eyes, breaking eye contact after a moment. She didn't understand what was going on. He was forthcoming with his apology, something that was long overdue. But why now?

She nodded, apologetically. But all she needed was for Derek to leave her alone.

He moved closer. "Do you forgive me?"

Derek could feel the tension between them. Samantha looked uncomfortable, yet he believed the right words would gain back her trust and everything would go back to normal.

Samantha stepped back, looking away.

"I'm sorry for hurting you," he said, kneeling down as he pressed his palms together for forgiveness. "I'm sorry. Please, Samantha, forgive me. I don't know what came over me."

Derek's lips trembled. Tears shone in his eyes. Deep down, he knew he'd hurt Samantha. He knew how much she loved him and yet he took her for granted. He knew the things he'd done to her were inhumane and would have landed him in jail for years if it weren't for the people he knew. But because Derek always had an out, nothing stopped him from continuing with the offense.

"I'm sorry," Derek repeated.

And Samantha, believing there was still little good left inside the man with whom she once fell in love, believed him.

"Okay," she said. "I forgive you."

Her heart sank as Derek clung to her legs. She used all the strength in her body to prevent a nervous breakdown. Samantha clenched her jaw, feeling vulnerable; she didn't know exactly *what* to feel. This was the first time she had seen Derek cry.

He looked up at Samantha. "Please don't leave me," he sobbed.

She examined his face. "I won't."

Little did she know what was coming in the weeks ahead.

***

It had been a few weeks since the annual charity event. Derek had been pleasing to Samantha. He'd taken her out on dates and bought her new jewelry, a new dress. On the weekends, he even helped Samantha with the dishes after dinner. When they lay in bed, he'd wrap his arms around her, wanting Samantha to feel loved and appreciated, like any woman wanted. But yet, there was still that demon that resided inside of him and it would take a miracle to destroy that part of him.

It was midafternoon, long before she was going to start preparing dinner. She finished stocking up the pantry knowing how Derek never liked the idea of food shortage let alone money. She planned to make a bubble bath for herself, listen to some soft music, followed by a pedicure, but Derek had something else planned for her.

Deep in thought, she was startled by the front door slamming shut. Frightened, Samantha cautiously walked out into the living room to see who it was.

And there he was.

Samantha's heart dropped. She leaned against the wall to keep from fainting.

Derek pressed the gun against Adrian's head. "Would you care to explain what has been going on, Samantha?" Derek said in a calm tone.

"I told you, there's nothing going on between us," Adrian mumbled.

Derek shouted from the top of his lungs. "I didn't ask you, did I brother?"

He kicked Adrian hard enough to make Adrian fall to his knees.

"Derek, please, put the gun down," Samantha begged.

Her heart raced. She'd never seen Derek with a gun or was even aware he owned one.

"No!" he shouted. "Tell me. What have the two of you been doing behind my back?"

Adrian looked at Samantha helplessly.

Samantha wondered, had she listened to Adrian that night,

would this all have been avoided? Thoughts zoomed across her mind. The what-ifs and could haves. There wasn't a technical and logical answer to the questions that were rumbling through her mind at the moment. Unpredictable as Derek was, it was unclear what he was capable of. He wouldn't kill his own brother...would he?

Derek knew exactly how to manipulate Samantha and he had done it well. Scheming a master plan was one of his proficiencies.

"Derek," she said, fumbling for words, "nothing is going on, I swear to you."

"I saw the two of you."

Samantha tried to swallow, but the back of her throat had become so dry, it was impossible. The truth was, she didn't know when and to where Derek was referring. Was it in downtown? Had he followed her outside of the city where Adrian met up with her for a wine tasting event? They had gone to the hotel down Peach Lane numerous amounts of times. Adrian had taken Samantha horseback riding out in the countryside. They went on a hot balloon ride. He took Samantha out on his yacht. They had done a lot of activities as well as making sure to keep their relationship as discreet as possible. But it still begged the question: Where did Derek see them?

Samantha knew the truth would always come to light and it was the only thing that would set her free. But she wasn't ready to face the reality, not yet.

She was pregnant. Given that Derek and her hadn't been intimate for over a month, she needed a chance to rekindle their romance before it raised red flags in Derek's mind.

Samantha always envisioned raising a family of her own. It was the plan Derek and Samantha agreed on, but soon after, when things started to change in their marriage, that dream had become a fantasy. She only imagined what life could have been like if she had babies. It was only after Adrian came into her life that her dream had come alive again.

"Where?" She tried to look confused as possible. There were many possible answers to his question.

Her heartbeat pounded through her ears. She couldn't think clearly.

"You know exactly where." His agitation grew. "Tell me what is going on or I will blow his brains out, right here, in front of you."

After quick thinking, she strategically responded. "We were discussing your birthday party. Adrian wanted to throw you a surprise party but I didn't know if it would work, since your birthday is on a weekday and you tend to come home a bit late. I wanted all of your friends and family to come, but I wasn't sure if it was possible." She paused for a moment. "That's it."

Derek let her explanation sit in his mind for a moment.

Samantha could see the sudden change in Derek's demeanor. A part of him believed Samantha. He had become less tense. He slowly lowered his gun, looking at Adrian, who had been silently thanking Samantha for the exceptional save she made, under the circumstances she was put in.

"Get up, Adrian," Derek ordered.

Samantha, wide eyed, watched as Adrian dusted himself off. He looked at her, and mouthed the words 'thank you'. She subconsciously placed her hand over her stomach. She still needed to tell Adrian she was carrying his child.

Derek chuckled as he looked at his gun.

CHAPTER 12

It was Tuesday morning and Evan awoke, kicking and screaming, drenched in sweat and heart racing. He sat up straight, looking over his shoulder to see a damp spot on his pillow.

Now he knew who Adrian was.

How could he do that? *How?*

The image of Derek pointing the gun at Adrian kept reappearing in his mind and sent shivers up his spine. Evan squinted his face, forcing the image out.

He sat at the edge of his bed, with his head sulked down to his chest. How could any human being point a gun at their own sibling? He was flabbergasted and his heart was still beating out of his chest.

Slowly crawling out of bed, he peered at the clock and just like every time he woke, it was 3:30 in the morning.

He stumbled to the bathroom, doing what he had to do every morning at 3:30. Evan flipped the light switch, then looked at himself in the mirror. He leaned forward against the sink. Derek was a piece of work. He wasn't a stable man, emotionally or mentally.

Evan turned the knob and waited as the water started to
warm up. He pondered the memory. There was a part of
Derek that was messed up and only an insight of his childhood
would help Evan understand why Derek found pleasure in
hurting someone who loved him. Adrian seemed the opposite
of Derek, which meant there was a difference in how they
were brought up. However, Evan had no insight of Derek and
Adrian's childhood, which put him in the dark.

There was a part of himself that he hated, even though he
was no longer Derek Will. Evan couldn't build a time machine
and go back in time and fix what he had done to Samantha,
but it was something he wanted to do. His stomach churned
in disgust.

After drying his face, Evan entered his bedroom, feeling
the need to get some fresh air. He pulled out his hoodie from
the middle drawer and slipped it on. He traveled down the
stairs, slipping into his sneakers then making it out through
the front door. It was peaceful outside. The night was cold.
The stars danced around in the sky, making the night all more
beautiful. Evan walked further and found someone sitting on
the curbside wearing what looked like a gray hoodie and pink
sweatpants, with their knees propped up. This was new. Of
all the times he'd come out during the middle of the night,
no one ever appeared to be out there. He was always alone,
which was nice. Skeptical, he walked in the person's direction.
As he neared, with the streetlights shining down, he realized
who it was.

"It's not safe to sit on the sidewalk all alone, you know?" he
chimed.

Shadow looked up and laughed under her breath. She
raised an eyebrow. "Then come join me and we can be rebels
together."

Evan crouched, planting his butt on the cold cement. He

left some distance between the two of them as a courtesy. "Rebels?" he said out of curiosity. "I get the feeling you weren't rebellious when you were a kid, huh?"

Shadow laughed. "It's that obvious?"

"I studied psychology. The way someone says something, their word choice, their body language, it all forms a language of its own," he said with a smirk.

"Oh jeez. I should be careful about what I say around you then."

"Let's just say I'm not a psychic."

"In my defense, I was the only child so my parents had high expectations of me. I did everything they told me to up until college. That's when I took a stand. Otherwise I would be some sort of doctor. I'm guessing you were pretty rebellious growing up, huh? Your parents probably looked forward to your bedtime." She giggled.

"My parents weren't around for it," he said, pausing for a moment. "They died when I was four years old, two weeks apart from one another. My grandma was the one who raised my sister and me. I did give her a hard time. I would jump from couch to couch. I tried to start a fire in the backyard with sticks a couple of times. I did a lot of little things like that."

She rested her chin on her arms and looked at him.

"You lost your parents when you were four?" she said with the slightest bit of shock in her voice.

He looked at her and responded, "Yeah."

"I can't imagine what you went through. You were *so* young." She examined his eyes for a brief moment. She didn't feel Evan was completely healed from his parents' loss—and to her, as someone who hadn't experienced the loss of a loved one, it was odd in a sad kind of way.

"I was."

They sat in silence for a moment not feeling awkward with

one another. They were perfectly content with sitting side by side.

"Why couldn't you sleep?" she asked after a while.

Evan contemplated how to respond. He simply couldn't tell her the truth, but didn't want to lie either. "I have a bad habit of waking up in the middle of the night. How about you? How come you couldn't fall asleep?"

Her mind jumped straight to Marvin's visit. "Life."

Evan laughed. "That was sitting at the tip of your tongue, wasn't it?"

Shadow giggled and gazed into his eyes that appeared more a darker shade of blue. She let out a deep sigh before she responded. "I guess." She studied his face. There was something about Evan that felt familiar. She gazed at him before continuing. "I just wonder if I made the right decision. Maybe you can help me since you studied psychology."

Maybe you can help me. That was something that was going to be stuck in Evan's mind.

He looked down at the pavement and then back at Shadow. "How can I help?

"My entire life, I grew up in a controlled environment. I did as I was told and the minute I started to do things that I wanted, there was friction and tension. I wanted to make my parents happy, you know, but I wanted to live my life too. I just have a habit of pleasing people and I forget about myself sometimes and I never learned how to confront an uncomfortable situation. I walk around it because it's easier to do instead of actually talking about the problem and resolving the core issue." She paused for a beat to collect her thoughts. "I moved here because it's far away from everything that isn't right in my life. I just don't know if I'm running away from my problems or actually making a decision that's best for me. I don't want to be running away from things, you know?"

He looked out into the neighborhood. His eyes panned down the street before focusing on the house right in front. "You said 'everything that wasn't right.' I don't think you're necessarily running away from your problems. You began to make your own choices at some point in your life. It's your parents who had the problem. Friction and tension was created on their end when you began to make your own decisions—and yes, it's an instinct to please your parents. However, you can always learn how to face problems head on and you probably have before but because the end result didn't go as you thought it would, you made a choice that led someone other than you to be unhappy. So it can feel like you aren't resolving the issue when in reality, you have. It just didn't go the way you thought it would, which makes it hard to decipher whether or not the issue's been resolved.

"But you said 'everything that wasn't right in my life,'" he continued. "That tells me that there's something deeper that you're dealing with that made you pick up and move here. Normally, people wouldn't move out of a city only because there was tension and friction between their parents."

Her mind immediately jumped back to Marvin. He wasn't right for her. *He* was the main reason why she'd moved to Lake View.

"Yeah, you're right but…"

"But what?"

Shadow sighed. "There's more to the story. I don't think I want to talk about it right now though."

Evan nodded.

Maybe you can help me. The words lingered in his mind.

"Okay, Shadow. We don't have to talk about it but if you ever want to, I'm right next door." He let out a soft chuckle and met her eyes. "Just don't be ashamed."

Shadow nodded. She then asked with a smile, "Since we're

out here, and we both can't fall asleep, you wanna play a game of twenty questions?"

The corners of his mouth turned upward. "Sure." He chuckled. "I've got a hunch you're gonna ask me some embarrassing ones."

She laughed, knowing how true it was. "C'mon, it'll be fun and I'll get to know you a little better. I'll start." She thought about her question. It had to be a good one. A question that would lead to some insight in Evan's life. "If you could go back in time and change one thing, what would it be?"

"That's a hard one," he admitted. Aside from the fact of changing his past life, there wasn't anything he wanted to change. "On the top of my head, I'd say…jeez…I can't think of one."

"C'mon, think harder!"

Evan laughed. Shadow had become more enthusiastic within the last few minutes—a side that was novel to him. She was like a playful schoolgirl and he liked it.

"All right. The one thing I would change if I got to go back in time would be the time when we went skinny-dipping. It was with my buddies and the girls we were seeing at the time."

"Skinny-dipping?" she teased. "I wouldn't imagine you as a skinny dipping kinda guy."

Evan smirked. "It was a *long* time ago. It was during my junior year at college and we decided to go celebrate after finals. One of my friends had the bright idea to go skinny-dipping. Long story short, after I went in, one of my best friends ran off with my clothes and not to mention, I brought the girl I was dating along too. I guess it was a good way to break the ice."

Shadow laughed. "Oh my god! That's so horrible!"

Evan chuckled. "Yeah. It was pretty embarrassing. I had to walk butt naked all the way back to the car, with nothing but my hands to cover up. My friend ended up giving me my clothes before we headed back only because he didn't want my naked butt touching his car seat. I was pretty pissed at him for about ten minutes." He grinned. "Now, it's my turn."

"Let's see what you've got."

"If you could pick up any talent and make money off of it, what would it be?"

"Singing. I *love* to sing." She giggled. "I always wanted to be a singer, but I don't have the voice. It's not horrible but it's not all that amazing either."

"A singer," he thought aloud. "Have you ever entered a competition?"

Embarrassed, she nodded.

"Did you win?"

"No, I didn't win. I came in second."

"Second place isn't so shabby. Wait, how old were you during the competition? It doesn't count if you were five or six."

She playfully rolled her eyes and looked out into the street. "I was a senior in high school for your information."

"If you came in second, then you must be really good, assuming the winner landed a record deal afterward."

"I don't know about the record deal but he's married with two kids now."

"Let's hear it."

"Hear what?"

"Sing something."

Her face flushed. "No way. Absolutely not."

Evan laughed. "Why not? It sounds like you're really good."

Shadow shook her head with the widest grin on her face. "I'm not going to sing. Ask me again in a hundred years or so."

Evan chuckled. "Fine. But I will get you to sing one day."

"We'll see," she flirted. "It's my turn now."

"Fine. Shoot."

"What's one thing that people don't know about you?"

"Umm...another hard one. Where do you come up with these questions?" He shot Shadow a boyish grin. Secretly he loved that Shadow wanted to know more about him, more than what was at surface level. "Let's see..." he wondered out loud. Evan thought about it for a moment. There were a couple of things that not a lot of people knew about him. "I still sometimes have trouble accepting my parents' death. As a psychology teacher, you would think it's something that would be easy to understand and accept, but I don't know why sometimes I have a hard time with it."

Shadow let his answer sit for a minute. "Maybe it's cause you lost both of them within a span of two weeks?"

Evan shrugged. "Maybe. I have a tendency to chase after reasoning. There's always a reason why things happen, right? I think I've been looking for the reason and that's why I've never gotten closure. Denise, on the other hand, accepted it a long time ago, which makes me wonder if there's a part of me that's in denial and that's why I haven't accepted their death. I mean, what reason did God have to take my parents away from us so quickly?" He sighed and looked at Shadow with a hint of sorrow in his eyes. He wanted answers he knew he was never going to get. "Do you believe in God?"

She turned to Evan with a half-smile. She rested her head on her knees and sighed. "To be honest, no. I'd like to though," she said, lifting her head, "but when I think about everything that has happened in my life, I don't see him there. If I did, I wouldn't have to go through so much alone, you know?"

"I get where you're coming from."

Evan learned more about Shadow in the next hour than a person would have on their first date. She had a sense of humor, was easygoing and adventurous. Evan admired who she was and became fond of her personality. He came to know how much she loved wine. She wanted to travel and explore the unknown parts of places that people overlooked. She loved simplicity over everything else.

Evan shared what it was like growing up and being raised by Grandma Venice. He shared the struggle of not having a male figure in his life, even though Mr. Brar filled that role over time. Yet, the love from a father for his son was something that couldn't be forged. Evan realized the shortcomings of not having parents in his life at an early age. In return, Shadow shared what it was like growing up in Pool View as an only child and having everyone at her beck and call. Her life and lifestyle indeed was completely different to Evan's and everyone he knew. But there were some things that clearly held her back, and he desperately wanted to know what they were.

Maybe you can help me. Those words had lingered in the back of his mind since that night.

* * *

Evan had been digging for hours out in the cold. It was 4:00 in the afternoon. The sun was barely visible and at times, it was fully naked, which not only brightened up his mood, but it made working out in the yard a lot easier. Had it been like this throughout the entire day, it would have made his work more bearable.

As he leveled the ground with a rake, he pondered his conversations with Shadow and Venice at the coffee shop.

Just like Shadow, Venice was keeping something hidden. Although it wasn't unusual for Venice to hide things from him or Denise, this time, she was willing to tell Evan the reason. It was odd. The question "why" lingered in his mind and he was forced to wait.

Lost in thought, Evan hadn't realized Shadow's cat, Mr.

Jingles, found himself roaming around in his backyard. Mr. Jingles caught Evan's attention as he grazed his leg, softly nudging Evan with his tiny head. Evan looked down and saw Mr. Jingles peering up at him, patiently waiting to be played with. Seeing the most innocent creature made him smile. Evan walked to the edge of the fence and rested the rake against it. Mr. Jingles followed, wanting Evan to scratch him behind the ears like the other day. When Evan did, the cat purred.

Evan enjoyed the company of animals. Growing up, as much as he wanted an Alsatian, Venice, terrified to the core of huge animals, especially dogs, didn't allow Evan to keep a dog. "I'm allergic to animals," she would say just to end a conversation about getting a puppy.

Evan observed Mr. Jingles, who sat down in front of him, his tail swaying side to side. Mr. Jingles looked at him as if Evan was expected to give him some sort of treat for being such a good guest.

I don't have any treats for you, man, he thought. *I wish I did. Where's Shadow by the way?* He stared deeply into Mr. Jingles' eyes, almost daydreaming about the cat's owner. He wanted to see her but didn't know how to quite go about it. Her resemblance to Samantha had made things more complicated, which only drew Evan more to her.

Moments later, Evan was standing in front of Shadow's doorstep, holding Mr. Jingles in one arm. He rang the doorbell and patiently waited for Shadow to open the door.

Seconds later, the doorknob started to turn. Shadow stepped out from the doorway, having eyes only for Mr. Jingles.

"I've been looking for you everywhere, mister," Shadow said with great relief.

Evan handed Mr. Jingles over to Shadow. To Evan's surprise, Shadow appeared to be as panicked as a mother who had lost her child at the supermarket.

"I found him roaming around my garden. If I knew you were looking for him, I would have brought him over sooner," he said smiling.

"Thank you so much for bringing him back," she said thankfully.

"Yeah, no worries."

"Moving to a new city and all, he's the only thing I've got here."

"I bet it's hard," Evan said, shoving his hands in his pockets.

Shadow smiled as she softly stroked Mr. Jingles' coat. "Would you like to come in?"

Evan waited a moment before answering, just so he didn't seem so eager.

"Yeah, sure," he responded.

Mr. Jingles mingled around as they sat across from each other in the living room.

Evan noticed there weren't any photos hanging up on the wall. Shadow's voice echoed in his mind. *I moved here because it's far away from everything that isn't right in my life.* What was it that she was running away from? *It's better to stay away.* Grandma Venice's voice seemed to push itself forward. There was something definitely missing and from what he gathered from their conversation seemed more of an acceptance issue with her parents. But it wasn't novel. There were always going to be some differences between the children and their parents. It was all part of growing up. So that wasn't it.

He went over his theories again in his mind. *Everything that isn't right in my life.* She moved six hours away from her parents because of their relationship? No. That didn't sound right or reasonable. Although everyone did certain things that were unreasonable in the face of society, Shadow's choices didn't fall into the norm.

There were still missing pieces to the puzzle.

Shadow looked to him with a smile. "So," she said, slapping her hands against her thighs, "what can I get for you? To be honest, my fridge isn't stocked, so I don't have much to offer, but name your drink and I'll see if I have it or not."

Evan chuckled. "Umm...if you have water, that would be great."

She smiled, getting up. "That I do have."

He looked down at his shirt, seemingly forgetting he had dirty clothes. He'd sat down on Shadow's couch without any hesitation as if it were his own. This wasn't good. He knew how women were, not to mention he'd lived with two of them most of his life. The glares and scoldings came rushing back, mostly from Venice. He'd had one girlfriend who had major OCD. That relationship ended with Evan getting the boot because he wasn't "clean enough," as she put it.

Shadow walked back into the living room with a glass in hand.

"Here you go." She handed the glass to him, and then sat back down in front of him.

"Thank you," he said, lifting the glass up in the air before taking a sip. He shifted his gaze to his dirty white shirt and jeans. "I apologize for potentially ruining your couch with my muddy clothes. I was doing some work out back."

Shadow threw up a hand, dismissing his concern, but showed appreciation. "When do you think you'll have it completed?"

Evan took another sip before responding. "I'm hoping, if everything goes as planned, to have the backyard all done by the end of winter vacation." He looked around the table. "Do you have a coaster I can set my glass on?" Grandma Venice always scolded him for not using coasters. Not that he cared for coasters since he didn't own any himself, but it was always nice to ask.

"It's okay. You can just set it there," she said.

Shadow rose from the couch and started toward the hallway. She turned around midstride. "Can I show you something?"

The way she spoke was eccentric.

"Sure."

He rose from the couch and followed her. He would have followed her anywhere, as a matter of fact. She was compelling.

Shadow stood in front of the back door that led out to the garden. Evan stood beside her and viewed the garden. There was nothing but tall grass and a little patio made out of cement.

Evan knew the old neighbors who now lived in Brickwood. Brickwood was secluded and quieter as opposed to Lake View. Mainly the retirees and people who enjoyed the countryside moved to the outskirts. It was a beautiful and peaceful place to visit in Evan's opinion. Zack's ice cream parlor became a major hit a few years ago, which attracted more people to the city itself. Now, more and more people were opening mom-and-pop shops in Brickwood, creating traffic to a town in which the people were happy without.

It didn't come to a surprise his neighbors didn't do much landscaping. They were old and most likely didn't care much about the appearance of the backyard. They had no kids, so no one really came around and most of their friends slowly moved to Brickwood anyway. It was only a matter of time until they made the move as well.

He shifted from one foot to the other. "Wow."

"I know. That's what I said when I first saw the place. How much would it cost for the landscaping?"

Evan subconsciously crossed his arms at his chest. His brow furrowed as he made basic calculations. "A few grand if you're looking at putting in some new grass and redoing the patio. You could probably make a raised flowerbed if you wanted in the corner and add a walkway in the middle. That's my professional opinion."

He knew he hit a home run when Shadow laughed.

"A professional?" she asked, raising an eyebrow.

Evan scratched an imaginary itch on his chin, trying hard to disguise his smirk. "I have the magazine to prove it."

He looked at Shadow with a boyish grin, unaware it was making Shadow nervous.

Shadow quickly looked away, feeling her cheeks flush. "A few grand huh?" She let her words sink in. She didn't have that kind of cash sitting in her bank account for landscaping. She still needed to buy more furniture to fill in the empty spaces. It didn't quite feel like home yet.

"Yeah. I know a guy who can do it for nearly half the cost but because he's so cheap, his schedule is often backed up. It all depends on how badly you want to fix that," he said, pointing at the weeds. "I can put in a good word for you and see if he can fit you in."

Shadow turned and faced him. She was taken aback by Evan's sincerity. "I would really appreciate that. Do you think he would be able to come in this week for a consultation? I'm guessing I'd have to book an appointment for a consultation, huh?"

Evan smirked. "I'm usually free in the afternoons for consultations."

Evan saw the expression on Shadow's face change from appreciation to utter disgust.

She shook her head and tried to hide the wide smile that only seemed to set in deeper every second. "I can't believe I let you pull one over me," she said.

Evan laughed. "But seriously, I can find someone for you who will do a better job than I can."

"I would appreciate that."

His eyes moved to her laptop with a pen and paper sitting beside it. "Let me guess. You brought work home with you."

Shadow looked over her shoulder and responded, "I'm working on a nursery for a new client and the specifics are killing me."

"What are the specifics?"

"They only want to use pearl white and gold as for their colors. So basically all the furniture is going to be white along with some other gold furnishings, like photo frames, and curtain railings. I'm thinking of a gold ceiling, which will make the room pop, and make the bottom trim gold too. It'll be different but unique, but the main issue I'm having is creating an efficient closet. That's what I'm stuck on right now."

Evan crouched to eye level and examined the sketches on the screen.

"Do you mind if I move some things around here?" He looked up at Shadow for approval.

"Be my guest."

She watched as Evan scrolled over to the closet and cleared her layout. Within minutes, she was looking at something completely different. Something even she wouldn't have thought of. Evan placed an island in the middle of the closet because it was big enough. He removed most the shelves and replaced them with two closet rails, making more room to hang clothes. On top he placed a board for storage and added built-in drawers on the bottom that lined the entire closet.

He gazed over at her, pursing his lips. "What do you think about that?"

Shadow was left speechless. She didn't want to admit it but Evan was a better interior designer than she. "How did you— how did you do that?"

"I just moved the mouse around and clicked here and there."

She placed her hands on her hips and shook her head. She

tried hard to muster her laugh, but failed. "You just know how to do everything, don't you?"

He chuckled as he rose, meeting her eyes. It was at this instant when he realized he'd never seen anyone so exotic and beautiful. Her eyes twinkled as she peered into his. Then all of the sudden he forgot the English language. There was a moment of silence. What he was about to do next took him by surprise. "Would you like to grab a cup of coffee sometime— or dinner?"

Suddenly he felt his confidence shatter into pieces. The worst that could happen was she'd reject him and then he'd have to give the awkward wave and smile every time they'd run into each other. Now, he'd wished he'd just kept his mouth shut. But, he had the feeling she liked him too. Then, there was a chance that he was wrong and Shadow was just being a nice host, a good neighbor. He looked away for a second, not trying to look too desperate or eager for a response.

Then she responded. "Yeah, I would love that."

The corners of his eyes crinkled as a smirk appeared across his face.

"How about sometime this week?"

"How about this Friday?" she said, maintaining eye contact. "I get off at 5:00." She slid her hands in her back pocket as they started toward the front door.

"Perfect. I'll pick you up at 5:30 then."

He smiled and reached for the knob.

Once he opened the door, the cold air crawled in. As he walked across the lawn, he turned back and waved.

Shadow waved back and closed the door behind her, feeling ecstatic. He had the ability to make her forget all about her worries and problems. She headed back to the kitchen table, and carefully looked over at the nursery. Evan left her amazed by how quick he'd changed the closet.

Shadow stared at her computer with a grin, putting the project on the back burner as Mr. Jingles sat and watched. She bit her lip as she thought about Evan and dinner Friday night. But before she could fantasize any further about her handsome next-door neighbor, she was disrupted by a knock at the door. Without a second thought, she quickly sprinted to the door.

When she opened the door, there stood Marvin with a devious smirk appearing across his face. As always, he was dressed in a suit and a tie.

CHAPTER 13

S hadow," he said with a malicious smile. Before Shadow could react, Marvin welcomed himself in, eyeing Mr. Jingles.

"What are you doing here?" She shut the door behind her, knowing she was powerless when he was around. Though she stood her ground, making sure it was obvious she was not going to take any orders from him.

"I see you've met your neighbor, Evan Storm." He paused for a moment, looking around the place, as if something was missing. "How come you haven't hung up any of our pictures, darling?"

Marvin knew exactly how to enrage Shadow and it worked.

She clenched her jaw, holding back the scream she had been wanting to let out the last time he came waltzing in.

"Why are you here?" she repeated, this time raising her voice.

Marvin ignored her question and made his way to the kitchen. The only choice Shadow had was to follow him. At this point, she wanted to strangle him. She imagined choking him until his face turned blue, but next to Marvin, she was a puny woman.

"It's funny how both of our jobs require us to work with clients," he said as he looked at the laptop screen. "Is your client a pain in the ass as well?"

"No. My clients are a delight to work with," she said, pulling her hair back, feeling her anxiety rise.

Marvin examined the walls—all empty. "How come your house is so plain? There's no personality here. It doesn't feel like a home."

Shadow crossed her arms at her chest, rolling her eyes.

"What do you want from me, Marvin?"

"What do I want from you," he said, thinking out loud. "What do...I...want...from...you... Now that's a question with a variety of answers, don't you think?"

"You're a very complicated person. So, yeah, I would think so."

"You need to come back to Pool View with me," he said, pacing back and forth, his head lowered. "We will get married. Mother will take care of all the arrangements, invitations, so on and so forth. Then we can start our family."

She cringed. "I'm not going back!"

"What was that?" He arched his face in Shadow's direction. His pupils dilated with rage.

"I said I'm not going back and there's no way in hell I'm gonna get married to you."

"Oh is that so, Shadow?"

Shadow stood with her arms crossed at her chest. She glared at Marvin with fear still instilled in her. "There's going to be no wedding. I'm not moving to Pool View. This is my home now and I'm not leaving."

Marvin shrugged. "Okay, if you say so. But let me make something clear," he said, slowly walking to Shadow with his hands in his pockets. "If you continue to stay here in this dump you call your new life, you will find yourself struggling to breathe. You're going to come crawling back to me because this place is only going to remind you of all the horrible memories. Evan, on the other hand, is going to wish he was never born."

Shadow's eyebrows furrowed, disgusted at hearing how pathetic Marvin was. His obsession with her had hit a new low.

"I'm not scared of your threats anymore, Marvin. You don't scare me."

"Well, it certainly seems like someone has been brushing up on their bravery skills." He chuckled, scratching the tip of his nose. Marvin's eyes lingered over to the couch, slowly bringing back his attention to Shadow. "I would rethink about getting cozy with your new neighbor, since it will not last too long."

Shadow marched over to Marvin, close enough to hear him exhale. "Get out of my house," she hissed through gritted teeth.

"It will be my pleasure," he whispered. "I hope you consider my offer, otherwise your life is going to become much more difficult, starting from this moment onward." He glared at Shadow with sincerity and continued, "I'm the only one who can give you a peaceful life."

Every fiber in Marvin's body wanted to drag Shadow out by the hair. He clenched his fist and resisted the urge to hurt her. With nothing else left to say, Marvin let himself out, with pride in his walk.

Shadow was left standing in the kitchen, trying to grasp what just happened. Just a few moments ago, she was merely enjoying Evan's company, and within moments, that memory was tarnished by Marvin's visit.

She slowly proceeded to take a seat. Everything was starting to hit her. Marvin was right. He would do anything in his power to tear her apart. He made people want to end their own lives—this is what he did for a living. And he *would* make Shadow surrender, which would be a piece of cake. He had his tactics and ways of getting Shadow to fall apart.

Deep down, Shadow knew the end was near. She could choose to put up a fight, and fail in the end, or she could just pick up and move back to Pool View.

Marvin would go to great lengths to send her a message if she didn't obey his orders, and now Evan would be caught in the middle of this.

Shadow folded her arms on the table and put her head down. *Why is this happening to me?* she asked herself. *What did I do to deserve this?*

Angry and frustrated, all she wanted to do was scream at the top of her lungs and for someone to come in and save her. Save her from the grueling living nightmare she was facing. That's what she needed. She needed saving. But there was no one she could turn to for help. She was all alone, and the thought brought tears to her eyes.

***

Later that evening, Mr. Brar wheeled his way out onto the porch to get some fresh air. He was bundled up in a scarf and a sweater. It wasn't as frigid as it was the day before but he didn't want to risk catching a cold. He examined the neighborhood. He was well aware of every person who walked down Knight's Drive, and he knew the type that sparked a red flag. Earlier, he'd seen a man driving an ice cream truck up and down the street, which he noted. It made Mr. Brar chuckle because he'd known exactly what time the ice cream truck came around the neighborhood. It certainly wasn't around this time of the day. It was obvious an agent down at the SEA didn't do a splendid job in hiring a second floor agent to do field work.

***

Evan walked out into his front yard with a cold beer to get some fresh air before heading back inside. He'd showered and changed into a clean pair of clothes after working on the garden for the past few hours. The only thing that was on his mind was Shadow. Her presence occupied a huge chunk of his mind. It seemed as if nothing else mattered. The essays sat in his office yet to be graded.

The cool breeze brushed against his face, making him feel refreshed. He observed, seeing no one in sight until he looked to his left and spotted Mr. Brar sitting on the porch, deep in concentration. He took a sip as he tracked across the grass. "How's it going, Mr. Brar?"

Mr. Brar responded without breaking his focus. "I stepped out to get some fresh air, son. How was your evening?"

"Oh, it was an interesting one," Evan replied, cracking his neck as he trudged up Mr. Brar's porch steps. He stood in front of the porch with one foot on the step. "I met the new neighbor."

That caught Mr. Brar's attention. He craned his neck sideways, looking down at Evan. "You did?"

"Yup," he said, lifting the tip of the bottle to his lips.

The conversation Mr. Brar had with Bruce lingered in the back of his mind. "What are they like?"

"She is…very unique," he said. The corners of his mouth turned upward as he took another sip.

"Unique? How so?" he asked, scanning the streets subtly with his eyes. He noticed something particular at the corner of the street.

"I don't think I can explain it."

Mr. Brar did a once-over at Evan before looking out at the street again. He didn't know the backstory of the new neighbor, but he was skeptical. "Son, is it safe to assume you're becoming fond of this new woman?"

A corner of his mouth lifted. "I am."

Mr. Brar pondered on Evan's response for a bit. Something didn't sit well with Mr. Brar. There wasn't much he could do or prevent from happening, but he'd hoped Bruce was getting to the bottom of this. He saw Evan grow up, attended his graduations and the birthday parties Venice threw for him before he'd become too old for party hats and balloons. He couldn't bear the thought of the SEA getting their dirty hands on Evan.

"I should get going. I need to get up early and work on the garden."

"How's the garden coming along, anyway?" he asked, peering up at Evan.

"Let's just say that I'm making progress." He chuckled.

"As long as you're keeping yourself busy, son."

Evan smiled. "Have a good night, Mr. Brar. You should go inside too. It's chilly out here."

Evan started to make his way over to his home.

Mr. Brar waved at Evan and replied, "I will, in a bit."

Mr. Brar sat in his wheelchair and pretended he didn't notice the man who'd been shuffling behind the trees in the corner of the street.

Mr. Brar worried about Evan just as much as Venice and Bruce did. He knew what happened to those who became an agent's target. Some were brutally murdered while others were often left with the thoughts of suicide because it felt like the only solution.

Evan was certainly in danger.

* * *

The rest of the week seemed to drag by for Evan. He had a lot to think of.

Venice stopped by the following afternoon as he was working

on the garden. To his surprise, she *did* share why she was so reluctant about Evan getting involved with Shadow. However, because Evan knew there was a chance Venice's vision could be wrong, he didn't take it seriously.

Venice, on the other hand, knew her vision was no mistake. What was going to take place in the near future scared her to death and Evan, who'd become optimistic, argued that nothing was going to happen. She'd given him the statistics of her visions that said so otherwise. Still, Evan blew off Venice, telling her there was a good chance she was wrong. Venice knew the only way to convince Evan was to tell him about Bruce, which she knew she couldn't do.

A little part of him was blind to the fact that Venice's vision could in fact be true. Evan had tunnel vision when it came to Shadow.

Evan analyzed his backyard with a beer in hand. He looked around, shaking his head. *What in the world was I thinking?* he thought. *To think I could do this all on my own.* His renovation included a bridge under a manmade stream, which flowed from a waterfall. He shook his head again in disbelief, thinking how much he'd underestimated himself. He chuckled as he stepped back into the kitchen.

He set his beer beside the gardening magazine he'd picked up before he started the entire project. He flipped through the pages wishing he hired someone to do the job. It became somewhat of a headache but kept him busy through the vacation.

The magazine made it look so easy. After digging up the place, he'd realized how big the responsibility was going to be. The maintenance to keep his garden fresh and clean was going to take a lot of work. He could hire a gardener to come in every week to cut the grass, clean the pond, and water the plants but from what he remembered, his mother did everything on her own. She took care of the garden. So why couldn't he?

He stood and weighed out each scenario.

He sighed, realizing he had imagined something so brilliant and peaceful but truth be told, this project wasn't cut out for a single person. At this point, he was considering just throwing cement all over in the backyard and calling it a day. Evan was determined to finish what he started except it was going to be *a lot* simpler than his initial idea.

He took another sip of his beer.

The grocery list posted on the refrigerator caught his eye. He moseyed his way over, snatching the list from underneath the green round magnet.

He'd compiled a list of things he'd run out of over the past couple of days. He let out an exasperated sigh. He hated grocery shopping to say the least. The long lines, items no longer in stock, chasing down an employee to find where the eggs were, or not being able to find an employee to begin with—it became a whole ordeal.

Just the trip to the Grand Foods Market in the central business district itself was a whole other story. The city couldn't have picked a better route to place stoplights, one after another. Every seven seconds, Evan found himself parked at another stoplight.

After changing into clean clothes and searching for his keys, he headed out of the house.

As he drove down Knight's Drive, the black SUV followed.

* * *

Venice awaited Denise's arrival at Bernie's coffee shop. Venice insisted on going to the fine Italian restaurant, Niki's, for dinner, but knowing how booked it would be, Denise opted for a less packed place to discuss some of the important things that were on her mind.

Venice studied the people who came in to grab a cup of coffee after work. Each and every one of them was facing some kind of problem—home, work, relationship problems, not making ends meet, late on the rent—everyone had something eating away at them. Some of them knew how to handle their issues better than most.

Not too long after, Venice spotted Denise navigating her way toward the table.

"Hello, darlin'," she said, studying Denise's demeanor.

"Hi, Grandma." It almost seemed as if she was forcing the words out. "How've you been?" she asked as she removed her coat.

"I've been good. How are you doing? How's Ryan?"

Denise sighed. "He's home now. I wanted to tell you that… well, I'm sorry I didn't tell you sooner," she said softly.

Venice shook her head in nonsense. "Don't be silly, darlin'. I know you really weren't mad at me."

Denise, wide-eyed, studied Venice.

There was a long pause before Denise spoke. "You knew Ryan was going to lose his memory, didn't you?"

Venice let out a sharp sigh. Her eyes scattered around the table. It was something that had been hanging over her head ever since Ryan's accident. All she wanted was to sit down with Denise and talk it through. Finally, she met her eyes and agreed.

"What would have happened if you *did* tell me about all of this before it happened?"

Venice didn't hesitate to answer. "Honey, Ryan wouldn't have survived." She paused for a moment, recalling the day it all hit her. She didn't want to believe it, but her gut told her otherwise. "Ryan losing his memory is better than losing Ryan altogether."

Denise sat there, trying to process everything Venice said. She tried her best to keep her composure. Her eyes glistened and with every passing second, she felt herself giving up. Suddenly she was in tears.

"Oh sweetie," Venice said, staggering over to wrap her arms around Denise. "Please don't cry, honey. Everything is going to be fine."

The people in the bakery started to look over, wondering what was going on. Some turned and looked away, while others still managed to stare with no shame.

Mind your business, she thought as she hugged Denise, rocking her.

"What am I going to do?" Denise wailed. "He doesn't even remember Nate. Like…what am I supposed to do?"

Venice wiped the tears away from Denise's face with the tip of her thumb, while continuing to give onlookers the stare.

Willow, who stepped out from the back room, caught Venice's eye. He had a mixture of sadness and concern across his face. Venice waved, gesturing everything was fine. He stood for a couple of seconds before going back.

"We'll do everything to help Ryan regain his memory," she said softly. "It's not going to happen in a day, but he'll remember his son."

Venice's throat started to constrict as she thought about the possibility of Ryan never being able to remember Nate. So far there was no vision of Ryan's fate, but all she could do was hope Ryan would eventually remember bits and pieces of his life with Nate.

Ryan still had a long road of recovery ahead of him. And that meant anything was possible.

* * *

Evan pushed the cart around down the aisle looking for cranberry juice. It was one of his favorites along with apple juice, orange juice being on the top of the list. He looked up and down, left and right, trying to locate the drink. Unfortunately for Evan, the Grand Foods Market rearranged the shelves a few days before.

Oh there it is, he thought, as the red plastic bottle on the bottom shelf caught his eye. He picked up two, placing them in the cart, knowing they would last for a few months before he ran out again.

Marvin turned the corner, also pushing his cart. He'd thrown random items in his cart as he kept a close eye on Evan and his every turn. He pulled out a box of granola bars off the shelf as he simultaneously peered in Evan's direction. *He is outrageously average,* he thought. *Dressed simply in jeans and a shirt. The man has no class whatsoever.*

Evan stood still for a moment as he checked the list. He scanned it, making sure there wasn't anything on the list he could get from the aisle he was currently in. Next on the list was packed cookies, which happened to be in the next aisle.

The old lady at the end of the aisle seemed to be taking her time. She had been standing there for the last five minutes, checking the labels and putting back the cereal boxes, unsure what she wanted for breakfast tomorrow morning. Evan pushed the cart around, heading back, knowing her indecisiveness would last longer and he didn't want to spend any more time here than he had to. He wanted to get his shopping over with as quickly as possible.

Marvin turned his attention back to the box of granola bars as Evan pushed his cart past him. He appeared to look concentrated on the label, but what he was really thinking about was beyond imagination. The horrible and cruel things he wanted to do to Evan, just for having introduced himself to Shadow, was enough to set the inhuman thoughts in motion. He sneered as he put the box away. He turned around and pushed the cart in Evan's direction.

Evan continued down the aisle as he looked for the Chips Ahoy! cookies he was fond of. He looked across the shelves. His neck craned to the side, noticing the blue cartons farther down. He pushed the cart with sudden ease, halting to a stop as he picked up two cartons of cookies.

Marvin subtly eyed Evan. He was tall, broad shoulders and narrow hips—the muscles bulged as he reached for another carton of cookies.

Well, I see why Shadow would find him appealing, he thought. She always did have a thing for men with muscles. It was disgusting. *Why do looks matter more than personalities?* He picked up a box of gummy snacks and salt and vinegar potato chips, placed them in the cart, which would then be left idly in an aisle for one of the employees to deal with.

Evan strolled down the aisle, looking right to left, wondering if there was something new to try. If anything interesting caught his eye, he would add it in the cart.

Evan reached the end of the aisle. As he passed by the registers, he noticed customers were slowly making their way to the lines. This tempted Evan to speed up and get everything on the list before having to stand in agony.

Like before, Marvin followed, only a few steps behind.

* * *

The sun had started to set. Kids in the neighborhoods began to head back inside after playing football or street hockey. It was dinnertime and Denise sat in her car as she pulled a compact mirror from her purse. She examined her face, making sure her eyes hadn't become puffy from all the crying earlier in Willow's bakery. The tip of her nose was a bit red, just enough to have it mistaken for a cold winter nose. But the rims of her eyes were visibly red.

She walked down Kentwood Drive to pick up Nate, who'd been playing at a friend's house, which was only a couple of houses down to theirs. She came to a gray two-story house, shutters in still creek color and the door painted in Blizzard white, with a white picket fence and professionally done landscaping.

As she reached the front, Denise pushed the doorbell, took a step back, and slipped her hands into her coat pockets. She looked down closely at her shoes, rubbing the heel against the cement as she waited for someone to open the front door.

Moments later, Greece Moore appeared at the front door. Her cantaloupe breasts were amped up to her chin, which Denise believed were fake, as well as the lips that were parted and turned up into a smile. No matter what day of the week it was, Greece was always put together, her hair either curled or straightened and she always made sure to wear some color on her lips.

Greece was married to a neurosurgeon, Zack Moore, who had freckles all over his pale face, eyes set close together, a curved nose, and bright orange hair. Denise always speculated Greece married Zack because of his income. Anyone would have thought so too just by judging the two by their appearance, but she never quite figured it out since they seemed to get along so well in the public eye. Quite frankly, she believed they belonged in Pool View, with their fancy lifestyle.

"Hi Denise!" Greece squealed in her heavy Southern accent. "How's your husband doing? I didn't get a chance to ask." The sympathetic look started to set in.

Denise didn't really want to get into the whole thing. Greece loved to share gossip. It would get around pretty quick—

another reason why Denise thought the Moores were better off in Pool View instead of here in Dusk View.

"He's doing better day by day," Denise responded, leaving out Ryan's memory loss. She didn't want any sympathy. It would only make it worse. "How's Zack?" she said, feeling obligated to ask.

"Oh, you know, just doin' surgeries left and right, saving lives." She chuckled as she twirled a strand of her hair like a young girl in middle school. "Oh, where are my manners?"— waving a hand—"Would you like to come inside for tea or somethin'? We can talk if you'd like."

"No. Thanks though," Denise said, almost forcing the words out. "Is Nate ready? I hope he didn't cause any trouble."

"Oh, hush now. He's a sweet little child. He's a delight to have." Greece smiled, subconsciously pressing her breasts together. "Nate!" she screamed into the house. "Your mommy's here."

Seconds later, Nate showed up at the door with Skylar right beside him. Skylar was dressed in a pantsuit; his curls jelled and dangled in his pale, freckled face. *Where was he off to?* Denise wondered.

"Hi sweetie," Denise said, tracking back to why she was here in the first place. "Ready to go home?"

"Yeah," he replied, stepping out with jacket in hand. It concerned Denise that Nate was quiet. Usually he was excited to see her, but not today. Something must've happened while she was gone.

"C'mon, put on your jacket or you're going to catch a cold," she said, ignoring her thought.

"But it's not that cold."

"Yes it is," she insisted.

"Kids," Greece chimed in. "This one never listens," she said, nodding in Skylar's direction. "I have to repeat myself a hundred times before I get him to listen."

Denise grinned as she assisted Nate with putting his arms in his sleeves. Denise zipped up his jacket and was ready to leave.

"Thank you for watching Nate, Greece," Denise said with a smile. "Bye." Denise headed toward the sidewalk, holding Nate's hand.

"Anytime, sweetie. We're always here for ya. Take care now," she said, waving.

Denise looked down at Nate, who kept himself entertained as he kicked around a stone the size of a quarter.

"So, what did you do today at Skylar's?" she asked, breaking the silence.

"Nothing." He sighed, kicking the stone once again.

She gripped his hand tighter, not wanting to press, but doing so anyway because it was in her nature to get to the bottom of things, especially with Nate. "What's wrong, sweetie?"

He let out another long, exasperated sigh. Nate wasn't the type of kid who went straight into detail about his feelings. If he felt like sharing, then Denise would get an earful; otherwise, she had to find alternate ways to get Nate to tell her what was really going on.

"Did something happen at Skylar's?"

Nate kept quiet, indicating something *did* happen.

"Did Mrs. Moore say something to you, about me and Daddy?"

Nate shook his head, no.

"Did Skylar say something to you?" She looked at him for an answer.

There was a long pause before Nate confessed. "Skylar and his dad are going hot air ballooning and they're going camping. He went skiing last week too." Nate's face wrinkled before he started to whimper.

They stopped in their tracks. Denise kneeled down, meeting

his eyes. "Oh, sweetie," she said as she pulled him closer, wrapping her arms around him. She fought back the tears, heartbroken, not knowing how she was supposed to handle this. "Why are you crying?"

"Daddy's not the same now."

"Oh honey, Daddy's going to recover soon. It's just taking him more time to get back into the spin of things."

"What…if…he doesn't?" he asked, gulping down his words.

"Oh, baby, he will. Daddy will. We just have to be patient. Everything's going to be okay." She pulled away, looking at his face, wiping the tears from his cheeks.

Nate wrinkled as nose. "Okay. Promise?"

"I promise."

* * *

After having to wait in the long line at Grand Foods Market, Evan managed to make a quick trip to Bakery Village on the way home after all. Fortunately, he was in and out in five minutes. He picked up the chocolate fudge cake he'd been craving; thankfully there were a few left.

Evan unloaded the groceries on the kitchen counter, stocking the pantry with fresh bread, a few boxes of dry pasta and sauce, pizza sauce, orange and apple juice, and chocolate chip cookies. In the fridge there was finally some cranberry juice and produce to last at least a week. He eyed the chocolate fudge cake, knowing he had to resist, but it was too good not to have a piece right now.

Evan tore the seal and grabbed a knife, a fork, and a plate and served himself a slice. He took a bite and his eyes fluttered in delight. *Oh my god*, he thought, *this is too good.* The whipped hazelnut frosting melted in his mouth as he started to devour the most satisfying thing he'd ever tasted.

And there, sitting in front of the back door, was Mr.

Jingles—watching every move. Only the cat's eyes moved as Evan traveled around the room. He placed the plate on the table, keeping his eye on Mr. Jingles as he went to retrieve a carton of milk from the refrigerator.

Evan turned the cap until he heard the snap indicating the seal was broken, and turned to the cabinets where he kept the glasses.

And Mr. Jingles sat and observed.

Evan poured himself a glass, putting the carton back in the refrigerator. He looked on as he held the glass up to his lips before taking a sip.

Mr. Jingles sat in position.

I wonder what he's thinking about, Evan thought. There was something about this cat that made him unordinary.

Eventually, Evan unlocked the door, sliding it open, letting Mr. Jingles in, who didn't hesitate to enter.

"Do you want some milk?" he asked, leaning over and scratching beneath his neck. Mr. Jingles purred and shut his eyes. He was enjoying it. Evan continued for a while before pouring Mr. Jingles some milk in a ceramic plate.

Evan crouched down and placed the plate in front of Mr. Jingles, who slowly leaned forward, sniffing the plate, and started lapping up the milk.

Evan's amusement came to an early end when the doorbell rang. He rose, making his way to the front door. To his surprise, Shadow stood at his doorstep, looking flustered.

"Have you seen Mr. Jingles?" she asked, cutting to the chase.

Evan was thrown off by her abruptness. "Yeah," he finally said. "He's in the kitchen."

Hearing those words brought Shadow relief. There was always a little part of her that believed Mr. Jingles was in harm. It was her first instinct, since nothing good ever happened since she met Marvin.

She followed Evan and as she did, a sudden sense of peace overcame her. There was something about him that made her feel at ease. Evan made her feel safe. She couldn't pinpoint it, but she certainly hadn't felt like this in a long time.

Mr. Jingles looked up as they entered the kitchen, then continued to indulge in the fresh milk.

"I came home after doing some grocery shopping and found him sitting out there. I wasn't sure if he was hungry or not but I gave him some milk anyway."

"Well thank you," she said, tucking her hair behind her ear. She looked at Mr. Jingles with a smile. "I let him out after I came back from work, so he could get some fresh air. He's just cooped up in the house all day until I get home, you know." She stood with her hands placed on her hips, staring at Mr. Jingles almost as if daydreaming. Her smile faded and was overtaken by concern. "I just get really worried about him. I don't want anything to happen to him."

Evan examined Shadow, sensing there was more to the story.

"Would you like some cake?" he asked, keeping the thought as close to his mind as possible. "It's really good." He grinned as the words slipped out.

Shadow eyed the cake, knowing she shouldn't indulge. She wasn't much of a fitness freak but she did make sure to keep her diet healthy. She had soda every once in a while and stayed away from candy as much as possible. It was a difficult diet to keep, but she tried, and that counted for something. At least that was what she told herself.

"Fine," she said, giving in mischievously.

Evan held eye contact for a moment, still finding Shadow to be surreal.

"You're going to love it." He pulled out a plate and fork, slicing a decent-sized piece. "This is the best of the best. No cake can compare to this."

She gave him a flirtatious look mixed with uncertainty. "This cannot be the best of the best," she answered, pursing her lips, trying to contain her giggle.

He scoffed. "Just wait until you try it."

"I'm going to regret this in the morning," she murmured.

"We all do." He snickered. "Do you want some milk with that?"

"Yeah, sure." She pulled up a chair, feeling comfortable.

"Some people like to drink 7-Up or Coke with cake. I tried it once. Let me tell you something," he said, pausing as he poured a glass of milk, "it does not go well with cake. Take my word for it." He placed the gallon of milk back in the refrigerator. "Milk is meant for cake. Like peanut butter to a jelly sandwich."

She met his eyes. "I'll take your word for it."

He sat down in front of her, moving his plate toward him. He glanced at Shadow for a moment as she dug into the cake. It sent shivers up his spine, just by having her in his home, sitting right across from him. Memories of his past came flashing back. The way she begged and pleaded for him to stop torturing her. It made his heart sink. How could someone be so cruel? It was inhumane. And the more time he spent with her, the more he was convinced she walked into his life for a reason.

"Wow," she said, her eyes widened. "You weren't lying." She pointed at the cake with her fork as she took a sip of her drink. "This tastes amazing."

"See, I told you."

"So," she began, her words lingering, "have you finished the garden yet?"

Evan let out a muffled laugh, cautiously swallowing the cake, not wanting to choke and possibly have Shadow perform the Heimlich or CPR. He cleared his throat with a slight grin.

"Are you mocking me?"

His eyes twinkled when he looked at her.

When their eyes met, it felt as if he was looking into her soul. It made Shadow nervous. The good kind of nervous—the one that made her want to sit in his lap and kiss his neck as she whispered sweet nothings into his ears.

She was attracted to him, in ways she couldn't explain. Sure, he was cute and he had a sense of humor, which was a huge plus. But most importantly, from the moment they met, she felt safe and comfortable. Given that her past relationship was with Marvin, it'd been hard for her to trust anyone.

Evan was different.

"Not really." She giggled. "The view's kinda doing it for me. What do you do all day anyway since you're on winter vacation?"

"I'll tell ya. First I wake up and make myself a cup of coffee. Then I have breakfast. After breakfast, either I'll go for a run or start working on the garden and then I'll take a shower and start making dinner. Then I'll sit down and read or grade papers. By then, it's time for bed."

Shadow looked at him with a mouthful of cake. "Wow. For someone with a lot of time on his hands, you don't do much, do you?"

Evan raised his eyebrows and chuckled. "You sure have a lot to say. I offer you some really good cake and this is how I get treated? In my own home?"

Shadow took a gulp of milk and set down the glass. She looked at him with a smile and beaming eyes. "I just would of thought you would've had finished working on your garden by now."

Evan laughed. He got up and put his dishes in the sink, and began to pull out the ingredients he needed to get dinner started.

"Since you think you know so much, why don't you come and help me?" He turned toward her, holding a cheese packet and ground meat.

"Yeah I can help you," she said, pausing for a moment, "and by help, I mean sit on a lawn chair and mentor you."

They broke into laughter.

There was a moment of silence and neither of them felt they needed to say something. Shadow gazed off into the backyard, wondering how Evan existed all this time without her knowing. She moved away from Pool View to start a new life, and the universe set her up next to Evan, maybe by far one of the dreamiest and genuine men she'd come across. *It's funny how life turns out*, she thought. *Everything I had to endure led me to where I am right now. Was it worth it? It definitely was.*

"I'm going to get dinner started. You should stay."

Shadow smirked before she took a sip of milk. She looked down at her plate, nearly empty. Her eyes moved to Evan, who stood in the middle of the kitchen waiting for an answer.

"What's for dinner?"

"You like tacos?"

"I certainly do."

"Tacos it is." He winked.

Shadow proceeded to get up from the table. "Do you need any help?" She carried her plate to the sink.

"You mean help as in watching and critiquing?"

Shadow turned around and looked at Evan after she placed her dishes in the sink. She exaggerated a sigh and placed her hand on her chest, her eyebrows furrowed. "Are you mocking me?"

Evan broke into a smile. "A girl with a sense of humor. I like that."

Evan's comment made Shadow blush.

"So, how can I help?

He looked at her with a sparkle in his eyes. "Just keep me company while I cook."

He gave her arm a gentle squeeze as he moved past her to retrieve the rest of the ingredients.

As he cooked, Shadow comfortably leaned against the counter. She watched as he diced the onions. As the meat cooked, he chopped the cilantro, the knife loudly hitting the cutting board. He was fast, which amazed her.

"Where did you pick up your kitchen skills?"

"Back in college. My grandma made Denise and I move into dorms and experience the college life. And we had to support ourselves. So, I worked at a restaurant as a server. During my breaks, I'd watch the head chef go wild in the kitchen. Cooking became a stress reliever. It would calm me down during the stressful times and it was fun to watch too. Then I'd come home and try to mimic the chef." He laughed. "I learned a lot from working as a server."

"That's so odd."

"What's odd?"

"Cooking is relaxing for me too."

Evan looked at her for a brief second before he began to pour the mixture onto the tacos. He smirked as he focused. "Putting in slices of bread into the toaster does not count as cooking."

Shadow genuinely gasped this time. "You're so evil." She playfully slapped his arm. She found herself grazing her hand over his upper arm. She could feel the definition of his muscles. When she looked at Evan, he'd been focused on the cooking portion that she wasn't sure if he'd even noticed her hands lingering.

He felt her hands remain and he quite enjoyed it. However, Evan remained nonchalant as he squeezed some lime on top of the meat and then added some chopped cabbage on top.

His feelings continued to develop. But before anything could happen, he wanted to tell Shadow about the memories. He needed to get it off his chest, but this wasn't exactly something easy to discuss.

"Are you telling me that you can cook an entire meal?" He asked, looking at Shadow with gentle eyes, "Without anyone's help?"

"Yes, I can, Evan," she said defending herself. "I can cook all by myself."

"We're going to have to see about that."

And all Shadow could do was smile and giggle. She hadn't enjoyed herself like this in some time. She'd forgotten what it was like to be around someone who radiated happiness and kindness. It was an environment that was going to let her blossom into the person she was meant to be as long as Marvin was no longer an issue.

"I don't know if you want wine with tacos, but I have dry rose. Coke and Pepsi are also available if you prefer that."

"Wine sounds great," she said.

After they'd finished, dishes were rinsed and put into the dishwasher. The night was still young. Shadow quietly sat on the sofa with her wine glass in her hand. When she craned her head over to the kitchen, she could see Mr. Jingles sitting in front of the back door, looking out into the garden. Then Evan came back with a box in his hand. He sat down next to her and opened the box in his lap.

Shadow set down her wine on the coffee table, curious to know what was inside. "I hope these aren't the remains of a skeleton you found when you were digging in the backyard."

Evan snickered as he removed the lid. "Seems like someone's drinking a bit too much," he said as he looked at her.

She looked back wide eyed and pretended to take offense. But the smirk didn't fool anyone. She leaned in and picked up the first picture on top. Ironically it was of naked Evan at two years old. "Well, well, well, what do we have here?" She waved the picture in front of Evan. Shadow could see the slight pinkish color appear on his cheeks when he realized the photo she was holding.

"Do you mind giving me that back?" He asked without making eye contact. The corners of his mouth lifted up and held out his hand.

"You've been making jabs at me all night. I think I deserve a little bit of fun."

Evan scoffed and looked through the box, pretending not to care about his naked baby picture.

"Would you run around the house naked when you were younger?"

"Yeah, I did and then I began running down the streets." He chuckled. "You wanna give me the picture back?"

Shadow pursed her lips and thought long and hard about her decision. Making Evan sit there, shy and embarrassed was the first she'd seen that side of him and she wanted to squeeze every ounce of joy she could out of this moment. "Here," she finally said and handed back the picture to Evan.

"Thank you," he said, his voice low-key. He took a quick peek of Shadow and she still wore a smile on her face, like a little kid who'd uncovered a juicy secret. "This is literally all the pictures we have from our childhood. All in this one box."

Shadow took another look at the depth of the box and realized there weren't many photos that had accumulated over the years.

"This is a picture of my parents on their wedding day," he said when he handed the picture to Shadow.

She studied the image for a moment. "Your mom was so beautiful. Your sister takes after her, you know?"

"Looks wise, yeah, but her mannerisms are more like my grandma's."

"You look like your dad. He was a good looking fella," she said as she gazed over with a smirk.

Evan and Shadow spent half an hour looking at the photos, not in any particular order. She looked at each photo and Evan would tell the backstory. He only remembered so many stories thanks to Venice. She was able to fill in the blanks to most of the memories the pictures captured. Besides, Evan was too young to remember half the things that went on back then.

"This is the last picture we have of the four of us before their deaths."

Shadow took the photo from Evan and admired the memories they must have created that day. All four of them looked happy. From previous pictures, Shadow could tell Evan's parents were very much in love by the way they looked at each other. It didn't sink in until now how big of a loss Evan must have endured when they died, even though he was young and maybe too young to understand.

"You don't appreciate time until it's gone."

"You were young. No one thinks their parents are going to die at that age."

"Yeah," he said in a somber tone.

He took the photo and placed it back in the box.

"So," he said after replacing the lid on the box, "what was the last straw that made you move to Lake View?"

Shadow leaned forward and rested her chin on her hand. The box of Evan's memories sat there taunting her about her own past. It wasn't that she didn't want to share with Evan about why she'd moved here. She didn't want to relive it. Shadow didn't want to be reminded of the fear that drove her away in the first place. Whether she told Evan or a random stranger she met on the street, neither would be able to do anything.

She sighed and then looked back at Evan who had his arm stretched out on the couch. He smiled back at her with a pleasant look in his eyes.

"You didn't murder someone, did you?"

She chuckled and shook her head before she leaned back into the couch, now closer to Evan. "I don't even know where to start," she finally said.

"What happened?" he asked softly, running his fingers through her hair.

"I felt trapped," she answered. She looked up at the ceiling, her heart pounding in her chest and she could hear the little voice in her head telling her it was okay. But a little part of her feared his reaction. What if Evan decided that he was going to become her knight in shining armor? She sensed he cared for her but that didn't mean she wanted Evan to lay his life on the line for her.

"What happened?" he pressed. "I know you're scared of something. The look on your face when you came looking for Mr. Jingles makes me think that you're not safe."

Her eyes flicked over to his. She shifted her body to face Evan. "He's all I have here." As she let the words slip out of her mouth, she knew it wasn't true. "He's the only one I've had with me for a long time." She took another long deep sigh before continuing. "I was engaged to someone who turned out to be this whole other person. I couldn't trust him anymore. I just wanted to be as far away from him as possible."

Shadow wanted to go into detail about how dangerous Marvin was and the fact that she wasn't even supposed to have any kind of contact with Evan in the first place. She knew she wasn't supposed to be sitting here next to Evan on his couch and releasing all the worries in the back of her mind. She wasn't supposed to be here *at all*. But something in her gut told her this was *exactly* where she needed to be. Plus, maybe Marvin was just bluffing. There was the possibility that he'd eventually get bored obsessing with Shadow and then move on to someone else. She didn't wish any harm upon another innocent girl, but at this point she was being selfish and if it meant that she had to be selfish to be safe, that's what she was going to do.

Evan understood why Shadow moved all the way out to Lake View. A new life, a fresh start. It's what people did when things went horribly wrong. Except that Evan didn't know how wrong things were. Evan, not knowing the volume of the danger Marvin was to him, suggested something that would only be a short-term solution. "You know what you should do? Get a cat door. He'll be able to come and go whenever he pleases and then you won't have to stress about him being cooped up in the house all day."

She hadn't thought about it, but it seemed like a good idea. "Yeah, I've heard of those screen doors with the built-in cat door. I'm gonna have to go down to the hardware store and get it sometime this week."

"I can get it for you and install it."

Shadow laughed at his gesture. "Are you the only professional available in town?"

Evan mocked her laugh, then let a small smile fade in. "They should put a warning label on the wine bottle clearly stating consuming this may make sweet girls sassy."

Evan hadn't heard someone laugh so hard as Shadow. Her head tilted back and she covered her mouth with her palm.

Shadow, who struggled to gain composure, wiped her eyes. For the first time in a while she laughed to the point of tears. Evan brought in light to her life where darkness once existed. Every ounce of fiber in her body wanted this to be the beginning to something far more wonderful than she could ever imagine.

"That is really nice of you to offer, but I'd be just holding you back from your project," she said, tilting her head in the direction of the backyard.

Evan peered into the backyard, knowing there was *a lot* of work that needed to be done. "It's no big deal," he reassured her. "I'm home all day anyway," he said, playfully nudging her. "Just think of it as a 'welcome to the neighborhood' gift."

"Are you sure?" she said, batting her eyelashes, deep down happy that he'd offered.

"Yeah," he responded. "I can get the door tomorrow and install it once you're home."

She nodded, liking the idea.

"Are we still on for this Friday?"

"You ask me like I've changed my mind," she gleamed. She softly grazed his hand that sat on his lap. When they hands intertwined, their heartbeats became in sync.

By far, this was the most perfect night of her life. And then suddenly everything that felt familiar about Evan came rushing back to her in bits and pieces. She looked at his face, his eyes, his nose and his lips. Her heart tore when she realized who she was looking at. Her eyes began to fill with tears.

"What's wrong?"

She forced a smile and said, "Nothing."

"Are you sure?" Evan asked, not convinced.

"Yeah, I'm sure."

"Okay."

She leaned in closer while keeping her hand interlocked with his. She finally found the missing piece to the puzzle and Shadow didn't quite know how to feel about it just yet.

* * *

Bruce sat in his office with Marvin's files spread out in front of him. He rubbed his face, exhausted. What was this guy up to? Twice, he carried out the same exact assignment. But why? Why was he going after Shadow Hex the first time? There was no indication on personal files about the motive for the assignment whereas client-based missions had thorough detail of the motive and exactly how the mission was supposed to be carried out. It was going to drive Bruce insane trying to figure out why Marvin was so interested in Shadow Hex. *Hex*, he thought to himself. The name started to sound familiar. Hex…he recognized it but he hadn't interacted with anyone with that last name from what he could recall.

Hex.

Bruce shifted to his computer, pulling up all the files associated with the assignments he'd done in the past. He typed in the last name in the search bar and waited for the results to pull up. Seconds later Bruce was staring at a white page. There was no one by the last name Hex he'd worked for. This was going to eat at him until the light bulb went off in his mind.

Hex.

Did he come across that name in the newspaper? Did he hear it as he passed by a conversation in the office? Bruce grunted as he continued to search.

Hex.

Bruce tried a different approach. He looked up Shadow Hex, pulling up her background information. Everything he needed to know about Shadow was right there in front of him. But it was no use. He wasn't interested in the girl—he'd never met her.

As he scrolled down, he came across a familiar name. He leaned in closer to the screen, making sure what he was seeing was correct. Suddenly, the light bulb flashed in his mind. *Roy*

Hex. Now he knew where he'd heard the name Hex before.

He'd met Roy once. A stern sixty-five-year-old man with the stamina of a thirty-year-old. The time he'd met Roy, Bruce felt intimidated by the way he looked at him as if he had a vendetta.

This was not good at all.

Bruce wanted to shut his eyes and hope all the thoughts running through his mind would freeze. But that wasn't going to happen. He was panicking. The room started to feel like it had been set on fire. His tie started to feel too tight around his neck. Loosening it didn't help.

Roy Hex was Shadow's father—who also happened to be the head of the SEA.

Bruce didn't have all the information yet, but now that Shadow was Evan's neighbor, the chances of Evan getting swept up in Marvin's assignment had become much higher.

He had to let Venice know that under no circumstance was Evan allowed to associate with Shadow. The farther away he was from her, the safer he was.

Whatever Marvin was doing concerning Shadow, having two agents linked to Shadow—one being the head of the agency—only meant one thing. Anyone who got in the way would end up dead.

Bruce leaned back in his chair, trying not to vomit. *Inhale and exhale,* he repeated to himself. *Inhale and exhale.* He quickly pulled out the trashcan from underneath his desk and puked.

He knew what they would do to Evan if he somehow prevented Marvin from completing his assignment. Bruce knew what the torture was like. He knew what the agents were capable of doing. Skinning their victims alive, burning their genitals, breaking their knees and collarbones, or paralyzing them so they would never walk again—he knew the torture.

Something had to be done.

CHAPTER 14

Bruce fidgeted in his seat in a windowless hall that had shiny dark mahogany flooring and a panel that sat five board directors. Before him was a piece of paper, which in great detail proposed for Marvin to take a step down as Agent 212 and take a leave of absence from the SEA.

He needed this appeal to work. This was the only way to stop Marvin dead in his tracks. With the board signing off on his request, Marvin was prohibited from working on any cases. He would be restricted from making any kind of connections with anyone at the agency. And of course all of this was going to be monitored, for precaution, just in case he slipped through the cracks.

As Bruce continued to fidget in his seat, in came the board of directors one by one, all dressed in black pantsuits, taking their seat at the panel in front of him, which was about five feet higher than he was. One of the directors was a brunette, wearing a black pantsuit, who sat at the end, fashioning long bangs, a bun, and red lipstick. She was fifty-eight but didn't look a day over thirty-five. The rest were men in their late fifties and early sixties, graying or balding.

The board members that sat before him had been agents at one point in their life. Now their responsibility was to attend meetings for the agency, handle issues within the departments, hire new agents, and ultimately promote who they believed was doing an exceptional job to the next floor. It was less messy and stressful. The excitement they had for going on missions for their clients had reached its peak. These were the individuals who had done and seen everything but weren't exactly ready to retire.

Bruce sat up straight, trying to keep his nerves calm. His eyes flicked to the brunette for a moment, feeling a bit of tranquility before looking away and focusing on the speaker who sat in the middle.

"Please state your name and your ID," said the agent in a husky voice. He had his hands folded, holding eye contact with Bruce, who looked like more of a cleaned-up version of an inmate at a court hearing.

"Yes sir," he answered and cleared his throat. "Bruce Storm, 513-510-231-958."

"Thank you," he said, looking down at the file in front of him. "We are here to help in whichever way we can. Our decision will be based entirely on the benefit to the whole and not to the individual. The sole purpose for this meeting is to hear your appeal and formulate a decision, which will be fair and final. Do you understand, Mr. Storm? If you have any questions, we can clarify before we get started."

"That won't be necessary."

"Please proceed," he motioned.

All of them looked at Bruce in a condescending way except for the brunette. Her eyes were soft and understanding. It put him at ease knowing she was there.

Bruce cleared his throat and presented his appeal.

"I had my boss sign a written statement that allowed me to

look into all of Mr. Stone's cases, open and closed. The case he's currently working on puts innocent lives in jeopardy. It will only create backlash and chaos with the public, which can be detrimental for our organization—"

"Mr. Storm," the man interrupted.

"Yes?"

"The agency can never be located. We cannot be tracked down. Mr. Stone's assignment will not in any way put our agency at risk for any kind of backlash or legal dispute because in reality, we do not exist."

Bruce nodded. "Yes, I understand that sir, but looking into Mr. Stone's files has raised some questions. The rules here at the Secret Eye Agency," he said, tapping his index finger on the table, "is that we do our work as well as we have been trained to do, if not better, keeping in mind that there is no tolerance for revenge. And I believe Mr. Stone is out to get revenge. He was on this same assignment once before until he was suspended from it. I believe—"

"Mr. Storm, you're a fifth floor agent, correct?"

"That's correct."

"Then I'm sure I don't have to explain to you the meaning of what a 'personal assignment' is."

"No, sir. You don't."

"Mr. Stone has the authorization to continue with his personal assignment."

Bruce was confused. "From who?"

"Mr. Stone has the clearance to go ahead and proceed with his assignment. That's all you need to know."

"This is absurd!" Bruce jolted out of his seat in rage. He planted his hands on the table and leaned forward. He looked at each and every one of the board members. None of them had said a word or made an impression whether or not they disagreed with the speaker. "He is a menace. He shouldn't

even be allowed to work here. Have you looked into his files?"
Again, he looked at each one of them for an answer. "Have
you?"

"No, but there is nothing more we can do. We listened to
your appeal, Mr.—"

"You didn't even give me a chance to finish!" he said, cutting
him off. "How about the rest of you? Aren't you allowed to
weigh in? Isn't this supposed to be a *fair* discussion and a *fair*
decision? Doesn't this agency exist to protect the people?"

The speaker spoke in a calm and collective voice. "Mr.
Storm, there is nothing we can do."

"Yes, yes there is something you can do. People's lives are
in danger, people who are completely innocent. This is not
how we do things around here. I know that, you all know
that." His heart picked up its pace. His fingers trembled and
for some reason it felt as if his body was frozen in position.
He couldn't seem to move. He remained standing. Before a
panic attack was about to set in, he shut his eyes for a brief
moment before glaring at the speaker once again. "Mr. Stone
can't continue—"

"Mr. Storm," said the speaker, raising his eyebrows, "you
need to drop this or we will put you on probation. This is an
order." He tilted his head toward the door with a stern look.

Bruce wanted to grab the man by the throat and choke him
until he turned pale. He slammed his fist on the table. "This
is bullshit! Innocent lives are going to fall into your hands. *You*
will be responsible for that," he said, pointing his finger at
each one of them. Bruce buttoned his blazer and wiped the
beads of sweat off his forehead with his pocket handkerchief.
"You will pay for this."

He headed out the door, feeling defeated without a fair fight.

As the door shut behind him, the brunette spoke, very much

with a powerful voice. "This certainly was not fair. He had no chance to argue his point."

The speaker looked down at the end. "You already knew this was out of our hands when he called in the meeting."

The brunette shook her head in disagreement. "This agency works in favor for the innocent. This isn't right."

One of the men from the opposite end spoke. "Is anything we do right? We were given an order and there's nothing we can do. Our hands are tied."

"Then what are the rules made for? If you can walk around them, break them every once in a while for someone else's best interest, then why don't we just allow every one of our agents to do whatever the hell they want? So what if they slit throats in broad daylight to send a message to the rest? That's what's going to happen if we let one slide just because we were given an order."

"She's right," chimed in another. "We give strict rules to our agents for a reason. It keeps them in line, and breaking the rules for one agent only means we'll be breaking the rules down the line for others as well."

"This was Mr. Hex's order," said the speaker, "and there's nothing we can do. It's out of our hands."

The brunette shook her head again. "We're all going to Hell."

"I believe we signed our death sentence to Hell the day we agreed to work for the agency."

The brunette leaned forward; glaring at the speaker, knowing for a fact there was something that could have been done on Bruce's behalf.

She, like the rest of the board, was instructed not to say anything during the meeting. Whether they agreed with the decision or not, for this case, they were asked to keep their opinions to themselves. And the brunette had been fighting to keep her voice locked in a cage from the moment she entered the chamber.

The brunette scoffed as she left the chamber, leaving the men to rethink what just happened.

* * *

Evan walked into the family room with a glass of water, wearing a fresh pair of clothes. He wanted to look good for Shadow when he'd see her later. It had been a while since he'd put in the effort to look good for someone else and even when he tried, a little part of him always felt he could do more.

There sat the box of memories next to an empty photo album. This time, he was going to at least finish one album. Evan knew he was going to get sidetracked with every bit of emotion the photos carried, and it was hard not to sit and just think of all the memories he'd had with his parents. At age four, there was only so much he remembered and photos helped bring back the little missing pieces.

Placing the glass on the coffee table, he propped open the box, placing the lid beside him on the couch. He sighed as he picked up a photo of Venice at his father's high school graduation. The one after was of Denise and her mother. Denise's smile looked just like their mother's. There was no denying the fact that Evan took after his father and Denise after her mother. One could say they were little miniature versions of their parents.

After spreading half of the photos all over the coffee table, Evan grouped them according to a timeline. He placed all the pictures of just his father and Grandma Venice and Grandpa Dean in one pile. Graduation pictures were in another pile. Photos of his mother and his father went in another. College graduation went in another and then wedding photos of his parents. A stack of pregnancy photos went in another one.

The ones that had Denise in them went into a separate pile. This was unquestionably easier than the project he started in the backyard.

Once all the photos had been placed in a pile, Evan began to slide each photo into the clear plastic pockets. Evan stared at each picture momentarily before sliding it into the photo album. One photo specifically made him grin: It was a picture of his mother, pregnant; his father had his hand placed on her belly, smiling at her as she looked at the camera, beaming. The look on his father's face said it all. He looked at her as if it was the first time he'd seen the love of his life. There was no doubt that his parents were in love.

He slipped the photo into the pocket, moving on to the next one.

It was half past five. He was almost done completing the third photo album and there was still one stack left, mostly of the ones of him, Denise, and Grandma Venice. Graduations, birthdays, and Denise's wedding—that was the most recent one he'd come across. If it hadn't been for Venice, they'd have only a couple of photos from the last twenty-seven years. He'd come to appreciate his grandmother's efforts to create memories so they'd have something to look back at.

Evan stepped into the garage, carefully carrying out the new screen door for Shadow. It was the first thing he did that morning before working in the backyard. It wasn't heavy, but the box it came in made it difficult to maneuver. He held the door with one hand and used the other to push the box upward then onto the hardwood floor. He slid it across the floor all the way to the front door. He picked up the business cards of landscapers that were available in the area for Shadow and put them in his back pocket.

He stepped outside and locked the door behind him. The sun was shining over Lake View but within seconds heavy gray clouds obscured the sky. Evan hoped for rain. He found an odd sense of peace when the rain pattered against the bedroom windows. If he was sitting in the living room watching TV, the sound of rain made everything seem more enjoyable and worry-free. It reminded him of the days where his mother would make hot cocoa for him and Denise and then huddle up on the couch to enjoy a good movie during the holidays.

Usually Lake View experienced rainy days, one after another, from November until mid-January. But this time around, there was no rain. When it appeared that there was going to be a chance of rain, it only happened to be a tease. The clouds would clear up with a brisk breeze and a cold temperature.

He tracked toward Shadow's house, carrying the cardboard box over his head and finding the balance was tricky. As it would lean forward, within seconds, it would lean backward, and he'd struggle to find the balance once again. Carrying the door made the walk from and to Shadow's house convey the impression that it was farther than it really was.

Once Evan stepped foot on Shadow's porch, he let the cardboard box lean against the house, and pushed the doorbell. Subconsciously he took a step back.

A moment later, Shadow stood in front of him. She looked stunning in her dark blue pencil skirt and white blouse. Her hair was curled at the ends, giving the strands a little bounce and volume.

She batted her eyelashes as she gazed at him through her sea blue eyes.

Evan was certain his heart skipped a beat when she did that. She smiled. "Hi."

"Hey," he said, shoving his hands in his pockets "Did you just get back from work?"

"No, I came home about an hour ago. I went shopping for groceries afterward," she said, pausing as she stood to the side.

"Come on in. I'm keeping you out in the cold."

"It's not that cold," he said, with a soft smile. Once the words slipped out of his mouth, he realized the cold breeze was starting to attach itself on the base of his cheeks and the tip of his nose. "On second thought, it kinda is."

Evan proceeded to pick up the cardboard box and Shadow moved out of the doorway automatically. Evan carried the box by his side and Shadow subtly walked behind him, admiring his broad shoulders and his biceps bulging through his shirt. She found herself smiling as she ogled Evan from behind. She didn't fail to notice his jeans fit snug around his rear and hadn't forgotten why Evan felt so familiar. Then her feelings began to sink in.

Finally when he reached the back door, Evan carefully set the box by the wall, next to the back door. He rested his hands on his hips, eyes fixated on the box.

"I got some landscapers for you," he said as he slid his hand into his back pocket. "Most of them offer free consultations."

Shadow, having been deep in thought, gave him a blank expression. She knew she couldn't change what she'd done but Evan reminded her of her mistake. She looked at what Evan was holding in his hand and then back at him.

"You okay?"

"Yeah, sorry. I was…I just in a whole other world," Shadow said, shaking away her thoughts. "What were you saying again?"

"I got some people who you can contact about doing your landscaping."

"Oh, thank you. You can just go ahead and put them on the table. I really appreciate it," she said, smiling.

Evan set the cards on the table and focused on the project that sat in front of him. He proceeded what he needed and analyzed how long it was going to take him to take the old door off and install the new one. After some thought, he came to the conclusion that it was going to take an hour—maybe even less, if he focused.

Meanwhile, Shadow unpacked the groceries she'd set on the kitchen counter. She subtly watched Evan, who looked deep in thought, as she set down the pizza sauce, then the cheese. Before she could voice her concern, Evan expressed his thought.

"You wouldn't by any chance happen to have a toolbox, would you?"

Shadow pressed her hands against the edge of the counter, pursing her lips.

"Actually, I do."

"You do?"

"Yeah," she answered, batting her eyes.

Again with the eyes! Shadow sent a vibration that ran through his body, making the hairs on his neck rise for a standing ovation.

Shadow passed by Evan as she made her way to the garage close enough that he could smell her hair. And it smelled like a flower garden. A few moments later, Shadow appeared, carrying a red toolbox. She set it on the table and waited for Evan to tease her.

"Well," he said, nodding, "I thought you were going to come back carrying a couple of tools painted in pink."

"I had those too," she chortled, "and then for a very short period, I wanted to become a handy-woman. I went out and bought a real toolbox. It was a short-lived passion." She grinned. "I can fix a lose screw and a water leak in the sink, but that's about it."

He raised an eyebrow. Shadow was something else. "That's more than what most women know how to do."

"You're just being nice."

"No. I'm just telling you the truth." He smiled.

"I hope you brought your appetite. I'm making pizza."

"As long as you have a fire extinguisher nearby, I'm game."

"Wow," she exclaimed, "you're a piece of work, aren't you?"

"I had a little too much wine before I came over." He winked.

Shadow broke into laughter. Without saying another word, Shadow threw up her hands, playfully showing defeat and went back into the kitchen. And Evan watched her walk away like a goddess.

After taking in the majestic view, Evan turned to the task. He crouched down, balancing on the heels of his feet as he set out to install the new screen door.

For half an hour, Evan listened to Shadow hum as he worked out on the patio, which made the cold bearable. He'd look through the kitchen window every now and then, watching her for seconds at a time. He was drawn to her like a moth to a flame. The way she gracefully kneaded the dough and cut the vegetables—he could tell she was in her zone.

Evan listened to her sweet humming as he unhinged the old door and got ready to install the new one. There were some moments where Shadow would slip in a lyric and then gradually slide back into humming. He unconsciously smiled to himself. She had a beautiful voice.

Being around Shadow made him genuinely happy. He was falling for her and it was simple as that.

CHAPTER 15

W hat's going on?" Venice asked, trying not to jump to conclusions. Bruce shook his head and flashed his hand as he paced back and forth in her office. His eyes were fixated on the floor.

Venice raised her eyebrows, knowing well enough to give him some space. Although it would put her at ease if he'd just come out and say what was on his mind. It made Venice antsy—sitting there, wondering what was going on.

She sipped on her coffee, knowing this had Evan written all over it. And the only thing she knew was that Shadow was no good for him.

She sat on the couch as Bruce continued to pace. For a brief moment, he stood by the window, peering out, looking side to side, as if he was keeping a lookout.

In silence, Bruce shook his head. Debating with voices in his mind, he turned around and stared Venice dead in the eyes.

"You have to take Evan away—far away from here," he finally said.

Taking longer than a moment to process what Bruce just said, she blurted, "What?"

"He's not safe here." He paused for a moment, staring off into the ceiling, like he was going to find the answer to his troubles hidden in there somewhere. "No." He slowly made eye contact with Venice, this time, wide-eyed, feeling he'd come up with the best solution. "We need to find a place where no one can find him. He's going to have to stay there for a while or…he can change his name, move away—start a new life somewhere else. He can move to Honey View or Rein View. They're both farther out. Actually, Brickwood is much better. I have a safe house out there just in case things got out of control, which they are. It's a small—"

"Bruce!"

"What?"

"You're talking crazy. Evan's not going to move away—not on my say so, anyway."

"He's going to have to," he objected. "He's not safe here."

Venice shifted in her seat, putting the mug down in front of her.

"Safe? What'd you mean he's not safe here?"

Bruce clasped his hands together and walked toward her. He maintained eye contact as he slowly sat on the couch beside her.

He sighed. "Remember when I told you I was a contract worker?"

Venice nodded her head, feeling she was about to hear the real truth.

He continued, "I'm not exactly the kind of contract worker you'd think I am."

"Oh?" she said.

"There's an agency." After a beat of silence, he finished, "I work as an agent."

"So what do you do as an agent? What's the name of the agency?"

Bruce sighed. He looked up at the ceiling again, knowing it was best if Venice didn't know but the time for the truth had come.

He fished for the right words but struggled. "I work for people. Upper class people who need...help resolving issues..."

"Okay," she said, closing in, trying to gather what Bruce was communicating. "What's the name of this agency? Maybe I can look it up and get a better understanding of it. "

"Here's the thing...you can't."

Now he'd just confused her even more.

"I can't?"

"No. The agency goes by the SEA, short for The Secret Eye Agency. It's hidden; no one can find it. You won't be able to search it on the Internet." He paused for a moment. "It's nonexistent."

As confused as she was, Venice shook her head, not accepting what Bruce was saying.

"That's impossible. There's no way—it can't be. How in the world is there some agency that no one knows about? And you can't even look it up on the Internet?"

Bruce sat in silence. He fiddled with his fingers, looking past Venice. Explaining the agency was one thing but understanding it was a whole other aspect.

"No one other than our clients knows that the agency exists, which are all upper class folks." When he said that, he met her gaze in all seriousness. "If you have money and you've done something wrong, and you need to cover up your tracks, *we* are the ones you come to. We control the issue. That's what we do. We *control*. It doesn't matter *how*. As long as the problem is being controlled—that's it. "

"Basically people throw money at a problem and it goes

away, because you work for an agency who controls the problem?"

Bruce nodded in shame.

In a comforting voice, Bruce explained everything Venice needed to know and how he'd joined the agency.

An agent had been keeping track of him. His every move. The places he went to. Where he lived. Who he interacted with. The group of people he surrounded himself with. Bruce was under investigation in order to see if he was going to be the right fit for the agency.

One sunny day, a man wearing a nice suit came and sat with Bruce while he had lunch. The man proposed the best solution to his problems with a significant amount of money to reel anyone in—it had been just six months since Bruce had left his old life behind him. Having no idea what he was getting himself into, Bruce agreed for an interview. As soon as he agreed, the gentleman called in two other men also wearing suits. Shortly after, Bruce was escorted into a black SUV. The men, sitting on both sides, asked Bruce politely to wear a shroud over his face. "We are not at liberty to reveal the location of the agency until after the interview," he remembered one of the agents saying. A part of him felt if he didn't obey the order, it wasn't going to end well for him.

With no complaint, Bruce slipped the bag over his face, seeing nothing but darkness. Then one of the men slipped on noise-canceling headphones over the bag, which played music of all sorts. He realized soon after that this ride was going to lead to a whole other life—a life that he couldn't escape from, even when he wanted to the most.

The ride hadn't felt long since he'd lost track of time while listening to music. The headphones and duffel bag were removed once he was sitting in the same chamber he'd gone to for his appeal, except this time, there was no brunette. And that was when the interview took place, explaining in great detail what the job description was for a Secret Eye agent. He was informed by one of the men if Bruce rejected their offer, he was free to go, but in order to maintain the low key of the Agency, they would monitor his every move until he took his last breath. It was clear Bruce had no choice but to agree. Before he knew it, he was being signed in as Agent 115 and started his first day in training the same day.

For the sake of his family, he left his old life behind but deep down, he couldn't leave it *all* behind him. Bruce managed to show up to both Denise and Evan's graduations—elementary, middle, high school, and college—he kept track of where they were going in their lives. Making sure they were safe was still his number-one priority. The only difference was he had to do it from afar otherwise he would have placed Venice, Denise, and Evan in jeopardy as well as their future families.

For the last two years, he'd contemplated whether it was a good idea to come back into their lives. Going back and forth about the right way to go about explaining everything to them, he realized there really wasn't a right answer. He had to just do it and explain everything along the way.

Bruce saw Venice's reaction. He reached and placed his hand over hers, giving it a squeeze.

Venice leaned into the couch, taken aback by everything she'd heard. Her eyes focused on the beige carpet, processing it all. Her hands began to tremble. She clutched her knees to keep herself from spiraling out of control.

She closed her eyes tightly as tears began to well up. She gripped on to Bruce's hand just as tight.

"I didn't hear from you for a really long time. I thought you were dead," she whimpered. "I wasn't sure if I'd ever know if anything happened to you. I couldn't figure out how to get in touch with you and I couldn't let Denise and Evan know about any of it. They were all I had after you left," she said, leaning over to the Kleenex box, pulling out a tissue. "Now you're here. You're here," she said, blowing her nose and using another one to wipe away her tears.

Bruce pulled Venice closer, kissing the top of her head.

"I'm sorry," he whispered.

They sat in silence.

At the time, going away for a while was a way for Bruce to cope with everything that happened. It was the easiest solution. Having his kids see him drunk, coping with the loss of his wife in odd ways, wasn't the way he wanted them to remember him.

Venice leaned forward and reached to grab another Kleenex to pat her face dry. With the crumpled tissue, she wiped her nose, stuffing it in her cardigan pocket.

"I can't protect Evan the way I was able to." She looked into Bruce's eyes, helplessly. "He's all grown up now. I can only talk to him and hopefully instill some common sense in him."

Bruce's focus was scattered all over the place. This was not how it was supposed to play out. He'd done everything he could to make sure they were protected. Evan wasn't supposed to end up in the middle of a battle—seeing Marvin's history, this indeed was going to be a battle Evan would not be able to win.

He pressed his hands together, bringing them up to his chin, knowing there was one card left to play. Bruce softly squeezed Venice's knee before getting up from the couch.

Venice's eyes followed.

He positioned his body toward Venice before reaching for the door. "There's someone who will kill Evan and he won't flinch when he does. I need to protect Evan from him and I'm going to do whatever it takes to make sure he's safe. You need to make sure he…listens and stays away from Shadow."

Venice nodded, not knowing what she had to do yet. "I'll see what I can do."

"Thank you."

Bruce quietly shut the door behind him as he left the office.

Venice navigated toward the window. She peered out into the busy street from the third floor and watched as cars drove past while pedestrians waited to cross the street. As a sense of relief finally entered into Venice's life, it went away just as quickly.

***

"Wow," Evan exclaimed as he chewed on a bite of pizza, wishing he'd waited just a little longer since the sauce underneath was still boiling hot—this wasn't the first time he'd done this. "This is really good pizza. I think it's safe to say that cooking is probably one of your areas of expertise since we didn't have to use a fire extinguisher or call the fire department. I was kinda worried for a bit," He grinned as he dabbed the side of his mouth with tissue, catching the bit of sauce.

"Very funny," Shadow said, holding a pizza slice in her hand and softly blowing over it. Shadow took a bite, feeling it was safe to do so. "Thank you for installing the door for me. I really appreciate it."

"It was my pleasure," he said with a boyish grin. "Now you won't have to worry about keeping Mr. Jingles cooped up all day."

Shadow nodded as she washed the pizza down with her glass of wine. Her tongue did a once-over on her lips. Evan halted and watched.

Evan sat back in his chair. All the memories of him and Samantha came rushing back in this one moment.

"What are you thinking about?"

He looked away for a second and then met her gaze once

again. "There's something I want to show you."

Evan looked down at his plate. There was one bite left, which he shoved into his mouth.

He excused himself as he rinsed off his dishes in the sink.

Shadow turned to face Evan in the kitchen. "What is it?"

He gave her a cheeky smile. "You'll see."

Shadow picked up her plate and glass, meeting Evan in the kitchen. She couldn't help but smile as she rinsed her dishes. "Where is it?" She grabbed the kitchen towel off the counter and wiped her hands.

They faced each other, close enough to smell one other's aroma.

"It's here in Lake View and we should get going before it gets too dark."

"Okay," she said with a grin. "Let me just get my coat."

"I'm gonna go get my coat too. I'll be right back."

Shadow nodded and hurried up the stairs to grab her long black military coat.

She quickly walked down the stairs, keeping a grip on the railing. When she neared the end of the staircase, Evan was already standing there in a black trench coat, waiting patiently.

He looked up as he heard the soft sound of footsteps approaching. Evan couldn't help but smile.

"You could have borrowed one of my coats." She smirked. "It would've saved you the trip."

Evan chuckled. "I don't want to have to question my sexuality again." He winked. He softly brushed his hand against her back. "Come on, let's go."

***

Bruce waited outside of the Secret Eye Agency in anticipation. He had no idea when Marvin would leave the premises, but he was going to wait until he walked out through the invisible doors. He paced back and forth in front of the intercom. Waiting an hour for Marvin felt like a century.

He stood still for a moment. The cold breeze brushed against his face as he pushed the dirt around with the tip of his shoe. Bruce contemplated the different ways this might go down. Marvin as he knew was not the type of guy to step down from a fight. Bruce didn't want to be violent. Surprisingly after all the years at the agency, his humanity remained intact. This was rare for agents who were on the fifth floor. In most cases, by the time agents reached the third floor, they already crossed lines which they knew they shouldn't have but the authority and the adrenaline rush after handling the issues for their clients, humanity didn't matter anymore to them. They did what gave them temporary satisfaction. For Bruce, as much as he wanted a peaceful confrontation with Marvin, he already knew that option was out the window. However, Bruce he was confident the leverage he had over Marvin was enough for him to back out of his mission.

* * *

"Oh my god," Shadow said, looking up, turning slowly. "I've never seen anything like this."

Weeping willow trees surrounded Cherry Park, making it seem like they were in a green bubble. Benches were placed half a mile from each other. Far into the middle, there was an immense lake. Joggers made their way around Cherry Park, running in the distance, far enough away that in moments, they were once again all alone.

"This is the most peaceful place in Lake View. I can guarantee you that."

"It's definitely peaceful," she said in awe.

Shadow was amazed by how Cherry Park made her feel like she was in an entirely different world.

Evan let Shadow take in the scenery before they walked to the nearest bench and sat side by side.

The lake was calm. No sight of ducks or geese, like Evan usually noticed when he'd come for a run.

"I've never seen anything like this before. I mean, there's nothing like this in Pool View. There are parks there, but definitely nothing like this." She absorbed the beauty and simplicity Cherry Park had to offer. The green grass surrounded them, as if it was a sign there was hope in her own life to see the light where there was once darkness. "Do you know why it's named Cherry Park?"

"As a matter of fact, I do. A long time ago, a married couple bought this land and they planted cherries here. When the husband passed away, his wife died soon after. Since they didn't have children of their own, no one was in line to claim the inheritance, so it went to the county. After about a year or so, maintaining the field became too much of a hassle. They ended up changing it to a park and planted all these beautiful trees here," he said as he looked around them.

"To sum it up, the name comes from the original plantation?" she said, turning to Evan.

He broke into a wide smile. "Was my story that long?" he said, staring off into the lake.

"Just a tad." She playfully nudged him. "Is it usually this vacant during the winter?"

His brows furrowed as he thought. "During winter, it's kind of unpredictable. Sometimes there are crowds of people scattered all over the place, everyone's doing their own thing and sometimes, it's like this. In the summer, it's a whole different scene." He paused. "It's really nice in the summer."

"It feels like we're the only two people who exist right now." Her words trailed into the thin air, each one sounding softer than the last.

Evan rested his forearm on top of the bench. "It certainly does." He paused for a moment and then looked at her. "This used to be a safe spot for me growing up. I'd come here just to think." He laughed. "I want you to know that you're always safe with me."

Shadow said nothing but smiled.

In silence they sat. Evan's mind jumped from one thought to another. He could see Shadow in the corner of his eye, enjoying the moment, the peacefulness. But he knew something in the past was hanging over her and for the life of him, he couldn't simply ignore the fact that there was a bigger picture.

"I have to ask…" The words trailed off. He didn't know exactly how to finish his sentence. He looked away briefly and gathered his thoughts. "Was he abusive?"

Shadow's body shifted, her attention back to the lake. She glimpsed at Evan, feeling a little ashamed about the truth to her reality, but the genuine caring tone in his voice pushed her to share her past.

"No," she said before she introduced who Marvin was, leaving no psychotic detail behind. Evan heard all the ups and downs the two had. How her parents sided with Marvin on things that meant to stay within relationships. The threats and how she managed to move out of their townhouse, without letting Marvin get a sniff of the scent that she was leaving for good. After Evan was caught up with Shadow's infuriating past, he felt like he'd been hit by a bus but somehow survived the tragedy.

For Evan, this was all a little hard to believe. It wasn't that he was under the impression Shadow was fabricating her past but because it truly seemed he was seeing a pattern here. Why was this happening to Shadow again? It was as if enduring pain and torture in her previous life wasn't enough that peace and happiness had no place in this life.

"Why can't you file a restraining order on him? He's clearly a loony and needs a restraining order."

"It's not going to work."

"What do you mean, it's not going to work?"

Shadow sighed. Merely talking about Marvin made her anxious. She rose from the bench, hands in her pocket. "I don't really feel like talking about this," she responded.

Evan launched forward. "You can't use the same excuse twice. So tell me, what's the whole story?"

"Are you the town's savior or something?"

Evan sensed the sarcasm but continued to press. "Is he threatening you?"

She threw her hands up in the air and exclaimed, "Can we not talk about this right now?"

"Okay, fine."

Her eyes narrowed. "Just because you have a degree in psychology doesn't mean you have me all figured out. And why is it so important for you to help me?"

Evan opened his mouth to speak then closed it. Telling Shadow about the memories of his past life wasn't going to accomplish anything right now. If anything, it would only make things worse. She would bombard him with questions—and was he ready to answer all of them? Did he have all the answers? No, but he knew one thing for sure: His feelings for Shadow had no correlation to his past life. He wanted to make sure she knew that before he brought any of this to light.

Evan stepped closer, knowing in his heart, he wasn't going to leave her on her own. Fate had steered him into the direction it needed to go and he wasn't going to let Shadow face this on her own.

"I know I don't have you 'all figured out.' But I'm not going to just sit back and let him have this control over you. I saw the fear in your eyes when you thought you lost Mr. Jingles. I wouldn't ever want to see you like that again."

Shadow looked at Evan with sympathetic eyes. A little part of her wanted to blurt out what Marvin did for a living. But Shadow knew Marvin would kill Evan if she did. She knew what the agency was capable of covering up. She'd heard too much from Marvin and was well aware of how little a restraining order would be able to do, let alone the police force. It was pointless.

As much as she loved the feeling that Evan wanted to help her, she wouldn't be able to live with herself if something terrible happened to him at her expense. Deep down, she knew Evan came into her life for a reason but feared that it was all too good to be true.

She looked at him with pleading eyes and took a step closer. "I appreciate you wanting to help, I really do, but you can't. It's just the way it is." She shrugged.

He studied her. *I'm supposed to help you.* He pursed his lips, and tilted his head forward. "It's getting late. We should get going," he murmured.

Shadow hesitated. She wanted to be clear about her concerns but the look Evan gave her said it all. His heart was in the right place and he was the only person she could trust. Those reasons convinced Shadow that Evan didn't belong anywhere near Marvin.

She started down the pathway alongside Evan, in silence.

* * *

Night was approaching. The wind started to pick up and the cold breeze brushed against Bruce's ears and nose as the leaves rustled across the pavement. It had been more than an hour since Bruce had been waiting outside of the agency. He kept his head lowered to keep his face from becoming stiff.

Bruce had a plan and was sure it would work.

When the invisible door opened, Bruce's head jerked up. *Finally.*

Marvin stepped out wearing a long black coat. He spotted Bruce in the far corner of the Agency's premises, idly standing by.

The towering trees made both of them look like miniature human beings. Both of them proceeded to walk in each other's direction.

Bruce stopped ten feet away from Marvin, knowing getting too close wasn't a brilliant idea.

Marvin didn't waste any time in small talk. "What do you want?"

"The personal assignment you've been working on, the one on your ex-fiancé. If you don't shut it down—"

"You're going to do what?" Marvin interrupted. He was amused. He took a few steps toward Bruce. What was he capable of that Marvin wasn't?

"First, I'll break her kneecaps. Then I'll suffocate her to the point where she thinks she's going to die…and stop. Then torture her again—and again, and then again. When I see the pain in her eyes and she begs me to end her life because she doesn't want to go through any more torture, I'll use a knife to slit her throat… very slowly. She'll die in more pain and agony. You wanna know the best part? You'll be there to watch it all. You'll have front row seats and you'll watch her as she screams for your help but you won't be able to do a damn thing about it."

Marvin stared at Bruce for an instant and roared with laughter.

It came as a shock to Bruce to see Marvin react this way. He was sure this would have angered him, leaving him with no choice but to shut down the entire assignment. Maybe not so easily, but this? Bruce didn't expect this.

"Pardon me," Marvin said, holding up his index finger as he tried to gather himself. Large tears brimmed his eyes. "You're going to kill Shadow?" He snickered.

Bruce remained silent.

"I haven't laughed like this in ages," he said, pulling himself together. He leered at Bruce with the devil's eyes. "You're not going to kill Shadow."

"What makes you think I won't?"

Marvin slowly circled Bruce, chuckling. He completed his round and met Bruce's eyes, standing closer than he was initially. "Evan," he whispered.

Marvin allowed Evan's name to penetrate his mind. He'd fathomed the fact that Bruce hid his family from the agency. Although Bruce didn't break any rules, he managed to keep his family from being used as leverage. It was a smart and strategic move in Marvin's opinion. But as Marvin comprehended life, he realized there were no such thing as secrets. One day, they would come spilling out and this secret Bruce kept was now going to be used against him.

Bruce's jaw and fists clenched simultaneously. Bruce was absolutely sure he kept his track clear and made sure there were no breadcrumbs on the trail. He grunted. "How do you know about Evan?"

"That's not the question you should be asking right now, Bruce."

"How do you know about Evan!?" His voice boomed.

Marvin got a kick out of pushing Bruce's buttons.

"Just like you dug through my past, I dug through yours," he said as a mischievous smile dawned on his face. "If you were to ask what my thoughts were, I'd say you were a coward for leaving your family after your wife, Geneva," he spoke, as his gaze remained fixated on Bruce, "started using again, and then had multiple affairs with men, driving her to end her own life.

You would think a man, a *real* father, would stick around for his children and take care of them, but you did quite the opposite. You ran away and left them with your mother." He shuffled for an answer, but Bruce remained quiet. "You thought you could save her, didn't you? You married her knowing crystal clear she had a history of drug use. You literally drove her back to her addiction." He continued to press, knowing the truth was making Bruce's blood boil. "It's sad, isn't it? When you think the person you love cares about you just as much, only to realize what they truly love is shooting up cocaine and getting high in the middle of the day. I wonder how Evan and Denise would feel if they knew the truth."

"You don't know anything about Geneva!"

"The correct way to put it is that I know too much," he said, clasping his hands together and blowing hot air into the cusp, "and I'm sure you would want to reconcile with your son sometime in the future. However, if you lay a hand on Shadow, I will kill him."

Marvin reeled back from a punch to the eye, which threw him off balance. Out of instinct, Marvin punched back— once, twice and then once more before Bruce managed to get a hold of Marvin's neck.

As Bruce proceeded to hold him in a chokehold, Marvin's eyes started to flicker. He started to lose feeling in his face. Just as Bruce thought Marvin was about to pass out, Marvin reached up to Bruce's face and began to gouge out his eyes.

Bruce grunted in agony and let go.

Marvin, free of Bruce, took a second before throwing another punch straight in the face. He charged at Bruce who'd struggled to find balance and socked Bruce in the ribs. It was one strike after the other.

Bruce, flushed, dawdled toward Marvin and used all his strength to take a swing at Marvin. He struck Marvin on the cheekbone, jabbing him twice before feeling the energy drain out of his body. And before he knew it, he took another punch to the face, making him fall to his knees.

Bruce lay on his back. The trees appeared to be green blobs. His body ached. He used every bit of strength left to get back up but each body part felt like an overdone noodle. His head throbbed with pain. His lip was ripped open, bleeding into his mouth. Eyes felt swollen and the sound of his wheezing came and went along with deep breaths exhaled by Marvin, who'd crouched near Bruce as he lay on the ground.

Marvin pulled up Bruce's head by his hair. "If you lay a finger on Shadow, *I'll* cut Evan's throat. Do you understand?"

Bruce used all his strength to look Marvin in the eyes, but for the life of him, he couldn't. Marvin appeared to come and go but his voice was clear as a bright and sunny day. The words slowly processed through his mind, but dispersed just as they began to soak in.

"If you touch Shadow, you'll never see Evan again," he hissed.

Marvin let go of Bruce's hair and watched as Bruce's face hit the dirt. He stood over Bruce, pulled a handkerchief from his pocket, and wiped away the blood from his face. The leaves swayed against the ground as the cool breeze moved through the premises. This day constituted what was to come.

***

Rain started to pour down just as Evan and Shadow reached Knight's Drive.

"This is the first time it's rained this winter," he said, looking up at the sky. A little grin surfaced as he slowly turned to face Shadow. "C'mon," he said, as he took Shadow's hand.

As Evan picked up speed, Shadow automatically began to sprint. In a way, running in the rain with Evan beside her felt liberating. She'd never done anything like this. Growing up, it was all about how a woman carried herself. She could see her mother standing in the distance, lips pursed, brows furrowed. She would never approve this free-spirited version of Shadow. A lecture would be in order if Shadow's mother ever saw her running down the street in the rain like a teenager. It was unacceptable.

When they reached Shadow's house, they stood under the roof. Shadow watched as little raindrops slid off Evan's hair down to his forehead, merging with little droplets on his face, sliding down his cheeks to his chin, and then slowly dripping to his shirt. His chest rose and fell with rapid breaths. Evan's arm softly grazed around her waist, pulling Shadow in closely. As the rain poured, and with no one in sight, Shadow tilted her head upward, looking deeply into Evan's blue eyes.

He moved his hand upward and softly grazed against her jawline as he gazed into her eyes. Evan leaned in, and before she knew it, she felt his soft lips press against hers.

It was electrifying and felt familiar. It brought back some of her good memories.

Shadow tugged onto Evan's hips as he gently massaged the back of her head, kissing her, feeling as if this was going to be the last time. The faint smell of her shampoo—a combination of orchids and roses—lingered, which caused his neurons to run wild.

When their lips parted, Evan looked at her, hugging her closer, knowing all he wanted to do was to keep his arms wrapped around Shadow. That's where she was meant to be.

"I'm not going let anything happen to you," he whispered.

At a loss for words, Shadow just nodded.

CHAPTER 16

His face still bruised and lightly swollen, Marvin sat at his desk, reminiscing the evening before. He could have killed Bruce if he wanted to, but his plans for the future were far too superior and having Bruce alive was much more satisfying.

A tall, slender man walked in as Marvin was deep in thought. He sallied forth, holding a manila envelope.

"Here you go, sir," he said as he handed over the envelope. "Is there anything else I can do for you, sir?"

The man stood with a tall erect posture, waiting for Marvin's response.

"Stand by for your next order," he finally said.

"Yes, sir."

He cocked his head toward the door. "That's all."

On order, the man quietly left.

Marvin pulled the pin forward, allowing the fold to release, then pulled out a set of photos.

They were pictures of Evan and Shadow from the night before, walking side by side, close in proximity. There were a couple of photos of them sitting on the bench. He saw the way Evan looked at Shadow. This made Marvin furious. As he flipped through each one, his fury rose, hating Evan's guts more and more. But the last one brought shock to his system. His eyes fixated on the picture that showed Shadow and Evan kissing. As he continued to digest the picture, he squeezed his eyes shut.

The image of them kissing was etched in his mind. Shadow and Marvin were meant to be together. They were meant to grow old together and her being with Evan, all of that was now impossible.

His eyes sprang open. Marvin picked up the phone and pushed the buttons on the receiver. Leaning back in his chair, a wary smile surfaced on his lips.

"I need a cell for containment to be ready and six field agents on standby."

Marvin put the phone down on the receiver. He pressed his palms together, feeling satisfaction trickle through his body.

* * *

Denise walked in through the front door, keys in one hand and a grocery bag in the other. She donned a ponytail and fashioned workout gear. Earlier, she went to yoga class before dropping Nate off at the recreation center. Denise signed up Nate for the recreation program to keep him productive for at least half the day, which was better than being glued to the TV all day or playing video games. Plus, Skylar and a few of Nate's friends were enrolled, which made the five, sometimes six-hour day for Nate bearable.

She walked into the kitchen to find Ryan sitting at the table with photos scattered all around. Setting the bag down on the countertop, Denise moseyed her way closer to Ryan.

"Hey babe," she said, peering over at the pictures. "I bought donuts and some of the other stuff you asked for."

"Thanks," he said, not taking his eyes off the picture. "Do you want coffee?"

Denise paused for a moment and then casually replied, "I gave up coffee after Nate was born. It was actually a bet we had…you had to give up drinking for six months and I had to give up coffee. Winner got out of doing dishes for three months."

Ryan looked up at Denise and responded, "I'm guessing you won."

She gazed into his eyes as if his answer had an underlying meaning. "So, any progress?"

His attention shifted back to the picture. "No. Nothing." He paused to collect his thoughts. "he's seven years old, right?"

"Yeah," she answered, taking a seat next to him.

"Seven years of memories, wiped away, just like that," he said, snapping his fingers.

"I know it's frustrating—"

"Denise," he said, slamming his fist against the table, "seven years! Frustrating doesn't even begin to describe how I'm feeling. I probably won't ever remember the past seven years of our lives together."

Her forehead creased. "Ryan, don't say that," she said softly. "The doctor said it was going to take some time before you regained your memory."

"And how long is that Denise? A year? Two? Five years? I don't remember that I have a son, Denise, don't you get that?" he said, sounding defeated.

Denise looked at him sympathetically, knowing whatever she said wasn't going to help, but she said something anyway.

"We are doing everything—"

"Don't give me that 'we' crap. I'm all alone in this. You don't know how I feel, Denise! You don't know how it feels to have something taken from you in an instant."

But she did. Her parents, *her pregnancy.* She knew.

"You're not alone, Ryan," she said, exasperated, "you're not alone, babe."

"Yeah, well, I feel alone," he responded, pushing his seat back then promptly getting up.

"Where are you going?" she asked, staggering to her feet.

"I need to go for a walk, to clear my head."

Denise hit panic mode. This felt too familiar.

She strode, following Ryan close.

"Let's just sit down and talk about this," she objected.

The night of the incident flashed through her mind. The conversation they'd had replayed over and over, reminding her of the words Ryan said. *Sit down and watch TV with me.* And every day, she wished she'd listened.

"I need some space, Denise," Ryan answered, walking out through the front door, his hands deep in his pockets. He shivered, wearing only a short-sleeve shirt and pants, as he walked down the path.

Denise watched as he walked away, her eyes wet, her stomach was doing somersaults. She couldn't help but think how she was to blame for all of this. If they hadn't fought that night, if she had just sat down with Ryan that night, like she was asking right now, the accident would never happened. Ryan wouldn't have ended up in the hospital. He wouldn't have gone into a coma and then have his memory wiped away.

One moment, she felt she had everything she'd ever wanted. Now, it felt everything was falling apart, piece by piece.

* * *

Marvin sipped on some scotch on a grand leather couch across from Roy Hex, who was doing the same. They sat in Roy's office, which was off limits to the rest of the agency with exceptions for the agents serving on the panel. Both of them exchanged only two sentences with one another. Marvin looked into his glass and made the scotch swirl.

"So," Roy started off as he looked at Marvin with content, "is she coming back home?"

Marvin gave it a moment. "I'm trying every card in the deck. Don't worry, she'll come back."

Crow's feet were the only signs of aging on Roy's face. He was in shape, far better than anyone in their sixties. His blue eyes sparkled as the sunlight bounced off his face. A beard he started fashioning just a few months ago covered his cheeks and chin.

When he smiled, dimples appeared on his cheeks. "Then you're not trying hard enough. She's an easy person to persuade. I thought you'd know since the two of you lived together for a year. Or was it more? I can't seem to remember."

"It was a year, sir."

"What's holding you back? You do remember the deal, don't you?"

Marvin shifted in his seat, feeling cornered. "Yes, sir."

"What's the deal, Marvin?" he asked as he set down the scotch glass.

Marvin cleared his throat. He responded as he stared at the carpet, "If I have Shadow's baby or get married to Shadow, I'll be able to take over the agency once you step down."

"I picked you out of the crowd of men here for a reason. I see potential in you but from where I'm sitting, it doesn't seem like you really want to run the agency."

"That's far from the truth, sir. I love your daughter and more than anything, I want to marry her. I want to have a family with her—"

"Then what's the holdup? Whether you love her or not, since this was a sham to begin with, you can only operate the agency if you get married to her." He paused for a moment before he continued. "Convince her that you're the only person in existence who will make her happy, far from what she could imagine." He crossed his leg over the other. "I want this to be clear. I can't hold this position open for too long. There are a few agents who are just as qualified. I can happily offer one of them the opportunity."

Marvin pressed his hands together, pushing the tips of his fingers between his eyebrows. Hearing there were other potential suitors for this position made him uneasy. He wanted desperately to run the agency. It would make him the most powerful and feared man. No one would dare to cross him. And this was a once-in-a-lifetime opportunity. This was his chance to make something out of himself.

"There is one problem," he said. "She's involved with someone else in Lake View."

"Is it getting serious?"

"From the looks of it, I'd say yes."

Roy leaned over to pick up his drink. "I don't care how you do it, but get rid of the problem...permanently."

"I have the situation in control now, sir. He won't be problem any longer."

"Good. And I suggest you do it soon. I already had the panel take care of your first problem. They weren't too happy with what I asked them to do. "

"I know, sir, and I appreciate you going out of your way to help me stall Bruce."

Roy raised his glass.

"To making this world a better place." Both of them took a sip of their scotch, knowing each was on the same page as the other.

***

It was late in the afternoon. Denise sat in front of the picture

Ryan had been studying before storming out. It was the picture of him holding Nate for the first time. Ryan wore scrubs and had a grin from ear to ear. She could see the happiness on his face—it radiated in the picture. Tears filled her eyes knowing there was a chance Ryan would never recall this moment.

What was going to happen to their family?

The doorbell rang. Denise scattered to her feet, pressing her eyes with her thumbs so there were no signs of tear trails on her cheeks.

Nate was standing in front of the door, accompanied by Greece.

"Hey Denise," she said as soon as Denise opened the door. Greece's upbeat personality never seemed to die down.

Denise shook her head in disappointment and mentally smacked herself on the forehead. "They get out at 3:30 today. I totally forgot." She sighed. She looked at Nate, who was bundled up in a jacket and scarf, mittens and boots. "I'm so sorry sweetie. I lost track of time."

"Is everything okay, Denise?" Greece asked with concern.

"Yeah," she forced out with a smile. The last thing she wanted was Greece over for a cup of coffee to talk about feelings. It would go on for hours and Denise simply didn't have that kind of time on her hands. "Thank you for picking up Nate. I really appreciate it."

"What are friends for," she said cheekily. "If you ever need anything, or want to talk, I'm always here," she added, flashing a smile before turning back and heading down the sidewalk.

Yeah, right.

Denise proceeded into the kitchen, where she found Nate looking over the pictures. She stood a few feet behind him.

"Are you hungry, sweetie?"

"No," he replied, eyes still glued to the table scattered with pictures of him, from when he was a child to months back.

"What did you have for lunch?

"Pizza. Where's Daddy?"

"Daddy went for a walk, sweetie. He should be back any minute."

Any minute. It had been a few hours since Ryan left the house. Thinking about Ryan, Nate, and the entire family ever since Ryan woke up from his coma had mentally drained Denise. Some days, she was fine and was able to function properly. Other days, she couldn't even remember what she had for breakfast, fifteen minutes after she'd had it.

All she wanted was to go to sleep and never wake up. This burden the universe had thrown on her, she wanted it to be done and over with.

Life wasn't supposed to be easy, but it wasn't supposed to be *this* hard either.

"What do you want for dinner?"

His back was still turned toward her.

She waited for an answer. Nothing.

"Nate, honey, what do you want for dinner? I can make spaghetti or sandwiches."

She realized Nate was crying. Her heart dropped as she jolted forward, reeling in Nate closer to her. She cocked her head and saw tears trickling down his pink cheeks.

"Nate, what's wrong? Why are you crying?" Deep down, she already knew the answer.

"Is Daddy gone again?"

As much as she wanted to fall apart and cry with Nate, she had to pull herself together for his sake. "No, honey. Daddy's not gone. He's here. He just needed to get some fresh air. He'll be back." She wrapped her arms around him as he buried his head into her shoulder.

Ryan had walked in soon enough to hear the last bit of their conversation. He stood in the doorway, making sure not to make a sound. He leaned against the doorframe, letting out a sigh. What was he supposed to do?

Ryan made it to the kitchen, where Denise still had her arms wrapped around Nate. The sudden sound of Ryan's footsteps startled both of them. Denise was too in tears. They looked up at Ryan for a moment.

"Come here, you guys," he said, wrapping his arms around them. "I'm not going anywhere."

* * *

It was almost half past five. Shadow walked out of the building, her purse hanging off her shoulder, feeling pretty good about herself. She scanned the parking lot before walking any farther. With a blink of an eye, she was bombarded by thoughts of Marvin. As much as she tried to fight the menace out of her mind, he had a habit of popping up. She was finally able to shake away the thought and reminded herself about what a great day she had. Most of it was spent thinking about the kiss. On several occasions she found herself trying to repress a smile as the previous night replayed in her mind.

Work life wasn't too shabby either. The Pences were happy with the final design she'd worked on, thanks to Evan. She had landed two other big clients at the end of the day. She now had four demanding clients, which was going to keep her busy. Things were starting to turn around for Shadow. She was feeling content and powerful, something that was novel to her.

It took her a moment before she heard the loud gallop-like sound coming from behind her. She quickly turned around to find a young slender man, who wasn't any older than twenty-one, running toward her direction. Her forehead creased in confusion. It was the same man who delivered the mail and made copies. He was also the first one before anyone else to leave but for the life of her, she couldn't remember his name.

"Hey," he wheezed.

"Hi," she said, looking at him with concern. "Is everything okay?"

"Yeah," he said, handing her a black clasp envelope. When he tried to compose himself, his asthma kicked in. "This came in earlier and I was informed to personally hand it over to you, but then I couldn't get a hold of you, and then I lost track of time. But, here it is. I'm giving it to you now."

All Shadow could manage to say was "Oh-kay."

The young man slouched over, wheezing and coughing. His eyes became watery and the veins in his forehead began to bulge.

"Are you sure you're okay?" she asked.

He nodded.

Shadow took a moment before she walked away, in confusion and concern. Why was this so urgent? Her pace became slower as she unclasped the hook. She pulled out photos of Evan running in the park. Her heart began to pound. The one after captured Evan at the hardware store, buying the cat door. Another picture was taken of Evan walking to the curb throwing out the trash.

The parking lot became blurry and nothing was making sense.

There were more pictures of Shadow and Evan together. One was of the two of them walking back in the rain from the park. Then there was the two of them kissing on her front porch.

Shadow felt herself standing still but everything around her seemed distorted. She could see the street, the cars parked in the parking lot. She could feel her heart begin to race. Her eyelids fluttered for a few seconds and then shut. Everything went black for a moment. The ground beneath had begun to spin. Even though cars were driving by, and a truck had passed by, the only sound she could hear was of her breathing.

This cannot be happening right now.

Shadow kneeled to the ground, pressing her hands against

the cold cement wanting the pain to end. She gasped for air, feeling suffocated.

Okay, just breathe. Take deep breaths. Inhale and exhale. No one is going to hurt you. He can't hurt you. He can't hurt you. He can't hurt you.

Fifteen minutes later she finally gathered herself and managed to get back on her feet. The photos Marvin had of them were spread all over the parking lot. Her body trembled with fear, not really knowing what to do. She didn't want to walk any farther but at the same time, she wanted to run.

A faint voice behind her made Shadow's heart stop for a brief second. She sluggishly turned.

"Are you okay, Shadow?"

It was the same young man who delivered Shadow the black envelope. He looked at her, mixed with emotions. Shadow starred at him, not knowing what to say. How long had he been there?

"I woulda called the ambulance," he continued, "but… you kept saying he'll kill you too." He hesitated, his brows furrowed. "Are we in danger?"

She could hear the panic in his voice, but struggled to say anything. Shadow shook her head then slowly picked up the photos off the ground, still trembling. She feared what was to come.

This was just the beginning.

* * *

"Hi Evan," Venice said as she walked through the door.

Evan closed the door behind her.

"What smells so good?"

"I was making enchiladas."

As they walked into the kitchen, Venice noticed the two plates and wine glasses set on the table.

"Dinner for two?"

Evan was in the middle of filling the enchiladas. Like always, the counter was a mess. There was cheese scattered, and little droplets of sauce around his workstation. The sink was piled with dishes but he was certainly enjoying himself.

"Yeah," he said, taking a quick glance at Venice before bringing his focus back to the enchiladas.

Grandma Venice circled around the table as Evan's back was faced toward her. "It looks delicious," she replied. "Who did you invite?"

Evan craned his neck sideways, not meeting Venice's eyes. "Shadow. I invited Shadow."

"Oh."

"'Oh'? That sounded enthusiastic."

"Actually, I came by to talk to you about Shadow."

This time, Evan turned fully, giving Venice his undivided attention. "What about Shadow?"

"Look, Evan, I think we need to sit down and talk about this."

His eyebrows furrowed. "Talk about what exactly?"

Venice reminded herself she was doing this for the right reason. She was saving his life, even though it didn't seem like it right now, but by what Bruce had told her, Evan was in real danger. She pulled out a chair from the table for Evan and took a seat. "Come ," she said, gesturing to the vacant chair.

Evan navigated toward the open seat. He sat down, with his eyebrows knitted.

"What's going on?"

"So, there really isn't an easy way to say this since it's obvious you've invested time in this girl, but she's dangerous."

"How?"

Venice stayed silent for a moment. Her gaze flicked to the kitchen as her lips pursed. Her eyes met Evan's. "Getting involved with Shadow...it's going to get you killed." She studied his face, looking for a reaction but Evan didn't blink hearing the word *killed*. "I had a vision last night. There was a man standing over you with blood on his hands. I don't know who it was but he killed you. You *have* to stay away from her, Evan."

Her eyes brimmed with tears. Venice had to make sure Evan believed her. Otherwise, he'd start to question her and she knew better not to let Evan question her. She knew lying was never the answer but somehow in the situation she was in, it seemed like the best option.

Time was critical.

"Now all of the sudden, you have a vision of my death." Evan looked down at his laps, fiddling with his fingers. It was making sense to Evan, even though he didn't want to admit it. "How does this have anything to do with Shadow, though?"

"I think it's someone from her past," she whimpered. "I couldn't quite figure it out, but it's someone from her past and you're standing in his way. I'm begging you, please," she said as she put her palms together, "you need cut her loose."

"How sure are you? Are you a hundred percent sure this is going to happen?"

"I'm a hundred percent sure," she said, reaching out for Evan's hand.

Hesitating for a moment, Evan leaned forward and gripped Venice's hand.

"Okay," he said.

"Okay?"

"Okay," he reassured her.

"Please promise me, Evan. I can't bear to lose you."

He placed his other hand on top of the other, reassuring her, "I promise."

Evan hugged Grandma Venice, appreciating the concern but he knew in his gut it wasn't possible for him to cut ties with Shadow.

"You have no idea how relieved I am to hear that."

His response lingered with a hint of guilt. "Don't mention it."

* * *

He's going to kill Evan and it's going to be all my fault. Shadow sat on the bathroom floor leaning against the wall, sobbing. She had her hand laid out in front of her, holding a blade in the other. She didn't deserve to be with Evan or to be loved by him. She reasoned with herself. She knew she wasn't going to be able to keep herself away from Evan. He held a special place in her heart, even though it had been a short time knowing him. She would only attract danger to Evan as long as she was in the picture.

Life no longer had a meaning. It only became a burden.

Her stomach churned with anxiety and her heart bled with pain. Shadow knew this was going to hurt but the pain would go away forever. Then at last, she would finally be at peace. Marvin would no longer be able to hurt her. She would be free.

Mr. Jingles cautiously entered the bathroom, seeing something so familiar. He approached Shadow, his yellow eyes wide. He rubbed his head against Shadow's arm, but Shadow paid no attention.

She had no will to live anymore. Everyone around her would always be in danger. *What's the point in living if I can't have a normal life?*

"I'm sorry, Mr. Jingles," she said, choking on her sobs. "I don't know what to do anymore."

She tilted her head sideways, getting a blurry view of Mr. Jingles, who meowed as if he understood what she said.

Mr. Jingles strolled out of the bathroom, walking down the stairs. He passed the kitchen, through the new cat door, and trotted toward the fence. He looked up at the fence and jumped upward, his claws digging into the wood. He reached the top, his hind feet slowly meeting up with the rest of his body.

He leered into the glass door into Evan's kitchen. He kept watch, finally seeing Evan enter and head for the sink. Mr. Jingles slowly proceeded to walk down the fence, jumping off a few feet away from the ground.

Mr. Jingles pranced through the mud to the cement area in front of the back door. He paced back and forth, hoping he'd get Evan's attention.

* * *

Evan wiped his hands with the kitchen towel, looking over the enchiladas. There were two more left he needed to fill. Then it would be the simple task of pouring sauce and cheese over them. All he'd have left would be putting them in the oven on broil for a good seven minutes. Though he remembered the enchiladas were supposed to bake for about twenty minutes at 350 degrees, broiling would be quicker and he was becoming hungrier by the minute.

Digging into his front pocket, Evan pulled out his cell phone, checking to see if he'd received any messages from Shadow. He'd asked her to come over for dinner almost half an hour ago and received no response.

Confused, he shoved his cell phone back into his pocket. He continued to prepare the enchiladas before placing them in the oven whilst the earlier conversation he'd had with Venice settled in the back of his mind. He couldn't stop thinking about the man in Venice's vision.

He had blood on his hands, her voice echoed as he filled one enchilada. *Blood.*

Grandma Venice's voice went in and out. *Strange man. It's someone from her past.*

Evan very well knew this strange man in Venice's vision

was Shadow's ex but it still wasn't going to stop Evan from seeing Shadow.

* * *

Mr. Jingles pawed at the glass door, head shifting side to side, wondering how he was supposed to get Evan to look over. His instincts were telling him something horrible was going to happen and knowing how Shadow acted when Evan was around, maybe there was something Evan could do. Even though he was just a feline, he was able to sense these kinds of things. When something was off, *something was off.*

Mr. Jingles kept a close eye on Evan, who still managed to keep his back turned. Impatient, Mr. Jingles began to howl.

Evan's head jerked sideways toward the kitchen window. Evan carefully listened to the trail of the cry, looking out the window seeing nothing but his backyard. Yet the cry had become louder.

Mr. Jingles spotted Evan peering out the window then stood on all fours. He began to pace back and forth, his eyes still focused on Evan. The movement caught Evan's eye. He wiped his hands on a towel and proceeded toward the glass door.

The moment Evan opened the door, Mr. Jingles entered and headed toward the front door, wasting no time. Halfway across, Mr. Jingles looked back to see if Evan was following his lead. Evan stood in confusion. Eventually he followed Mr. Jingles. Once Mr. Jingles was at the front door, he meowed as he looked up at Evan. *Open the door. You have to save her.*

From basic intuition, Evan opened the front door, letting Mr. Jingles out. Evan stood in the doorway as Mr. Jingles began to trek toward his home. Less than halfway, Mr. Jingles stopped in his tracks and looked behind him to make sure Evan was following. But he wasn't. Again he meowed.

"You want me to come with you?"

Mr. Jingles meowed again.

Not sure what to think of this, Evan closed the door behind him and walked behind Mr. Jingles, still perplexed.

Once they reached the porch, Evan pushed the doorbell, sliding his hands into his pockets. He stood there wondering why Mr. Jingles had come to take him to Shadow's home. As they waited, Mr. Jingles stood on his feet with his front paws pressed against the window, peering in. The shades had been turned.

Evan took one look at Mr. Jingles' behavior, feeling as if it was odd. Evan knocked, starting to feel anxious. Mr. Jingles paced back and forth, wide eyed. He began to cry, just like he had done before.

"Shadow, open the door!" he shouted, feeling uneasy.

His gut urged the suggestion something horrible was about to take place. He couldn't help but to think it had something to do with Shadow's ex.

***

Shadow sat in her bathroom, tears running down her cheeks, listening to Evan's shouts from upstairs. He couldn't help her. Even if he attempted to, he'd get himself killed *or* Marvin would mentally torture Evan just like he was doing to Shadow. That was no way to live a life with Marvin in the picture. And she certainly didn't want to put him through that. Evan didn't deserve a life full of misery. She pressed the blade against her wrist knowing this would end it all.

"Shadow! Listen to me," he yelled in a panic, "you've got to trust me when I say this. I will *not* let anything happen to you. That's my promise to you. You have to trust me. Please open the door and we can talk about what's going on. Just please... open the door." He pressed his head against the door, shifting from scenario to scenario.

His mind jumped to the cat door he'd installed. Evan ran past the window and peered over the fence, on a slight tiptoe. Instantaneously, he remembered he'd hinged the door from the inside, rather from the outside, which meant one thing; it would be impossible to unhook the door and enter. He walked back to the front of the door.

"Okay, that's fine. If you don't want to open the door, I'll just call the police. They'll be here in three minutes and you're going to have to answer questions. I know you don't want to do that."

Evan pulled out his cell phone, ready to dial.

* * *

Blood poured out, trickling down from the sides of her wrist. She let out a long sigh of relief. But that didn't last. She continued to hear Evan's voice ring in her head. His persistent pounding continued to nag at her, with each pound seemingly getting louder and louder. With haste, Shadow surged to her feet, feeling dizzy.

She climbed down the stairs, pressing her wrist against her side. After taking the last step, she wiped away the tears and abruptly opened the door. There stood Evan, frantic, with his fist midway in the air.

Slowly putting his hand down, he gathered the view before him.

Shadow's eyes were lined with redness, her cheeks flushed. He hadn't seen someone in so much pain.

"If you don't stop harassing me, I'll call the cops on you."

The words went through one ear and flushed through the other. He studied her face, her stance, the way her right arm seemed tenser than the left. Everything around him became dead silent. Her lips continued to move but he heard nothing. Evan's eyes flicked back to Shadow's right arm. Still, it seemed tense, palm formed into a fist. The red that began to seep into her beige skirt caught his attention.

Without giving it another thought, Evan lunged forward and took her hand, facing the bleeding palm upward.

His eyes, filled with fury, met hers.

"What the hell are you doing, Shadow?!"

She said nothing. Even though she no longer wanted to feel any kind of emotion, oddly enough, she felt the disappointment and anger from Evan.

Mr. Jingles looked up at Shadow. He knew she'd been through more than she could handle. Loving her was his duty. Five years ago, he was once an abandoned kitten on the street in the middle of the night. He knew what lonesome felt like. That specific night, hunger for food had exceed hours and when he felt fear overcome his mind, Shadow picked him up during her evening walk and pressed his tiny body against her soft and warm neck. Suddenly, his racing heart had become steadier and his cry for help faded.

She rescued him. Now it was his turn.

Mr. Jingles he walked back into his home, his body grazed against her legs, knowing Evan would one day take his place to love and keep her safe.

Evan firmly grasped her other arm, as he closed the door behind them.

"C'mon," he said, tugging on her arm, leading her back to his place.

"Let go of me!" she protested.

Evan continued to ignore as Shadow tried to struggle free.

* * *

Shadow sat on the toilet seat cover as Evan pulled out the first aid kit.

Evan kneeled down in front of her, observing how deep the

cut was. Luckily Shadow had just missed the artery. He held a towel under her arm as he poured rubbing alcohol over the cut, stinging Shadow to the core. She winced.

"I forgot to mention it was going to sting," he said through gritted teeth.

He wrapped the ends of the towel over the cut and pressed against the cut as he singlehandedly opened the big bandage. Removing the towel, Evan placed the beige bandage over her cut, rubbing it back and forth, making sure it was secure. Over it he wrapped around a white PowerFlex bandage, making sure it was just tight enough that it didn't block the blood flow but secure enough to prevent any further bleeding.

"Okay, that should do it," he said, clipping the end, running his hand over to make sure the ends stuck to one another. His eyes roved to hers. She looked up and met his and this was the first time she'd seen worry, fear, and anger in someone else's eyes. But it was all formed in a different kind of way. It was because he cared. She looked away, feeling embarrassed and weak.

CHAPTER 17

They sat on the sofa with their dinner plates in hand. Evan had his feet up on the coffee table, and Shadow was curled up on the couch as her plate rested on her thighs. It had been a silent dinner. But in their minds, their thoughts about the last hour ate at them. Neither of them wanted to dissect what happened yet could sense the situation still lingering over their heads and feeling the need to address it.

Evan leaned forward, reaching for his glass of Coke. After he took a sip, he cocked his neck sideways, getting Shadow's attention.

She was just about to take another bite, but she could knew what was coming—the dreaded question.

"Why?"

Clearing her throat, she put her fork down on her plate.

She adjusted her position, getting a better view of Evan's face. "It's the only way to end the pain."

Evan looked away, bringing his focus to the coffee table and then back to his glass of Coke. One of the tiny bubbles that formed against the edge of the glass popped. He took a deep breath and looked back at Shadow.

"What problem is it going to solve?" he asked softly.

Shadow took a breath, wanting to give him an explanation, but then said nothing. She bit her lower lip with uncertainty.

"It doesn't solve anything. Even though it's your own life and you can do whatever the hell you want...suicide's not going to solve anything. It's only going to hurt the people that love you."

"I guess I haven't made it clear then. I don't have anyone in my life that cares enough—"

"That's a load of bull," Evan said, cutting her off. He set his unfinished plate on the coffee table and sprung off the couch. He ran his fingers through his hair, looking everywhere but at Shadow. "The last time I was *that* terrified was when I found out my dad died. I was only four and I realized I didn't have any of my parents anymore. They were gone and they were never coming back. And today, I thought the same thing was going to happen again. I don't know how I fell in love with you, I wasn't expecting to, but I did." Tears shimmered in his eyes. "I know it's selfish of me to talk about what I've lost, but you...I can't lose you. Protecting you has crossed my mind so many times for different reasons, but loving you? I don't have a reason for falling in love with you." Evan unconsciously ran his fingers through his hair again, feeling weight being lifted off his shoulders mixed with anxiety about what was to come next.

This wasn't the way he'd imagined telling Shadow that he was in love with her.

"Well," she said, her eyes flicking to her plate, not knowing what the right response was. Memories of the past came flooding back. She took a moment before she spoke. "I think it's best that we keep our distance. It'll be better for the both of us."

Her eyes brimmed with tears.

"Why? Give me a good enough reason."

"Okay," she said, placing her dinner plate on top of the table. She looked at him dead in the eyes and started, "My ex-fiancé is a secret agent. He works for a non-existent organization—and when I say non-existent, I mean that no one knows that it exists, literally. He tortures and kills people for a living. He's been keeping an eye on the both of us. He's been blackmailing me with pictures of you, me, and us and there's nothing anyone can do about it. As long as I'm anywhere near you, he's going to come after you and you don't want that, Evan. *I* don't want that."

Shadow arose from the couch saddened.

Evan studied her as the earlier conversation he had with Venice ran through his mind.

"What if I told you that I already knew that?" he said with a faded smile. "I mean, I didn't know about the whole secret agent stuff, but I knew getting involved with you would probably get me killed."

"What? How?"

"This is gonna sound ridiculous," he began. "Well…my grandma is a psychic. She had a vision about what was lying ahead for me. But she's not always right about these things."

Shadow let it register in her mind before she continued. "Did she say anything else?"

"No, that was about it," he said, leaving out the part about not seeing Shadow again.

"Wow. There's just a lot of information for one day. It seems like today is a first for everything, huh?" she said, looking up at him, mainly thinking about what he'd said earlier. She paused for a moment. The thought made her curious. "Why do you want to be a part of my life? I don't understand it. Especially since it can get you killed."

Evan sat back on the couch and looked at Shadow seriously.

His heart was racing. "You probably don't believe it and I don't expect you to because of everything you've been through, but I love you. You have this aura that pulls me in. All I want to do is be there with you and give you everything you could ever imagine or at least try to."

Shadow was taken aback by Evan's answer. Everything felt unreal, as if Shadow and Evan were merely just actors in a romantic movie. She moved back to the couch. "I...I don't know what to say," she said softly. Memories of Evan flashed through her mind. A part of her felt guilty for not sharing what she knew. She didn't deserve him. "You are a crazy man."

Evan chuckled but deep down, he wondered if Shadow felt the same way about him. Truthfully, he wanted to hear her say those words but it wasn't something that happened overnight, which begged the question: Why had he fallen in love so quickly? Was it a psychological way of fixing what he'd done to her in their previous life? Or was it because he really was in love with Shadow, for who she was?

He shook away the thoughts. His brows knitted in a frown as his eyes lingered on the white bandage wrapped around Shadow's wrist.

"How many times have you..." His voice trailed off.

Shadow directed her attention to where Evan's eyes were focused. "Today was the first time I actually went through with it," she admitted. Times of the past came flashing by when she sat and cried wanting to end her life. Her eyes welled up with pain.

As hard as she tried to keep her emotions in control, she broke down right there, in front of Evan. Shadow let her head sulk close to her chest. Her shoulders became stiff and before she moved to wipe away her tears, Evan wiped them away for her. He pulled her in close, and wrapped his arm around her.

He kissed Shadow on top of her forehead.

"I'm not going to let him hurt you anymore," he whispered.

She slid her arm around his waist as she rested her head on his chest. This was where she felt the safest.

Evan ran his hand through her hair while his mind lingered to what he'd done in his previous life. He wanted to share that with Shadow but so far there hadn't been the perfect time. He couldn't do it now because Shadow was in a fragile state and when they were having a good time, he didn't want to ruin the moment. The more he thought about it, the more it felt like it was better left unsaid. At the same time, he didn't want to keep anything from her either.

"You're so beautiful inside and out. I don't know why anyone would want to hurt you like this."

Shadow pulled away, and met his gaze. She thought about what he said for a moment.

"I read something online once and it kinda struck me: Sometimes we pay for the sins we don't remember." She let out an exasperated sigh. "I probably hurt someone in a previous life and maybe I'm paying for it now." Her mind jumped to the snippets of what she remembered. "It's my karmic debt, I guess. I started doing a lot of research on it after everything in my life stopped making sense to me."

Evan studied Shadow, impressed by the fact Shadow believed in karma, more so that she had poured herself into research. But she didn't deserve this. She didn't deserve to be emotionally blackmailed to live her life in constant fear. Not in this life or in the previous one. Understanding karma was hard. It only made sense to someone who knew the whole story, which neither of them did.

He shook his head in disagreement. "But you don't deserve this. Not at all," he said as he peered into her eyes.

"Yeah, well, the universe disagrees."

Shadow sighed. "I should get going. Thank you for dinner.

The enchiladas were really tasty."

"Absolutely." On cue, Evan rose to his feet. "Let me walk you home," he said, offering his hand.

The slightest smile came across her face and just as quickly, it faded away.

The night had set in hours ago. The sky now filled with stars and galaxies. They walked hand in hand, quietly down the sidewalk. The shadows created by the streetlights walked farther and farther away, creating an elongated image of two people holding hands, each of them deeply hoping this night had started off differently.

"How about I pick you up tomorrow around six-ish for dinner?" he asked as they reached the front of the house. "I'll take you to my favorite restaurant, Niki's."

They faced each other, Shadow still feeling a little bit of shame for what happened earlier.

Shadow thought. "I don't think it would be a good idea."

Evan reached out for her hands and held them in his. "Why? 'Cause of him?"

She searched in his eyes. Evan made her feel the most comfortable yet it all seemed too surreal. She remembered the look on his face when he was crouched on the bathroom floor, putting a bandage over her cut. He cared for her more than she could comprehend and that terrified her. She didn't want anything to happen to Evan.

"Yes, and your grandma's vision."

"My grandma's vision isn't always correct. I promise you, nothing's going to happen."

"You don't know that Evan," she insisted. "Don't you understand how evil he is? I don't believe he has an ounce of humanity left in him. Your grandma's vision couldn't be closer to the truth. He *will* kill you."

"Then I'll fight him."

Shadow was frustrated—Evan didn't comprehend what she was saying. "Evan! Can you please listen to me? I'm being serious here."

"I am listening to you," he reassured her. "I'm just not going to let anyone dictate what I can and can't do with my life. I respect your concerns but if I want to have dinner with you, then I should be able to without having to worry about what's going to happen next. And so should you, if that's what you want."

Shadow smacked her forehead. "You just don't get it, do you? I'm not exaggerating—"

Evan pulled her closer to him. "What do you want? Do you want to have dinner with me tomorrow and enjoy a wonderful evening or do you want to stay cooped up inside in fear? Huh? Which one is it?"

Shadow studied his eyes. Even though he wasn't smiling, she could tell how happy he was. She let out a heavy sigh. "You're crazy. You're absolutely crazy." Shadow slipped out of his arms and turned toward the door.

"So I've heard." He chuckled.

Before she could get any further, he pulled her back in. "What do you think you're doing?"

She shot him a confused look.

"I don't get a goodnight?"

Shadow looked into his eyes, reaching for his soul. With the faintest voice, she said, "Goodnight."

He kissed her on the top of her forehead. "Goodnight, Shadow. I'll see you tomorrow at 6:00."

She opened the door and looked back with the slightest smirk. "Okay."

He waved goodbye and walked back the path alone after she closed the door behind her.

***

That night, as Evan lay in bed wide awake, all he could think of was the similarities in Shadow's life now and in the previous life. She was married to Derek, who made her life a living hell, and now she was escaping the same life. Even now, escaping didn't help much. She was being followed, watched, and tracked, and so was he. She was still living in fear just as she was in her previous life.

After a while, going about it in his mind over and over about the same thing, Evan finally concluded that he was the only person who could help her. *Mr. Jingles is all I have*, her voice echoed.

Slowly he drifted into a deep sleep, dreading to be woken up by another memory.

CHAPTER 18

Push!" yelled the midwife. Samantha's head rested on a pillow, her legs spread wide as she lay on her bed covered with towels. Her hair was drenched in sweat, and beads of sweat trickled from her forehead to her eyebrows.

The midwife peered down below, telling Samantha once again to push.

Samantha grunted as she did what she was told. As she squinted, using all her strength to push, she could see Derek standing in the corner next to the bathroom.

Derek appeared glum. He brought his arms up to his chest and crossed them. He knew his life was torn apart by Samantha's infidelity as she was giving life to Adrian's baby. His *brother's* baby. He hadn't felt this much betrayal and hurt in his entire lifetime.

This was supposed to be *their* baby. Instead it wasn't. Even though he'd forgiven her, he was still torn about the decision he'd made.

"You're almost there. Just give me one more push!"

Samantha, out of breath, grabbed on to the towels and

craned her head upward and pushed once again. It was all the energy she had left within her.

Then there was a cry. That magical cry.

The midwife looked up at Samantha, who was spent and gave her the news. "It's a boy!" The midwife smiled as she cut the umbilical cord. She wrapped the cord and put it aside. Then she proceeded to clean the baby boy.

Samantha's heart pounded with exhaustion. She breathed and cried with happiness. "Can I hold him?"

Derek could see the smile that surfaced across her face when she asked to hold her son.

The midwife looked in Derek's direction, almost as if she was asking for permission. He nodded as his hands slid in his pockets.

Samantha saw their exchange, but didn't think anything of it.

After cleaning the baby, the midwife wrapped him in a blanket and handed him to Samantha.

Samantha held him and tears of joy ran down her cheeks. After longing to meet her baby, the time had finally come. He was the tiniest human being she'd ever seen. He looked at her with his big blue eyes, a head full of light brown hair, and rosy lips. He continued to stare as she stared back, smiling. It was the most beautiful moment Samantha ever encountered throughout her entire life. She managed to laugh as she held his little hand.

The midwife started to stitch up Samantha while she enjoyed her time with her newborn.

"Hi," she whispered to him with a wide smile. "I am so in love with you, little one. You are so precious." She sniffled and giggled. "I can't believe you're mine."

Samantha's smile slowly turned into a frown. She started to shed tears, overwhelmed with the joy. It had been a long time since someone other than Adrian made her heart dance with joy.

She smiled again, thinking about all the wonderful times they were going to have together. She would teach him how to draw, color, sing the alphabet, read, dance—everything a mother was supposed to do.

"I already have a name picked out for you."

The baby looked back at her, forming what looked like a little smile. It almost seemed as if he understood what his mother was saying.

Derek and the midwife exchanged looks. He nodded at the midwife, who had been casually watching as she gathered her things. She approached Samantha, holding out both arms.

Confused, Samantha's lips parted in the midst of asking a question but before she could say anything, the midwife had already taken her son from her arms.

The midwife looked at Samantha, feeling guilty for doing this, but she had been given strict orders and if they weren't abided by, her husband would receive her head on a silver platter for dinner.

Samantha's stomach turned into a knot. Her heart started to break, piece by piece. Everything in the room seemed to move rapidly. Her heart pounded louder and louder, and she couldn't hear what Derek was saying to the midwife as she was on her way out. She wanted to scream for help, but the words were lodged in her throat.

Her baby was being taken away from her and *Derek* had everything to do with it.

"Wait, wait!" she mumbled through her sobs as the midwife walked out of the room. "Come back!" she begged in the faintest voice. "Please," she managed to say, "come back with my baby."

Derek shut the door behind the midwife. He faced the door,

knowing what he'd done was the best, for *both* of them. He slowly turned around, with his hands in his pockets, thinking.

"I'm sorry," he mumbled, the rim of his eyes now pink.

She looked at him but he was blurry through the tears. Her lips quivered as she wailed. She covered her eyes with both of her hands, not wanting to look at him.

He minced toward Samantha. He was concerned for her. Derek knew this was the ultimate hurt. But he loved her. His eyes started to well up with tears, but they only reached the surface as he controlled himself, not wanting to get too emotional.

He knew sending away her baby wasn't right. Part of it didn't make sense, but then there was another part that made him see the reasoning of all of this. If he had let Samantha keep her baby, the child would grow up in a home where love once existed. He didn't want the child to grow up with a father who would lash out and then snap back like nothing ever happened.

When Derek saw Samantha hold the infant, it brought back memories of his childhood and the way he lived his life from shelter to shelter. And then from home to home when his foster parents could no longer take care of Derek because of his sudden outbursts and violence. He remembered the pain from not being wanted, from being rejected by his biological parents, who didn't want anything to do with their own flesh and blood. Adrian was their beloved child, the good one. He always seemed to get everything Derek wanted.

There was also a part of Derek that feared of being left alone. Samantha had become his savior the moment she walked into his life; the only way he knew Samantha would stick around was if she was constantly in fear. It was the only way he learned to keep anyone around. Fear kept people on their toes. It's what made Derek powerful.

Derek sat beside her, knowing she would hate him for the rest of his life until he died, and *that* he was okay with. As long as she never left his side, which she wouldn't, he was okay with her hating him.

Suddenly…

* * *

Evan sat straight up. He wasn't terrified, nor was he drenched in sweat like all the other times he remembered something from the past. His eyes darted toward his alarm clock: 3:30. His heart sank as he replayed the memory of Samantha giving birth only to have her child be taken away from her. Evan shifted to the side, his hands planted on the edge of the bed, as his feet touched the floor.

There were so many questions that no one had the answers to, and that gutted him. What happened to the baby? Where did he go? Did he kill Adrian? Why was Derek so intent on making sure Samantha never experienced happiness? What made Derek like this?

Evan took the clock and threw it across the room. He felt helpless. Why was he so cruel to Samantha? Why did he remember this? What was the meaning behind this memory? He took a pillow and shoved his face into it, screaming at the top of his lungs.

He wanted this nightmare end. He didn't want to remember what he'd done to Samantha. This wasn't who he was now.

Evan staggered across the room and picked up his alarm clock. It was hardly damaged as he examined it all around. He placed it back on his nightstand and proceeded to the bathroom. After taking a leak, he shuffled through his dresser and pulled out a gray hoodie. Using both palms, he rubbed his face up and down, trying to look alive.

The neighborhood was silent and the streetlights made

everything lively. He plunged his hands into the deep pockets of his sweater, leaving the hood hanging down his back.

Exhaling, the water vapor in Evan's breath condensed into little droplets of liquid and ice, forming a tiny fog, disappearing into the thin air. He stood at the end of the curb, looking up at the night sky, alone with his thoughts.

He recalled the night where he'd sat with Shadow on the curb. *Maybe you can help me.* Those words hadn't left his mind.

At times, he failed to understand how life worked. The good people somehow ended up with lives that seemed unfair. Evan realized why someone in Shadow's position would rather kill themselves than live another day of torture and misery, but that wasn't how it was supposed to be.

He looked up, seeing the stars were just little specks of dots from the corner of the sidewalk. There were so many uncertainties out there in the universe; no one had the answer to everything. It wasn't possible. The human mind was capable of comprehending to a certain extent, and the rest was just a gray area, yet to be understood.

With what he knew so far, Evan began to think of the future. Earlier conversations with Venice and Shadow started to curdle. As long as he stuck around with Shadow, he was already on his deathbed. And it was something that didn't sink in just yet. A part of him still believed Shadow's ex was incapable of killing him and Venice's prediction could be wrong. If the odds were in his favor, he'd live...but looking at the bigger picture, karma was waiting for him around the corner.

Other than losing both parents at the age of four, his life had been pretty mellow and easygoing up until this point. So maybe this was how he was going to pay for torturing Samantha. As much as he didn't want to believe it, it did make sense and he would have to come to terms with it at some point.

Evan inhaled a deep breath as he tried to divert his mind to other thoughts that didn't revolve around Shadow or his past. The essays sat on his desk that needed to be graded but procrastinating and working on the garden pushed the duty far down the list of things to do.

With the tip of his shoe, he kicked around a tiny rock. In the last few days, life had become overwhelming.

"Why are you up so late?"

He turned around, and saw Mr. Brar. He was wheeling down his driveway to the sidewalk, wrapped in a black cotton robe and blue silk pajamas. He wore a white turban and his oxygen tank hung off the side of his wheelchair.

Evan smirked. Seeing Mr. Brar was always a delight.

"Couldn't sleep. Why are you up so late?"

"Same. I think I had too much coffee before I went to bed. I read for a little bit, hoping I'd fall asleep, but when I looked at the clock it was 3:30. Tried to fall asleep but couldn't. So I thought I'd come out and enjoy the silence."

Evan nodded, feeling they shared the same boat.

"What's on your mind, son?"

"Ah, nothing really."

"If there is one thing I can share with you is that we can worry and think all we want, but at the end of the day, what's going to happen, it's gonna happen. No matter how hard we try and stop it," he said, letting it resonate in Evan's mind. "So." He cleared his throat. "What's on your mind?"

Evan sighed. "I told you I'd been having dreams of my previous life, right?"

He nodded. "You sure did. I think it's insane you can remember stuff like that. I can't even remember what I had for lunch yesterday. It's a blessing, you know?"

"A blessing and a curse in disguise." He chuckled. "The woman I was married to in my previous life is my next door neighbor," he said, running his fingers through his hair. "And I'm in love with her."

"But—" Mr. Brar started.

"Venice warned me not to get too close to Shadow because she had a vision. At first she didn't sound so serious, but yesterday she came by and told me she'd seen me dead in her vision. Then later, when I was having dinner with Shadow, she told me how her psycho ex-fiancé is a part of this secret agency and he'd been keeping tabs on the both of us."

Mr. Brar felt like he was hit by a truck. Everything he observed on Knight's Drive was making sense now.

"Basically, I'm a dead man as long as I keep seeing her."

Mr. Brar's mind was brought back to the time he'd worked for the agency and the things he'd done. If an agent got ahold of Evan, he was indeed going to end up dead. There was no way Evan would survive at the hands of an agent.

"This secret agency she mentioned," he said, locking eyes with Evan, "she didn't say anything else?"

"No, not that I can remember."

"I see," he said, his words trailing off. His eyes traveled to the lighted part of the sidewalk for a bit before he turned his attention back to Evan. "If you want my advice, I would suggest staying away from the girl. She's telling you her ex is an agent and keeping tabs on you…that's dangerous," he said. "You're too young to die, Evan. Die for a greater cause if you want, but not for this."

Evan sighed. No one seemed to understand him.

"As a Sikh, wouldn't you say if someone had the ability to remember who they were in their past life, it was only for a reason?"

"Yes," Mr. Brar responded, getting a hint of where this conversation was heading.

"Then why would I meet Shadow just months after I started having the dreams?"

"It could all just be a coincidence, son. Your dreams of your past life could serve as a reminder of what not to do in this life. It doesn't necessarily mean that you have to put your life on the line. There's more than one way to look at this."

"True, but she's in danger. And when you know someone needs you, you don't walk away like a coward afraid of what will happen to you in the process."

Mr. Brar was taken aback by Evan's reasoning. He couldn't have been more proud to see the little boy he saw growing up to be such a warrior. But he couldn't let Evan do this. There was so much of life Evan was supposed to experience. Reunite with Bruce. Get married. Have kids. Grow old with the love of his life. He was too young to go and it was going to break his heart just as much as anyone else's if Evan's death came too soon.

"I think you should listen to your grandmother. She knows what she's talking about. It's going to tear her apart if she found out what you were up to."

Evan shot back with a quick response. "But I have to do what's right—"

"How do you know this is right?" he asked. "You have a choice and you're not making the smart choice. Life is about making smart choices."

Evan was beginning to become irritated. No one understood where he was coming from and a part of him didn't expect anyone to understand either. No one knew the amount of guilt he carried around for what happened in a different lifetime. Maybe it didn't make sense or there wasn't a logical explanation to it, but in his heart, he knew this was what he was supposed to do.

"Life's also about taking risks. I can't leave her."

Mr. Brar aggressively shook his head in disagreement. His brows furrowed.

Given that Evan had respect for Mr. Brar, he didn't have the heart to argue with him. He knew Mr. Brar was coming from a good place, but he needed to do what had to be done, whether or not anyone was on board with the idea.

"Think about it. Sleep on it for a couple of days. At least do that. Can you do that for me?"

Evan hesitated for a bit before he nodded in agreement just to please him. This was the second lie he'd let someone he cared for to believe.

"Son, I'm gonna head inside now. The cold is getting to me," he said, turning the wheels to his wheelchair.

Evan nodded, needing to be alone with his thoughts.

Mr. Brar wheeled away toward his driveway. "Lord, why are you doing this to me?" *It doesn't seem like life gets any easier when you get old, does it?*

Mr. Brar hurriedly picked up the phone from the receiver on his nightstand and punched in the one number he always dreaded dialing.

Pick up! Pick up!

Moments later, Mr. Brar heard a muffled voice on the other end. "Bruce?"

"Yeah…everything okay?"

Mr. Brar took a long pause before responding. "It doesn't look good. Evan's got this crazy idea that he needs to protect the girl. You need to get this under control."

"I've been up all night trying to figure out how to put an end to this. The thing is, the girl, Shadow, she's Roy's daughter. Her ex-fiancé, Marvin, is a fourth floor agent."

"Roy as in Roy Hex? The man running the whole damn operation?"

"Yeah, so this shit ain't gonna be easy."

"You know what's going to happen, don't you?"

"That's the last thing I want to think about."

There was a beat of dead silence. The horrendous thoughts crossed both of their minds.

"It's not over yet, Bruce. There's still time to take this Marvin guy out."

"That's the only option I have now. There's nothing else I can do at this point. I'll probably never see Evan or Denise again but it'll keep everyone safe."

"Give me a ring if you need help."

"Yeah. Thanks, Mr. Brar."

Bruce pushed the button, ending the call. He turned to his side, barely reaching the tip of the drawer. He shifted closer just enough to reach the inside of the drawer to put his burner phone back in its place, then shut it.

He lay on his back with one arm resting behind his head, the other on top of his chest. For some reason, suddenly, a rush of hot air began to fill his body. Bruce pushed the sheets aside with his feet. A teardrop escaped the side of his left eye. Life for Bruce had been one huge roller coaster ever since Geneva died. He was at a constant battle trying to figure out what he'd done to deserve everything he'd been through. Aside from the fact he left his two children in the care of his mother twenty-seven years ago, he was still a good man. He always tried his best to do the right thing. He'd never wanted or had put anyone in pain.

Or had he? If he did, it was some lifetime ago that he possibly couldn't remember.

Shifting from one side to the other, he finally sat up, knowing there was no way he was going to get any sleep tonight.

He got dressed and went to work.

CHAPTER 19

"How've you been?" Venice asked, cozying up next to Ryan on the couch after breakfast.

Ryan refused to see a therapist. He was stubborn to admit there was a problem. Venice decided she was going to try to help him as a friend, rather than a specialist.

Denise was in the kitchen cleaning up and insisted on doing it all on her own. Nate was at Skylar's house for another play date. Everyone agreed Nate needed to be preoccupied with other things. They still hadn't told Nate the severity of Ryan's accident.

Ryan wore one of his gray thermals and jeans. He picked at some imaginary lint before turning to Venice and meeting her eyes. "I don't know how to answer that question." He pondered the thoughts he'd had in the last couple of days, none of them leading in a positive direction. "I don't know," he sighed. He rested his head back on the edge of the sofa, looking up at the ceiling, hoping the answers to his problems would appear.

"When you look at Denise, how do you feel?"

For this question, he'd already known the answer. He said

with a smile, "I feel lucky."

"You feel lucky. Why does she make you feel lucky?"

His eyes fixated at the ceiling, he answered, "She always put me first. I don't remember a time when she hasn't put her needs aside to help me or listen to me when I had a horrible day at work. She's just amazing. She's selfless, caring—she's my rock, Venice."

She nodded, agreeing. "Do you remember anything from that night, right before the accident?"

"I was walking. I was pretty pissed at Denise…"

"Why?"

He tilted his head in Venice's direction. "I don't remember. I know we had a fight but I don't remember what it was about."

Venice thought hard about Ryan's answer. It raised many questions of her own. Why hadn't they talked about the itty bitty things that led up to the fight? Why was the main reason behind this tragedy overlooked?

"Denise!" she shouted. "Come in here, will ya darling."

Denise was leaning against the kitchen sink. She'd just put away the last dish in the cupboard along with the rest of them. She'd heard the entire conversation since the two of them couldn't bother whispering and the walls, well, they weren't as thin as everybody thought. Denise was dreading to have this conversation with Ryan. Confiding in Evan and Venice was easy. They weren't there the day Denise and Ryan had a major outburst. They didn't know the entire truth behind the argument. And this was why it was easier to talk to them about than with Ryan.

Running away from the issue wasn't going to solve anything, but right now, that's what Denise wanted to do.

Denise entered the room nonchalantly. "What's up?"

"Sit down, dear," she ordered nicely. "There's something the two of you need to talk about."

Hesitant, Denise walked across the room, placing herself in the chaise, angled in a way that both Ryan and Venice were visible. She curled up, knowing what was coming.

"Why is it that you two haven't talked about the fight?"

Ryan and Denise exchanged wide-eyed looks.

"I don't know." Denise shrugged.

Venice looked down at her watch. She rose from the couch, having planted the seed. She patted Ryan on the shoulder as she walked past behind him, heading toward the front door.

"Both of you guys need to get everything out in the open." Her eyes flicked from Ryan to Denise, with a serious look painted across her face, and then back at Denise. "You can't avoid this."

After the door closed behind Venice, Denise and Ryan sat in silence. Denise prompted to biting her fingernails out of habit. Ryan shifted around on the couch, feeling the dynamic of their relationship had somehow changed without realizing it.

He patted the empty space next to him. "I don't bite."

Denise flashed a soft smile. She remained where she sat and took a moment to gather her thoughts.

"I was pregnant," she began, "I was excited when the test turned out to be positive. I even went to the doctors just to make sure a hundred percent. I knew how much you wanted another baby. I knew how much you wanted a big family and I wanted to give you all of that, but..." And then suddenly, trying to keep her composure started to become a challenge. She looked past Ryan, eyes brimmed with tears. Her voice cracked as she spoke. "But before I could even tell you, I'd lost the baby. I don't know how, but I felt it. I went to the doctors to confirm it. He said it could happen to anyone. After that, I started becoming more involved with work..."

Ryan's heart sank, feeling a heavy pressure on his chest. "Denise..."

She took a deep breath and wiped away the tears with her forefingers.

"You thought I was having an affair. I understand why you'd go there, now. But back then, I couldn't wrap my head around the fact that you'd think I'd cheat on you, you know?" She looked down at her lap, where her hands fidgeted. Finally, the burden was lifted off her shoulders. Although, she still worried about how Ryan would react with this news.

"I love you so much, I wouldn't do anything to jeopardize our relationship," she went on. "That day, things got out of hand. You left the house, raging, in the rain. My gut told me to run after you, but I didn't. About an hour later, I found out that you were hit by a drunk driver."

She looked up, tears streaming down her cheeks.

"There's so much regret just from that day alone. Sometimes I don't even know what I'm doing. It's like I'm doing things just to get through the day. Nothing makes sense. I feel like... all our lives are torn apart and if I had just gone after you that night, we wouldn't be here right now."

Ryan was blindsided by the truth but what hurt the most was that Denise had gone through all of it alone. He got up, walked over to Denise and sat on the armrest, pulling her body closer. He kissed the top of her forehead as he reached for her hand.

"I know there's nothing I can do or say that's going to make all of this better. I'm so sorry. So sorry," he said and hugged her tighter. "None of this is your fault. You hear me? You're always trying to tackle everything on your own, Denise. And I know where it comes from so I can't blame you for wanting to make sure everyone else around you is okay but from here on out, let me take care of the family. Let me take care of you."

Ryan never realized how much Denise took upon herself to make sure everything flowed smoothly. It was in her nature to have things done in a certain way. A perfectionist. But at the end of the day, Denise was just like everyone else. She was only human. She had gone far beyond her breaking point months ago.

"You're my warrior and I don't know what I did to deserve you, I really don't. I'm so grateful for you, for us, and we're going to get through this. That's my promise to you."

He lifted up her chin, wiping away the tears, feeling the bond of their relationship strengthen.

"I love you, babe," he said, hugging her tighter.

"I love you, too."

* * *

That following morning, Shadow sat in her office. Laid out were photos of herself and Evan from the evening before. She looked at each one carefully, being reminded of the entire night. Shadow propped up both of her elbows on top of her desk, with her hands pressed against her temples. She knew the message Marvin was sending her. Still, a part of her wanted to run away, far away, where tracking her down would be nearly impossible. Changing identity was a thought she pondered on. Right now, it was the easiest solution, but every time she'd convince herself running away was the best option, Evan's words came to mind.

I will protect you.

Shadow picked up the picture of the two of them walking back from Cherry Park. She hadn't noticed this at that time, but a picture most certainly was worth a thousand words. Evan was looking at her the way she'd seen new couples look into each other's eyes when they were beginning to fall in love. And she missed the moment. Ironically, Marvin had given her the photo that captured it for her. She couldn't seem to wipe away the smile until reality hit her like a thunderstorm.

Whether or not Evan listened to her, it didn't make the fact that he was still in danger any less important. She was in danger too but Marvin wouldn't lay a hand on her. She contemplated moving to a whole new town, somewhere that was secluded and quiet. It seemed like a great idea, but after rationalizing it, she knew she would be constantly on the run because somehow Marvin would manage to find her. As long as he was out there, she would always be looking over her shoulder.

She peered over at her wrist. She'd changed the bandage this morning after taking a shower. It nearly brought her to tears, remembering the look in Evan's eyes when he cleaned the wound and wrapped it with care. If it hadn't been for Evan, it would've been the night where it all would have ended. But she felt the universe had another plan, which of course involved Evan. His timing couldn't have been more perfect.

* * *

Marvin walked down the brightly lit hallway of the Secret Eye Agency with a black folder in hand. As he approached the room on the right-hand side, he pushed down the door handle, entering a conference room with six agents, all waiting to be filled in for this new assignment Marvin ordered. Each agent had his or her own black folder, sealed. On order, they were able to break the seal and see exactly what they were getting themselves into.

"Sorry I'm late," his voice boomed throughout the room. He made his way to the front where he set down his folder in front of his seat. Marvin unbuttoned his black blazer and placed it over the head of the chair. After he rolled up his sleeves, he booted up the laptop and began. "As you know, each one of you was hand-selected for this assignment; otherwise you wouldn't be here right now. Now, the pay for this specific assignment is indicated on the last page in your folder, but you will have to break the seal before seeing it. If there is any hesitation in your mind that you do not want to work on this assignment, or want to work for me, you have the right to walk away. Once the seal is broken, there's no going back."

Marvin looked around the room. There was no hesitation. Everyone sat quietly, anxious and ready to be informed about the assignment they agreed to take part in.

His eyes scanned the room, making sure everyone was on board. "You're free to break the seal," he said after a moment.

Marvin plugged in his USB stick, pulling up a file onto the flat screen behind him.

"Sir, this is Agent 513," exclaimed one of the agents from the far left, as he looked in the file, then met Marvin's eyes.

Marvin crossed his arms at his chest. "And?"

"Sir, if it's one thing that I know, it's that our own agents are off limits. I may be only a third floor agent, but our own agents are never a target."

"If this assignment wasn't signed off, you wouldn't be so heavily compensated for your work."

The agent scuffled to the last page, noticing the sum of money he'd make on this assignment. It was enough to take a year off from the agency and travel, if he wanted to.

The agent looked back at Marvin, satisfied. "Sir, what do you need us to do?"

Marvin smirked. He knew the pay grade for this assignment would have every agent in the force crawling at his door.

"Turn to page two and you will find everything you need to know about the missions and assignments Agent 513 has ever been on. He indeed is an intelligent man. We have to be five steps ahead of him," Marvin started, pondering over their brawl. Bruce was still strong but the men he had in this room were twice as strong. "That's why this assignment will run only for two days, day one being today. You will gather all the equipment today—all the equipment that we've been cleared for is on the second to last page. If you look behind me, you'll see the perimeter of Agent 513's home. Memorize it."

Marvin led the meeting about the entire assignment, from the beginning to the end. The plan would ensure Bruce would have no way to interrupt Marvin's assignment. Once Marvin completed his assignment, Bruce was going to be a free man. Marvin wanted to make it crystal clear to Bruce about what happened to people who got in his way.

Marvin looked through his folder, making sure he hadn't missed any important information.

"Although this is a simple assignment, Agent 513 is highly trained, as you can see from the file. He will put up a hefty fight, which may result in using some of the defense equipment that has been cleared for this assignment. However, no excessive force can be used against Agent 513 since he is highly valuable to the agency. In other words, he needs to be alive. Are there any questions?"

One of the agents from the left side of the table spoke up. "Sir, what is the motive for this objective? There is no indication why we're on this assignment. In all fairness, I believe we are entitled to know exactly why we're doing what we're doing."

Marvin hated when anyone questioned his authority. He slid his hands into his pockets, holding back his bitter and arrogant response. "Look at the last page for me."

He waited as the agent turned to the end of the file, looking at the compensation. "Sir, this is the pay grade?"

"If we wanted you to know the motive, it would have been stated in the file, wouldn't it have?"

"Yes sir."

"For reasons I cannot discuss, your compensation is as high

as it is so there are no questions. Do you understand what I'm saying?"

He nodded.

Every agent was trained to think outside of the box. They were taught to ask questions, wonder the what-if's and constantly be on their toes for any surprises that may come their way. Not knowing the motive for this assignment put each agent in their very own box of darkness. It would make the good agents question their morals and values, even though they worked for an agency that sometimes disregarded common ethical values.

"Know your target inside out. I expect all rules to be followed once he steps foot into the agency. I've sent each one of you a file," Marvin said, pointing at the flat screen. "Study it. Have an execution plan by tonight. Tomorrow, each one of you is expected to have Agent 513 back here at 8:00 sharp." Marvin studied the room for a bit as he pursed his lips. "Follow all protocol once releasing him. I advise everyone to get started on this right away. I'll be in my office if there is something that is unclear. Once the assignment is complete, your managers will have your review by next Friday."

Marvin left the room with confidence. Everything was set in motion. In less than two days, he would have Evan take his last breath and finally be with Shadow, the way it was meant to be.

* * *

When Venice entered her office, she spotted Bruce standing by the window. She didn't catch his attention until she shut the door behind her.

Bruce turned around swiftly. "Hey." Bruce pursed his lips as he moseyed his way toward Venice.

"This is a nice surprise," she said, laying her purse on the couch. She leaned in, wrapping her arms around Bruce.

Bruce slowly pulled away, placing his hands on her shoulders, looking into her eyes.

Venice immediately sensed something wasn't right. "What's wrong?" she asked, taking a step backward.

Bruce took her hand, navigating Venice toward the couch. They both sat down, looking at each other face to face.

"I don't know how to say this, to be honest." Bruce took hold of his head, as his elbow pressed hard against his knee, holding Venice's hand with the other. He stared at the rectangular coffee table, feeling guilt and anxiety mixed with many other emotions he fought back. "I came here to say goodbye, for good this time."

Confused, Venice asked, "What do you mean 'for good'?"

Bruce cleared his throat. "I have to protect Evan." Bruce forced a smile, trying to make the best of this moment but explaining it all to Venice was much harder than he had anticipated. "The agency I work for...is more corrupt than good. Shadow's ex-fiancé is one of the agents that works at the agency and he's after her for god knows what."

"And Evan is involved with Shadow," Venice stated, her voice trailing off.

"Yeah," Bruce sighed. "He's been keeping tabs on him too. It's just going to be a matter of time before he gets to Evan. That's why I've got to put an end to this."

"But why does protecting Evan have anything to do with you saying goodbye?"

"I don't know what's going to happen to me, Mom. The chances of me coming back are *very* slim. I don't want to give you hope that...I don't want you to wait around like before." His tears were reaching the surface.

"No..." She whimpered. "You can't leave me again, Bruce," she cried. "You can't!"

"I'm sorry for all the pain that I caused you. I'm sorry I

didn't come by as much. I'm sorry we're in this mess to begin with."

Venice fell into his arms, feeling her world falling apart.

For the first time, Bruce cried as he held Venice in his arms. "I'm sorry." He buried his face in her shoulder, not wanting to let go. He'd gotten used to the idea he was finally going to come back into their lives and begin to make things right, but the universe took that chance away from him.

Venice's cry slowly turned into light sobs, which then transitioned into heavy sighs. She rested her head on his chest, wiping away a trickling tear.

"Sometimes I feel our family's been cursed. Every time something good comes along, something bad is creeping up around the corner."

Bruce let out a wailing sigh. He wiped away the moisture from his eyes with the back of his palm. "There's something I need you to do." He looked at her with a sorrowful face.

"What is it?"

Bruce pulled out two red envelopes, one addressed to Denise and the other to Evan. "I need you to give these to them," he said, handing them to Venice.

Venice looked at the names, then looked at Bruce. "What did you write in here?"

Bruce clasped his hands together as his focus went back to the coffee table. "It's my apology. I explained everything that happened and why I made the decision to walk away from my responsibilities. I left out the part about Geneva's affair, though. They don't need to know that. She wasn't in her right mind. It's only going to tarnish their image of their mother. I hope they understand at some point in their life."

His eyes flicked back to Venice, who held on to the letters.

She bit her lip and smiled. "Okay," she said softly.

There was a moment of silence between them. They could

hear Candice answering a phone call.

"You know I love you, right?"

Venice nodded through her glossy eyes, still wearing the smile. "Did you ever remarry?"

"No."

"I think he loves her," she said after a moment.

"Shadow?"

Venice nodded. "But loving her comes with a price. It seems like it always does."

"Love is a dangerous fuel for our soul. It can kill us, but in parallel, we all crave it."

Venice glanced over. "After today, I hope you get the peace you've been looking for."

Bruce pondered the thought for a moment. He nodded his head subtly.

"Is there anything I can do for you? Is there anything else you need me to do?"

Without any hesitation, he said, "I'd love it if you could spend the rest of the afternoon here with me."

"Absolutely," she said. She got up off the couch. "Let me tell Candice to cancel my appointments."

Bruce rested his head back, feeling a sense of relief but also the pain of never being able to see Evan and Denise ever again. It still felt like a punch to his gut.

* * *

When Friday afternoon rolled around, it had been a nice sunny day, aside from the fact it was still winter and the cold breeze was yet present. Evan stepped out of the shower, grabbed his towel off the towel bar, and dried himself off. With his palm, he wiped the fog off the window and hung the towel on the bar before heading off into the bedroom.

He pulled out a fresh pair of briefs from the top drawer and put them on. As he shuffled through the next three drawers, he pulled out a black thermal and jeans.

Later, as he passed by the garden, he appreciated the progress that was taking place. The grass and the bricks for the walkway were scheduled to be put in Monday morning. Meanwhile he was going to start getting everything else in order. Sooner than later, the garden would be finally complete.

He'd imagined spending evenings with Shadow, having barbeques in the summer, sharing stories from their childhood—he'd pictured them growing old together. A part of him believed that no one was capable of taking that away from him even now though he knew who Marvin was and what Venice predicted.

Before he headed to the front door, he made sure the oven was off and the back door was locked.

He rang the doorbell and waited anxiously for Shadow to open the door. He heard the locks turn, then the door slowly opening away from him. Shadow stood in black booties and dark faded jeans, a royal blue military coat over her white blouse, and her wavy hair down to her shoulders. In her hand, she carried a black clutch.

"You look absolutely stunning," he declared with a hint of excitement in his eyes.

Shadow thanked him as she stepped out and locked the door behind her.

"How was your day?"

Shadow thought about the pictures. As much as she wanted to share that part of her day with Evan, leaving it out felt necessary for now. "It was good." She looped her arm into his.

He broke into a smile as they walked out to the sidewalk where Evan had parked his car. He kissed her before he opened the door for Shadow, and to his surprise, she was taken aback by his gesture.

A wide smile quickly appeared. "Aren't you quite the gentleman?"

"It's hard not to give a princess special treatment." He winked.

"Oh jeez." She blushed. "You really know how to make a woman feel special."

Shadow shook her head and chuckled under her breath. It had been a while since someone made her feel worthy of special treatment. And in the back of her mind, she remembered what she'd done to Evan.

He smiled, closing the door once she sat in the passenger side. He walked around, getting into the driver's seat.

"How was your day?" she asked, shaking away the thoughts.

He looked at her as he pulled his seatbelt over his chest. "It just got better," he replied. "How's your wrist?"

Shadow pushed back her coat sleeve. "It's healing, slowly."

"I'm glad to hear that."

Shadow leaned over, placing one hand around his neck, and pulled him in by the edge of his coat. She kissed him and ran her fingers softly through his hair before meeting Evan's eyes. Every fiber in her body wanted to whisper the words "I love you" but the pictures from earlier made her hold her tongue.

Marvin.

Evan turned on the ignition and put the car in drive. He cranked up the heat before making a U-Turn and headed down Knight's Drive. "I was thinking earlier…" Evan began. "There's this creamery outside of Lake View. Have you heard of the city Brickwood?"

"No," she said, shaking her head, "I can't say I have."

"The ice cream at Zack's is mind blowing," he said. "It's about a two-hour drive from here. They have a vineyard nearby too and a beach about twenty minutes away from a nice hotel. It's actually where Denise and Ryan got married—I mean on the beach." He glanced at Shadow, who'd been watching his facial expression as he spoke. "I was wondering," he said, hesitating, not knowing exactly the kind of respond Shadow would give, "if you wanted to go away for a weekend and get away from everything…"

Evan left Shadow speechless. *Is this too quick? Is this what people do these days?* She was hesitant. But just a moment ago, she found herself wanting to say those three words. The longer she pondered over the invitation, the less sure she was. Though, a weekend getaway with Evan sounded nice and romantic.

"Do you mind if I think it over?" she asked, biting her lower lip.

His forehead furrowed. "Oh yeah, of course," he said, throwing a hand in the air.

The dead silence filled the car. Shadow looked over, seeing Evan's cheeks slowly fade from the color pink. She put her hand over his arm that gripped the steering wheel.

"It's not that I don't want to go…" she said. "It's just that I've never been treated like…like this before, you know?"

The corners of his mouth lifted. "Start getting used to it then." He took her hand and kissed her soft skin. "We can go whenever you're ready. I'm not going to force you to do anything or go anywhere you're not comfortable." He wanted to make sure his intentions were not coming off the wrong way. He knew there was a large portion of trust that was taken away from Shadow. In order for Shadow to trust him, Evan wanted to make sure Shadow felt and knew she was in control.

Shadow looked at their hands. They somehow interlocked with each other without her realizing. She smirked and fancied the way their hands looked together.

"When is your vacation over?"

His forehead wrinkled with uncertainty. "In three more weeks. In total, we get five weeks."

She nodded and turned her attention to the road. Then the

car's interior fell into silence once again.

"Can I ask you a question?" Shadow's eyes remained focused on the road ahead of her.

Evan looked over at Shadow for a quick second. "Yeah, of course."

"Do you believe in reincarnation?"

He thought about the memories. "Yeah, I do." Evan's hand slowly slipped out of hers. He looked over at Shadow, whose focus remained on the road. "Do you?"

Shadow didn't answer right away. She mustered her thoughts before saying anything.

"Yeah," she said quietly. "Don't you ever wonder about the past? Like, who you were and what you did, the kind of life you lived?"

Evan began to feel a little uncomfortable. It was almost as if the universe was presenting the perfect opportunity for him to come clean. "Uhmm...I do sometimes."

Shadow faced Evan. "What if you could remember who you were in your past life? Wouldn't that be interesting?"

"Yeah, it would." He could feel his heartbeat thumping in his wrist.

"I feel like it would be able to answer a lot of questions about things that happen to us in this life. Don't you think?"

"Maybe. You never know." In the back of his mind, Evan entertained the thought of telling Shadow about his memories. He glanced over and asked, "What would you do if you did remember your past life?"

"I honestly don't know. I'd freak out and wonder what the reason was for being able to remember. It's not like everyone is given that gift, you know? How about you? Would you want to know?"

Evan puckered his lips, trying to find the best way to answer. "That's a good question. I think it's a pretty cool idea but I think I'd be better off not knowing."

Shadow let his words digest in her mind as she turned her attention back to the road.

The streetlights shone through the windows as they entered the city.

Shadow looked out the window. The town was alive with people, coming and going from restaurants, shopping, dancing at the clubs, enjoying a cold one at the local bars. Most of them were couples or groups of teens enjoying a Friday night on holiday.

Evan drove down two blocks before moving over to the left lane.

They pulled into the parking lot and drove down the lanes to find a parking spot. After a few minutes, Evan found a shopper heading back to her car and pulled into her parking space once she left. He navigated the gear into park and pulled the break. He pulled the key out of the ignition then peered at Shadow. She looked back with her sparkling blue eyes.

"We're finally here."

"I'm excited to try the food here."

"It's really good. Hopefully it's not too packed right now."

Luckily, they were seated right away. There were only limited number of tables that were still vacant. They sat at the table, draped with a white tablecloth.

Shadow briefly read each item from the menu, then scanned over the list of drinks. Without taking her eyes off the menu, she said, "I heard there's a fine ice cream parlor in Brickwood, Zack's. Not sure if you've heard of it, but I was hoping you would want to go with me one weekend."

As she peered over her menu, Evan broke into a stifled laughter. He put the menu down. A wide grin dawned on his face. His eyes sparkled with amusement.

Shadow slowly lowered her menu. She too was grinning.

"I'd love to go with you."

"It's a date then."

"Our first or second?"

"That depends on how well today goes." She winked.

"All right, all right." Evan chuckled and nodded. "Is there anything you like?" he asked, looking over the menu.

Shadow's eyes went down the first page as she held the menu in front of her. "The pasta primavera sounds good," she said, scanning the other items. "What would you recommend?"

Evan's eyes shifted to Shadow and then his heart took a leap. His pupils were wide and he felt as if someone was beginning to suffocate him. Derek stood behind Shadow with the same malicious smile. His hands slowly wrapped around Shadow's neck.

The music in the restaurant stopped playing and the sound of the conversations around them fell in dead silence.

Evan lunged forward. "Get your hands off of her!" Instead of grabbing Derek's hands, he grabbed Shadow's neck.

Suddenly, the music and conversations came back to life. People turned their heads at Evan's sudden outburst. All they saw was a man fighting off someone who wasn't really there. It took Evan a moment to realize what was going on. One of the waiters rushed to Shadow's rescue just as Evan let go of Shadow's neck.

Shadow gasped for air, terrified of what overcame Evan.

"Miss, are you all right?"

She looked up at the waiter, forehead creased and nodded. Her heart beating out of her chest, her eyes flashed back to Evan. His hands were gripped tightly around the table. His forehead wrinkled in terror. Evan slowly backed away from the table, his fingers now loose.

The manager of the restaurant walked over to their table and shifted his gaze from Shadow to Evan. "Sir, I'm going to have to ask you to leave."

Evan was in shock just as much as Shadow was. "I'm so sorry," he said to Shadow, his voice hoarse.

Evan walked out of the restaurant as onlookers watched, whispering among each other about what they'd seen. He didn't care what they said about him. His mind was still trying to comprehend what just happened.

Evan paced back and forth in the parking lot. He ran his hands through his hair over and over, frustrated with himself. He tugged at his hair, feeling Derek was somehow beginning to control his life. Something that was impossible began to feel possible and that started a fire in the pit of Evan's stomach. This was all a delusion and Evan let it get the best of him.

"Frustrated now, are we?"

Evan turned around and there stood Evan's demon. Derek.

CHAPTER 20

Bruce was in the kitchen pacing back and forth. He fought with his mind about his decision and the possibility of never being able to see his children again. Currently his main focus right now was getting rid of Marvin for good. Now, that was an easy mission but Marvin was a hard man to go up against. Marvin was almost half his age and he had more strength than Bruce. That was clear the day when the two of them had gotten into a brawl on the agency's premises. The one major difference between Marvin and Bruce was that over time, Bruce had become slower. He wasn't as quick to jump back on his feet as he used to. It took him a few seconds longer, and *that* made all the difference between the two of them.

He leaned against the kitchen counter, arms crossed at the chest. Tonight, when Marvin was fast asleep in his home, Bruce was going to end the life of Marvin Stone. It was going to be a clean job, one that would bring peace to his mind.

He looked at the pot boiling on the stove. For the past few days, Bruce couldn't keep anything down other than oatmeal.

The thought of Evan being in the hands of an agent made him hurl.

Meanwhile, agents surrounded the premises, keeping all areas covered as the other two sat in the black sedan, ready to go on order. One of the agents carefully unlocked the front door, minimizing the sound as much as he could. He signaled the other to enter. Both stepped inside, carefully stepping on the wood floor. To the right, there was the living room, and on the opposite side was the dining room. Straight down the hallway, the kitchen was on the left, across from Bruce's bedroom.

Bruce's house wasn't old but it wasn't fairly new either. The only sound to come from Bruce's home was from the hallway. It made loud creaks, even with the slightest pressure.

In the black sedan, the agent sat in the passenger's seat with a tablet in hand, giving direction to the agents on Bruce's whereabouts.

"I wonder what this is all about," he said to the driver.

The dark-skinned chauffeur spoke in a deep voice. "I don't know, man. Have you seen Bruce's file? It's clean, man. Every mission he's been on, he gets the job done without having blood on his hands."

"And...?" asked the other agent, keeping his attention focused on the screen. "That just means he's too scared to get blood on his hands. Marvin is the real deal. He's what we need more of at the agency."

"Do you even know what the purpose of the agency is?"

"Target is present in the kitchen, facing northwest," he said into his microphone.

The agents cautiously started to navigate to the hallway.

"What did you say again?"

"The agency was founded to protect the people from the bad guys, but Marvin...he *is* one of them."

"I don't care, man." He chuckled, still being attentive to the screen and watching carefully. "The paycheck for this assignment is going to get me loaded, man, you know what I'm sayin'?"

The dark-skinned agent scoffed.

"Why you being so uptight about this, man? You didn't have to do this. You had a choice."

"Nah, we don't have a choice. I'm only here cause I got bills to pay and support my kid."

"You have a kid?"

"Yup. He's gonna be five this month. Gotta save up for college. I don't want him ending up here, like me."

"Ah, come on. It ain't that bad, man," he said, looking away from the screen, meeting the agent's eyes. "Get out when you've saved enough to be set for life. That's what I'm gonna do."

"It all depends on your assignments and missions. We're not gonna get ten of these kinds of missions."

"True. But I'm sure your other assignments and missions ain't all that bad."

The driver glanced at the screen and then faced forward, placing his right hand on the steering wheel. "Yeah, you're right," he mumbled.

"Shit!" the agent shouted. "Bring in backup! I repeat, bring in backup!"

The driver's attention shifted to the screen.

"Straight down the hallway to your left!"

The two agents who'd been circling the home dashed toward the front door.

Bruce had stabbed one of the agents in the stomach. The kitchen floor was covered in oatmeal and pool of blood from the now unresponsive agent. He lay on the floor, limp. His face reddened by the hot oatmeal Bruce had thrown in his face.

Bruce threw a punch at the other agent. Bruce trained him during one of the boot camps the agency held. Agent 322 was pretty damn good. After all, he had learned from one of the best.

Agent 322 staggered to his feet and lunged toward Bruce with full strength. Bruce took a punch in the stomach—once, twice and then one right in the face. Bruce lost his balance with the last punch and his vision became a little blurry but that didn't stop him from giving up. He stumbled forward with a fist, trying to fight back.

Agent 322 shoved Bruce in the corner of the kitchen and jabbed Bruce in the stomach two more times. Bruce grabbed hold of Agent 322's neck, tightening his grip but once the other agents entered the kitchen, they separated Agent 322 and Bruce. Within a split second, Bruce was shoved to the ground. Bruce struggled to break free, but the pressure of one of an agent's feet against his back kept him firmly planted on the ground.

All he could think of was Evan. It was over.

The three agents exchanged uncertain looks with one another. No one was supposed to get hurt, let alone killed. This wasn't going to end well for anyone on the job.

"Call the agency. They'll send over agents to take care of this," the agent said, looking over at the dead body.

Bruce heard the scattered voices. His eyes slowly opened. Everything was slowly coming back into focus. He felt his hands being cuffed and shortly afterward, he was being peeled off the ground.

Moments later, Bruce was walking out into the dark night with the two agents holding a firm grip around his arms. The headlights turned on and so did the engine. Bruce got into the sedan following the first agent without any fuss. The following agent sat on his left side. The fifth agent stood outside of the vehicle.

"You guys go ahead. I'm going to stay back until the other agents come," he said, tapping the window then walking back into the home.

The agent cautiously looked into the rear view mirror at Bruce, who was looking right back.

Bruce gave him a glare as he fidgeted in the back, as they headed back to the agency.

* * *

Evan stood before Derek in the parking lot as if they were going to settle an overdue feud. He threw up his hands and stepped forward, his heart beating a little faster now. "You're not real!" He hissed.

People who were coming and going starred at Evan and made sure to stay as far as possible. As far as anyone knew, he was either on drugs or was having some sort of mental breakdown.

Derek chuckled. "What are you doing with her? You're going to hurt her Evan. Just like you did before."

"I'm not you! Not anymore. And you don't scare me anymore."

"Keep telling yourself that, Evan. Deep down, you're still the same person in a different time, in a different body, a different life. Stay away from her. You can't save her. You're going to hurt her."

"Stop saying that!" he hollered. "I'm not going to hurt her!"

Shadow walked out of the restaurant to see Evan going ballistic.

She proceeded forward with caution. "What...is... happening to you?!"

Evan quickly looked in Shadow's direction. He was speechless.

Shadow stood far off but still close enough where Evan

could see the horrified look in her eyes. She was on the verge
of tears. She'd never seen someone out of their mind like this
and to witness Evan go crazy terrified her. Who was Evan
really? What was he hiding from her?

"Answer me!"

He opened his mouth and then closed it.

Her voice quivered when she spoke. "I want an answer," she
demanded.

Evan took a few deep breaths. He needed to gather his
thoughts. "Okay, okay," he said calmly.

"Let me go pay the bill and I'll explain everything."

"I took care of it."

He pursed his lips. He scanned the parking lot before
meeting her eyes and gave her a pleading look. "Where do
you want to go?"

"Home."

"Okay."

For the entire ride back, neither of them said a word to one
another.

Shadow struggled to wrap her head around what happened
at the restaurant. With a blink of an eye, everything changed.
This night made her question everything about Evan. She
questioned her own judgment.

Once they pulled into Knight's Drive, Evan parked his car
by the sidewalk. Before he took off his seatbelt, Shadow was
already out of the car. The door slammed shut. Evan, who
refrained from puking on the drive over, took a deep breath
and stepped out of the car. He slowly walked over and met
Shadow on the sidewalk, making sure to keep his distance.
He could tell by the look in her eyes that she didn't want him
anywhere near her, which he understood and respected.

"I wanted..." he started but couldn't make out the rest of
the sentence. He let out a deep sigh, knowing whatever or

however he explained himself, it wasn't going to end well. "I wanted to tell you but I wanted to wait until the time was right."

He scratched his head, still unclear about how he was supposed to tell Shadow the truth.

"I actually remember who I was in my past life. For the past six months, I've been waking up from these night terrors early in the morning. I've been reliving a part of my life that I'm disgusted by. I beat up my wife. I made her life miserable."

He took another sigh feeling the anticipation of ripping off the band-aid. He couldn't stretch out the truth any longer.

"It makes my heart ache to know what I did in that life."

He looked at Shadow, whose eyes were wide and filled with concern.

"You were my wife, Shadow."

Her eyes brimmed with tears. She took a moment before saying anything.

"You remember your past life too?"

His eyes widened. It felt as if someone had punched Evan in the face. "Yeah... We both remember then..."

She nodded. "Well...isn't that something." She wiped away the tears from her cheeks.

Evan ran his fingers through his hair. "How come you didn't say anything?"

"The same reason why you didn't say anything. You wouldn't have believed me," she said, pausing for a moment. "What did you see in the restaurant?"

"I saw the old me...about to strangle you. I swear I didn't mean to hurt you."

She had delusions just like Evan years ago. Over time, they went away on their own. "Makes sense."

Evan stood quiet for a moment.

"But we get another chance——"

"No, Evan, we don't."

"Yes, we do," he insisted. "We remember these things for a reason. The universe is giving us another chance, Shadow. I want to take that chance."

Shadow looked out into the street, knowing in her heart what was best for both of them.

"Our circumstances are different now. Being in each other's lives is only going to help rewrite history."

Evan scoffed. "Is that what you really believe?"

"I want to," she said, looking back at him. "It's easier. No one gets hurt this way."

"You're wrong. I don't believe the universe put us in each other's paths for no reason—"

"That's the problem. We believe two different things. Marvin is the *biggest* reason why you and I shouldn't be around each other. On top of that, your grandma's vision is *another* reason why we should keep our distance from each other. It just makes sense."

"It doesn't make sense. Look at it—"

"How doesn't it make sense?!"

"Because I remember things from a previous life, and so do you. Don't you see? We were brought together for a reason. We owe—"

"Evan," she pleaded, "stop. I don't want to hurt you again. The universe is also telling us what will happen if we do stay in each other's lives."

Evan ran his fingers through his hair. "This isn't fair."

"And when has life ever been fair?" She looked around the street, feeling sadness overwhelm her heart. "I know how I treated you in my past life. I don't want to go through this cycle again."

"We're different people now. We'll do things differently. Clearly, we have a lot to talk about."

"Why are you being so stubborn? There's nothing to talk about."

Evan shuffled around to find his keys. "You're letting fear cloud your judgment."

"No, I'm not. *You're* the one who's not thinking right."

Evan pursed his lips. "Think about the first day you met me up until now. If there was even a second where you thought I wasn't good for you, then I'll let this go. I don't need an answer right now. You can tell me tomorrow when we talk."

He could see Shadow was irritated with him as he walked closer to her. "I love you, Shadow," he said as he kissed her on the forehead.

Shadow stomped her foot out of frustration. "Why aren't you listening to anything I'm saying?"

"Because you're afraid of what can go right when you've been used to having everything go wrong," he said as he walked down the sidewalk, leaving his car parked where it was.

He had a lot of questions but for the sake of both of them, he needed some time to wrap his head around everything that happened.

* * *

Bruce was stripped down after they entered the agency. It was protocol, regardless of the fact he had nothing on him. Wearing the white jumpsuit made him feel almost like a prisoner; color being the only difference. His hands were cuffed in front of him. He was led by one of the agents from the black sedan while two others remained by his side in case Bruce decided to do something stupid. Walking down the bright white hallway reminded Bruce of the times he'd come down here to check on his clients who were in danger. An agent who believed their client was at risk, brought them down to the basement for a short period until they believed it was safe. Bruce never imagined himself being sent into the dungeon, as some called it.

The leading agent opened the door to a windowless room. He looked Bruce straight in the eye, where swelling on the right side of his face had begun to appear.

"You'll be here."

"What's he going to do?" Bruce asked before entering. The agent standing in front of him looked past Bruce to the agents behind him, unsure of how to answer his question. All the agents except for the driver shot back blank faces. Bruce looked back and analyzed each one of them, knowing none of them knew. He turned around and entered the white room.

The agent motioned the driver to accompany Bruce while they received the say-so from Marvin to release Bruce from the premises. Quietly, the driver joined Bruce in the room, closing the door behind him.

Bruce looked down at his cuffed hands and then slowly met the driver's eyes, who stood in front of the door. He was a six-foot black man, a shaven head and eyes that pierced with intimidation. However, Bruce knew who he was. This was Agent 431.

Bruce's eyebrows crinkled and eyes widened. "I'd kick your ass if I wasn't locked into these damn cuffs. How the hell did you let this happen?"

"Look, I tried to do the best I could. I tried to distract him," he said. "You're the one to talk. Killing an agent, you know you're gonna be suspended for that, right?"

Bruce looked around the room. There was a bed in one corner and another door that led to the bathroom. That was it. If he had to spend a couple of days in the room, Bruce was certain he'd fall into some sort of depression. Nothing severe, but the bright walls and no windows would indeed have an effect on him. It would have an effect on anyone, to be frank.

He walked to the corner of the room with his heart in the pit of his stomach.

"Yeah, I know," he responded, glancing over at the driver. "I should have picked a different guy to be my lookout."

"Man, do you know how hard it is to distract someone who's glued to the screen like they're watching porn? The guy looked away from the screen twice. Only twice, man." He held up two fingers as if it wasn't clear enough.

"If you knew what you were doing, this wouldn't have happened. I wouldn't be in here, cuffed, while he's out there!"

"Look, I'm sorry. I don't know what you want from me."

"He's not really good at picking agents to do his dirty work, is he?"

The driver shook his head, ignoring the comment. "Whatever, man. You came to me. Not the other way around."

"And I paid you a shit load for this job. I guess it's safe to say I won't be getting my money back."

"Hell nah," he said, shaking his head.

For a while, both of them remained quiet.

Bruce scoffed. "How long am I gonna be in here for?"

"Don't know, man. I'd let you out, but the way this operation is ran, ain't nothing I can do. He's got agents outside of the premises just in case you find a way to break out."

Bruce lowered himself, dropping to his knees in front of the bed. He pressed his palms together as his fingers pressed underneath his chin.

"This wasn't how it was supposed to go," he said in a soft voice.

All Bruce could think about was what was happening right now. His conscience reminded him of the only possibility that would occur with Marvin in charge: The death of Evan. Bruce lowered his head, trying to get the thought out of his mind. He didn't want to think about it. But over and over, he kept picturing himself at Evan's funeral and regretting *every* single decision he'd made that led him up to here.

CHAPTER 21

Marvin sat at the desk, looking through a stack of pictures in a box. To his surprise, there were a lot of pictures of Geneva. She was smiling and looked as if she was enjoying herself with her family, but the real story behind it all—behind the attempted suicide, which was off the records, or the affair—was never brought to light. After the realization of what really had happened, it made Marvin more curious about the Storm family. So many secrets and lies. He wondered how Evan would take all of this.

As he thought, a mischievous smile lit his face.

Marvin walked upstairs to have a look around. There were only three rooms. The one right next to the staircase remained shut while the other two doors were wide open. He turned the knob, hearing the latch retract, and pushed the door inward.

He walked in with his hands in his pockets. He stood in front of the dresser, where a few photo frames sat of Bruce and Geneva. One of them was of their wedding day and one of them with Denise and Evan. He looked around the floor, noticing it to be spotless. It was evident that Evan was in this room often and had no plans on changing it.

Marvin chuckled as he walked out of the bedroom. Evan was in for one big surprise.

***

Evan stood in the middle of his driveway, but couldn't manage to walk any farther. Shadow was already inside her house. He peered at his front door, not wanting to go in. His mind replayed the last hour over and over. Bits and pieces of his past flashed through his mind's eye in slow motion, reminding him of how he'd hurt Shadow. He wondered what she'd done to him in a life that he didn't remember. Slowly he walked to the curb, and sat down on the sidewalk feeling overwhelmed.

His belief of why Shadow entered his life no longer sustained him now that he knew she too remembered her past and disagreed with his belief.

Nothing was making sense. Was this how it was supposed to end? For what reason did Shadow walk into his life then? Perhaps Shadow was right, but a part of him still didn't want to let go of the possibility he and Shadow were meant to be together in this lifetime. Now that he'd fallen in love with her, everything became complicated. After a long debate in his mind about the "what about's" and "what if's," Evan got up from the sidewalk and brushed himself off. He wasn't going to get the answer right this moment but he wasn't going to give up either. There was still tomorrow.

Evan proceeded to walk toward the front door, fiddling with his keys as he tried to keep a positive attitude. He looked down at his keys, swinging away the ones that didn't unlock the front door. The third one he pushed through the lock, turning it to the right and then back to the center. Evan simultaneously pulled out the key from the doorknob and pushed open the door, closing it behind him.

He slipped out of his shoes at the front door. As Evan headed down to the kitchen, he removed his coat and threw it over the couch. His eyes slowly began to adjust to the darkness as he walked into the kitchen. Evan searched for the light switch with his hand.

Just as he was about to flick the switch, he was held in a chokehold, restricting him from oxygen. His head jerked around, trying to gasp for air. Evan tried to pry the perpetrator's arms off his neck but slowly he felt his body slipping away. He tried to fight the drowsiness as much as he could. Suddenly, breaking free didn't seem too hard.

"No, no, no," he said in a tired voice as he drifted into unconsciousness.

Evan's eyes slowly shut and his body went limp.

***

Several hours later, Evan woke up to find himself tied to a chair, his head drooped to his chest. He felt dizzy and everything was a blur. Evan lifted his head up, trying to figure out what was going on. Looking around him, he couldn't see anything. It was still dark and his eyes were slowly adjusting to his surroundings. He was in his kitchen. Evan began to feel the soreness around his shoulders and wrists. As he tried to move his feet, he realized they were tied to the chair. His heart began to race.

Afraid of making any noise, he twisted his hands from side to side, trying his best to loosen the rope around his wrists. He pushed his rear against the back of the chair, managing to slide the chair against the hardwood floor. Evan grunted as he pulled his hands farther away from the back of the chair, in hopes of loosening the rope, but again, he had no luck.

But he continued to struggle to break free.

His head jerked backward in agony. What was going to

happen to him? Who was behind all of this?

Footsteps pattered down the staircase. As the sound of each footstep neared, his heart began to pound louder and louder.

The footsteps drew closer.

Suddenly the light switch flipped on. The kitchen never seemed so bright. Evan squinted. The lights burned his eyes and he felt the beginning of a migraine.

A calm voice came out of the darkness. "You're awake."

The footsteps appeared out of the dark. Evan craned his neck to see someone he recognized. His eyes widened and the brightness of the lights were no longer a bother. How could this be? This man looked like a spitting image of Derek's brother, Adrian. But this wasn't Adrian. It couldn't be. Evan continued to stare at the stranger.

Slowly the conversation he'd had with Venice started to come back to him. The stranger who she'd seen in her vision. Shadow's ex who'd threatened her, who'd been keeping tabs on both of them.

The puzzle was slowly coming together. Evan realized who this man was.

"You're still a little woozy there." Marvin shoved his hand into his pocket, pulling out a syringe and holding it up in the light. "Propofol. This is what they use before surgeries on patients so they don't feel a thing. *I* had to use it because you're a big guy. You work out six times a week. Every day you go for a run, but you have been slacking ever since you have been on winter vacation. I did my research," he said in a reassuring tone as if this was going to make Evan feel better about anything that was happening. He stood staring at Evan for a moment, not saying a word. Then he chuckled to himself. "Where are my manners."

He held out his hand in front of Evan. Quickly a solemn look faded over his eyes when his attention jumped to the ropes wrapped around Evan's hands. He slid his hand into his pocket. "I didn't get a chance to properly introduce myself. I'm Marvin Stone, Shadow's fiancé."

Evan clenched his jaw, knowing it was only going to get worse from here. "That's funny since you guys aren't even together anymore."

Marvin pondered this. "That's very well true," he finally said. "However, we'll be together soon enough." He smirked. "It's eerie."

Confused, Evan asked, "What's eerie?"

"In a lot of ways, you remind me of your father. He does not give up when he should and neither do you."

"I don't know what you're talking about."

Marvin proceeded to the table, pulling up a chair in front of Evan. He chuckled to himself. As he looked at Evan, a malevolent smile crept across his face.

"Oh, that's right. You think your father is dead. He died in a car accident when you were four years old, correct?"

Evan was speechless.

Again, Marvin chuckled. The look on Evan's face was priceless and it was just about to get better for Marvin.

"Your father is very much alive, Evan."

Evan shook his head. "That's not true. My grand—"

"Let me stop you right there," he said, cutting him off. "Your father is alive. I understand it's hard to believe since he has been dead to you since the age of four. However, do you want to know what boggles my mind? Your father didn't even attempt to reach out to you in all these years. It's horrible, if you ask me."

Evan's eyebrows furrowed. "What do you want from me?" He fidgeted in his chair, wanting badly to break free.

"You're not at all interested in hearing more about your

father? What he's been up to all these years when you thought he was dead?"

Marvin waited for a response, but Evan sat there with his lips pursed. He knew deep down inside, this was killing Evan.

"Did you know that your mother was a heroin addict? Actually, let me correct myself. She was a user *before* she met your father and then after she had you, she started using again and became an official addict." Marvin wore a puzzled look that faded with a grin. He chuckled softly to himself before he spoke. "Why would anyone get involved with someone who is a drug user? I don't understand. I am mind blown by the fact that your father chose your mother, even after knowing the fact she had an addiction to drugs, which *only* became worse after she started sleeping around." He sighed to himself. "If she hadn't associated with drug addicts herself, I believe she would still be alive today. I bet you didn't know your mother left a suicide note on the kitchen counter the day she killed herself, did you? Her death was no accident. I believe everyone is entitled to the truth. I do, however, apologize that it's coming from a third person."

Evan clenched his jaws. He didn't know what to believe. Had Grandma Venice been lying to him and Denise this entire time?

Evan glared into his evil eyes. "People like you always have proof."

Marvin pulled out his cell phone from the inside coat pocket. "Of course. I am a man of my word." He placed the phone in front of Evan.

Evan leaned forward, feeling his heart stop for a moment.

"That is his picture ID. Proof that he works at the agency. We're colleagues at a very secretive agency." Marvin swiped the screen with his fingertip, exposing Evan to more pictures of Bruce. "I wasn't bluffing like you hoped I was."

Evan's mind went blank as he stared at the photo of his father.

"Enough with the history lesson," Marvin said as he picked up his phone. "Let's switch gears. You and Shadow. Now, that really angered me. You stood in the middle of our relationship, Evan. I warned her, over and over, and she very well knows what I'm capable of. I don't know why she didn't listen. I love her, so I can't hurt her...but you, my friend, I can hurt you. You clouded her judgment. Now, she doesn't know who is right for her—which is me, obviously."

Evan tugged against the chair, trying to loosen up the rope. "You're a psychopath," he grunted.

Marvin chuckled. "That's exactly what your father said when he came to see me. Not only are you like your father, but there's quite a bit of resemblance between the two of you. I'm sure your grandmother has told you that in the past amid the other lies."

"What do you want from me?!"

Marvin leaned over the table and whispered, "Nothing. I came here to get some things off my chest and to...well, put an end to my problem. I wasn't going to kill you in the beginning, but then your father started becoming nosey," he said, pursing his lips, "so I'm doing this to let him know that he shouldn't get in my way either. Do you understand what I'm saying?"

"I don't have the comprehension to understand a maniac," Evan hissed.

"Don't worry. I'll be out of your life shortly, but before I do anything, I would like you to know this all could have ended differently."

Evan lowered his head and closed his eyes. Right now, all he wanted was to wake up at 3:30 in the morning, drenched in sweat, and realize this was all just a dream.

"This *still* can end differently. You have the choice to make a different decision."

"That's the problem. I don't."

Evan raised his head, squinting as he looked into Marvin's eyes. All he saw was Adrian but with Derek's characteristics. This was what Derek had done. Anything that didn't sit well with him, he'd make sure the outcome was in his favor and anyone who betrayed him would know not to ever cross Derek. Ever.

"Yes, you do. You always have a choice."

"I don't," Marvin said, shaking his head. He frowned but the look in his eyes showed Evan Marvin in fact didn't care for Evan's comments.

"Let's think about this rationally. If you get rid of me, would Shadow *ever* forgive you? Think about it for a second. You've warned her repeatedly, but she hasn't listened. Taking me out of the equation is simply going to make her hate you even more. Is that what you want, Marvin? Do you really want Shadow to despise you?"

"She may hate me for a little while, but she'll get over it. I've known her a lot longer than you have. She gets over things quickly and once I'm done with you, it's just going to be a matter of time until she comes back to me. She'll forget you ever existed."

Little beads of sweat began to form near Evan's hairline and his throat felt like it was on fire.

Marvin stepped back into the darkness for a moment. Out he came with a gasoline carton and a matchbox. Evan's eyes traveled around the room as Marvin proceeded to walk toward the table. He placed the carton and matchbox on the table, in front of Evan.

"I took the liberty in writing your suicide letter. It's sitting on top of your dresser upstairs."

Evan's eyes remained focused on what was sitting in front of him. "What did you write?"

"Nothing too drastic. Just plain and simple. To the point."

"No one's going to believe I did it."

"Perhaps, but with the evidence, they're not going to have any choice *but* to believe you did it."

"How so?" His heart expanded as it beat louder and faster, overbearing Marvin's voice. All he heard was words. The thought of this being the end of his life overwhelmed him and everything around him felt scattered.

"I'm going to give you an injection, which will cause you to start to lose consciousness. You'll be too weak to fight the medication but will be aware of everything that's happening. I'll proceed to untie you and leave you here as your kitchen burns in flames, but before the fire spreads to any other room in the house, someone will notice the smoke and call the fire department. By the time they come to save you, you'll already be dead. And your father will be released from the agency just in time to find out what happened to his precious little boy. He'll learn his lesson and I'll start my life with Shadow. Sounds like a marvelous plan, doesn't it?"

It was starting to sink in that this was the end of his life. Moments that he'd spent with Grandma Venice, Denise, Ryan, and Nate flashed in his mind. Evan's eyes glazed as he began to think about Shadow. His heart fell into the pit of his stomach. This wasn't how it was supposed to end. He wasn't ready to leave everyone and everything he knew behind.

"Help! Somebody help me!" Evan yelled at the top of his lungs.

Marvin laughed at Evan's attempt to save himself.

"Somebody help me!" He tugged at the ropes that were wrapped around his wrists.

His face scrunched trying to break free but Marvin had tied

the ropes too tight for Evan's strength.

"You're wasting your breath, Evan."

Evan didn't want to burn to death. He tugged and tugged, wrestling with the chair from behind, desperately wanting to flee. "Somebody help me! Somebody help me!" Evan continued to shout from the top of his lungs, hoping someone would hear him. His veins bulged across his temples and his face now pink from all the strength he was using.

Marvin took out a syringe from his pocket and removed the cap. He held the needle up to his face, admiring the sharpness and strength it contained.

Evan's chest moved rapidly up and down. He was out of breath and sweating. He grunted as he tried again to loosen the ropes, using all the strength that was left in him.

Marvin moved closer to Evan, peering over him with the needle in his hand. "It's time."

"No, no! Please don't! Somebody! Help me!"

Evan felt the needle poke through his skin. His eyes closed and he screamed again, as loud as he could. His veins protruded at the side of his throat. "Help! Help!" he pleaded. "Somebody please…help me…"

Within seconds, Evan began to feel lightheaded. He felt the ropes around his ankles loosen and then after, his wrists started to feel freer.

"Your father will learn his lesson," Marvin claimed, proceeding with his plan.

The room had become blurry. He tried to keep his eyes open and not let his mind shut down, but with every passing second, he felt his body slowly slipping away from him. "You're… going to…pay…for…" he murmured, as his head sank lower to his chest.

Marvin picked up the gasoline carton and popped off the cap. He proceeded to pour gasoline over the stove, the countertop, and all over the kitchen floor. After pouring the last drop, he approached Evan, who appeared unconscious. "Sleep tight, don't let the fire bite." He chuckled.

Marvin picked up the matchbox and scraped the match against the coarse side of the box. With one swipe, a tiny flame appeared. He took two steps toward the kitchen, and threw the match near the stove. Marvin watched as the flames slowly started to rise from the emptiness. He turned around and bent down, picked up the ropes he used to tie Evan's hands and feet, and threw them into the flames. As he turned away, he looked at Evan, feeling a sense of satisfaction.

He wore a smirk as he walked to the front door. Everything was falling into place.

CHAPTER 22

Bruce's knees started to ache. He hadn't done this in an extremely long time, mainly because he never figured he needed to do it. He had his hands propped up on top of the bed and palms pressed together. Bruce closed his eyes as hard as he could. He pressed his forehead against his hands, not knowing where to begin.

"What the hell are you doing?"

Bruce cocked his head in the agent's direction, not making any eye contact, and responded, "I'm praying."

"Praying? It's gonna take a big ass miracle to turn around whatever the hell Marvin is up to."

Bruce clenched his jaws. "Just…stop talking."

Agent 334 rolled his eyes and remained in position.

Once again, Bruce closed his eyes. He cleared his mind and focused on one thing: Evan.

"Hey," he whispered, "I know I haven't talked to you in… well, a really long time, and I'm going to be brutally honest with you. I didn't think I needed you back then. We're probably not on the best of terms and I'm not even sure if you're listening right now, but I don't feel like you were there when I needed you. My life was a mess and you weren't there to help me—it's beside the point." He took a deep breath, and gathered his thoughts. "Right now, you're all I have and...this is hard for me to do," he said, beginning to feel his heart open up. "My little boy is in danger. I'm in here locked up unable to do anything. I love him, *so* much. And I know *you* know that. I had plans. I was ready to face the reality and tell my kids the truth. I wanted to make things right. Please, just give me a second chance. Please let me make up for everything I did to my family. If Evan lives, I promise that I will quit the agency and do better, become a better man and help others who truly need it, and do it the right way. I'm making that promise to you and all I need in return is Evan to be safe. I beg you."

Bruce remained with his palms pressed together, feeling helpless for the first time in his life.

CHAPTER 23

Mr. Brar looked at the alarm clock on his nightstand. To his surprise, he'd been reading for the past two hours. *That* rarely happened. It had been a while since Mr. Brar read a good book, and this particular one had reeled him in.

It was a love story that mirrored the love he and Ekam had. Mr. Brar read this book five times now, in the past five years. It was something he'd done on the anniversary of Ekam's death. Reading the love story reminded him how amazing Ekam had made his life. Not just joy, but hope that true love did exist and he was the lucky one to experience it.

He let out a yawn as he laid the book on his nightstand. He lay in bed, with one hand under the pillow and the other on his chest, his thoughts focused around Ekam. She was one of the most supportive, energetic, and compassionate human beings he'd ever met. Sometimes Mr. Brar felt she saved him from falling into the dark hole. Given all the missions he'd been on, there was no doubt a person's life was capable of changing at the SEA. The blood on his hands for handling business for someone else, the torture, the screams and desperation to live another day—it haunted him with each sunrise. He vividly remembered every day after work, he'd take a shower just to feel less dirty. He knew the water didn't wash away his sins, but somewhere in his conscious, he felt a little better after stepping out of the shower.

When Mr. Brar was at his lowest point in life, the SEA crept in, presenting the perfect solution to his financial problem. The SEA had been keeping their eye on Mr. Brar for months as he juggled two jobs, struggling to make ends meet. When the time was right, they recruited who would have been one of their best agents yet. Ekam kept Mr. Brar sane. He lived and breathed for her.

Mr. Brar shifted back and forth on his sides, trying to get comfortable. After a few failed attempts, he gave up and roamed over to his window, passing his wheelchair and oxygen tank. Arms crossed at his chest, he peered out in his backyard. Right across, the neighbors were still up. At least their kids were.

The Butlers had three children—one boy and twin girls. The girls were finishing up high school and the boy would be graduating in the spring from middle school. Mrs. Butler was an interior designer at Storm Inc. and Mr. Butler was an engineer in the tech industry. Mr. Brar envied the Butlers; even behind closed doors, they truly were the picture perfect family.

Mr. Brar knew everyone in the neighborhood—their likes and dislikes, where they did their shopping, the people they didn't get along with, who their relatives were, whether they had kids and where their kids went to school, who their friends were—it came with the territory. At times, having all this information was overwhelming. Being an excellent agent required a memory such as Mr. Brar's.

Standing in the quiet, cold dark was peaceful. Mr. Brar

leaned his head against the windowsill. He wore a white T-shirt and navy striped pajamas, like always.

Before his mind was able to wander off into the world and its problems, the flickering yellow light caught his eye. Mr. Brar gazed over at Evan's house, where the kitchen was visible. He was taken aback by what he was witnessing. The kitchen was up in flames. From a distance, Mr. Brar could see Evan was hunched over in a chair. His heart immediately jumped out of his chest.

Rushing to grab his phone, Mr. Brar dialed Bruce, hoping he'd pick up. He dashed back to the window, as the phone continued to ring. *C'mon, c'mon, c'mon, Bruce. Pick up, Bruce. Pick up!* It went to voicemail. He dialed Bruce again, only to catch his voicemail again. Mr. Brar's fingers started to quiver. Something wretched had happened and his gut assured him it all was linked to the SEA. *God dammit. Somebody pick up the goddamn phone!*

Mr. Brar dialed 911. *C'mon, c'mon, pick up.* While holding the phone close to his ear, he jolted toward the treasure box set in front of the bed, where his bathrobe remained. He staggered downstairs as he slipped into his robe and wheeled out his wheelchair to the door, carrying the oxygen tank in the other hand. No one in the neighborhood knew Mr. Brar didn't need the wheelchair or tank. It was all a ploy.

"911, what's your emergency?"

"There's a fire across the street and someone's trapped inside," Mr. Brar relayed breathlessly. He rattled off the address.

"We'll send fire trucks and paramedics. What's your name, sir?"

Mr. Brar hung up.

He hurried into the kitchen and grabbed the spare key he was given from the cabinet. Before leaving, Mr. Brar phoned

Venice, telling her of the situation in a ten-second call.

Mr. Brar sprinted across the grass, his heart racing. When he reached the front of Evan's home, he jabbed the key into the doorknob. Once inside, Mr. Brar entered a deadly environment. Smoke snaked around him. He heard the roars of the flames from the kitchen. Subconsciously, Mr. Brar covered his mouth with the inside of his elbow. It would only be a matter of time before it would become useless.

It was going to take exactly twenty-two steps to reach the kitchen. From there, it was more trial by error.

Mr. Brar pushed forward, squinting through the heavy air, and continued to hold his breath.

He'd taken ten steps so far. There were twelve more to go. His lungs begged for air, but Mr. Brar ignored the human instinct of survival. He was going to get through this. Certainly he would be able to get Evan out of the house under a minute. The ambulance he called was going to be here in three minutes. The clock was ticking. It had been already twenty seconds.

Mr. Brar pressed onward as if guided by an invisible hand. The flames roared even louder as he approached, which meant he was getting closer to Evan.

Still holding his breath, Mr. Brar began to feel faint. This was not good.

Fourteen steps were taken. Eight more steps to go.

He battled with his mind, which was starting to give up. Still ignoring the thoughts of death, he moved forward with eyes closed. The heat licked his face and his bare hands.

Evan. He needed to save Evan. He'd promised Bruce he would look out for Evan, even if it meant putting his life on the line. Nothing was going to stop Mr. Brar.

There were only four more steps to go until he would reach the kitchen. The table was to the right. As he slowly crept into the kitchen, his knees began to spasm in pain. He grunted in agony. Putting the pain aside, he staggered to the right, hand out trying to get a feel of Evan's body. Mr. Brar moved his hand in slow circular motions, hoping to get a hold of something. A hair, his ear—anything.

Nothing.

He stepped forward, now doubting his count. He moved forward with one hand covering his mouth and the other in front of him hoping to find Evan in the next couple of seconds as time was ticking.

Nothing.

He staggered around the area, with his heart in his stomach. He continued to search and cringed every time he felt nothing but the heavy smoke. Finally, after a few seconds passed, he felt the hair on Evan's head, wet with heat. It had been already a minute and a half. Mr. Brar uncovered his face. "Evan! Hang in there…son."

Mr. Brar began to cough as he inhaled the poisonous air.

"Evan, Evan…stay with…me…son…I'm going…to…get…you out…of…here," he coughed.

He stood Evan on his feet, feeling faint himself and wrapped Evan's arm around his neck. Evan's head dangled against his chest as Mr. Brar brought him out, staggering over to the grass and laying him down.

It'd taken Mr. Brar two minutes and forty-five seconds to get Evan out of the home. The ambulance and fire truck were going to be here any moment.

Leaving Evan astray on the front yard, Mr. Brar darted back into his home and changed into a fresh pair of clothes, ones that didn't reek of smoke. Walking into the bathroom, he washed his face then patted it dry. He propped himself in his wheelchair with his oxygen mask to keep the suspicion of who rescued Evan at bay. As he fixed himself, the sirens of the ambulance and fire truck started to near.

When Mr. Brar wheeled himself out onto his front lawn, neighbors started to step out of their homes to see what was going on. Some stood in their doorways while others gathered in the middle of the street, asking one another whether Evan was still alive. Some pointed at the paramedics, wondering why they wore a red uniform, a question that would linger and soon slip away with other important thoughts.

It was the SEA. Paramedics and firefighters were called to the scene. They would treat Evan at the Lake View Hospital on the tenth floor, only accessible to the SEA.

The paramedic put an oxygen mask on Evan as the other checked for his heartbeat.

Firefighters were already starting to hose down the kitchen while the neighborhood watched.

As Mr. Brar approached one of the paramedics who was overlooking Evan, he saw the burns that were uncovered on his feet.

"How is he?"

The paramedic turned around and took a quick glance at Mr. Brar before he turned his attention back to Evan.

Mr. Brar raised his voice. "I said, how is he?"

The paramedic was stolid as he turned around again to look at Mr. Brar. "First degree burns on his face and neck. He's got second degree burns on his feet and legs. It's painful, but he'll survive."

Mr. Brar watched as the paramedics carefully turned Evan to his side, sliding the stretcher underneath him.

Moments later, the ambulance was driving down Knight's Drive with Evan in the back. The firefighters were still hosing down the fire. Two of them, in their red fire-retardant uniforms, trooped their way back to the truck.

Mr. Brar looked out on to the street. Some of the neighbors started to go back into their homes as some still stood, shivering in their nightgowns, wondering what happened. They too wouldn't know the real truth.

This brought back Mr. Brar to the day he had tortured and burned an innocent girl just to send a message to her father for his client.

He slowly coasted himself back indoors. He closed the door behind him and removed the mask. That was all he could manage to do.

Evan would survive, but things could have been much worse. He could've lost Evan tonight. The more the thought started to sink in, his heart began to feel what he learned to make numb. He sat in his wheel chair and cried. The last time Mr. Brar cried was when Ekam passed away.

CHAPTER 24

Venice studied the ground intently as she paced back and forth in her long gray pea coat, in front of Lake View Hospital. The tip of her nose had frozen. Her breath puffed out through the translucent air.

She'd been waiting for the ambulance to arrive for the past twenty minutes—it felt like a lifetime. Mr. Brar hadn't gone into great depth about exactly what happened but whatever it was, she was definitely not prepared for it.

She peered through the glass doors as she walked by. The receptionist at the front desk was taking a call. A nurse was wheeling an old lady back to her room. Her stomach was doing a somersault, waiting for the siren of the ambulance to near and when it did, her heart dropped.

When the ambulance arrived in front of the hospital, Evan was wheeled out on a stretcher. Venice squealed after seeing the visible parts of his body that were covered in burns. She stood, paralyzed. She could only look for so long before she turned her back to the ambulance. She had to crouch to the floor to prevent a panic attack.

Evan.

That couldn't be him. There was no way.

As they rushed into the hospital, one of the paramedics—a tall, slender, white male—towered over her for a moment before crouching down to her level.

"Are you Venice Storm?" His blond hair glistened in the light.

Venice nodded as she gulped. "Yes, I am." Her eyes flooded with tears. "Is that Evan?"

"Ma'am, I'm going to need you to come with me," he began in a heavy Russian accent, "Evan is in critical condition. For further details you have to discuss with the doctor. Come with me please."

He jolted inside the hospital, with his red coat waving behind him. Venice followed closely. The paramedic sprinted to the left, turning the corner. At the end of the hallway, there was an elevator—a black elevator, different from all the silver ones she was used to seeing at the hospital. He aggressively pushed the button, while looking above the door. The elevator was stuck on the tenth floor.

He grunted. "C'mon," he said, slamming the button with his palm.

Ignoring his temper, Venice asked, "How did this happen?" Her lips quivered.

"I don't know. We got a call, so we came. I don't have the details, ma'am. Sorry."

"How bad is it?" she whimpered.

The truth was, Evan's heartbeat dropped on the drive over. They needed to resuscitate Evan and time was not on his side.

"He's got second degree burns," he confessed, keeping his attention focused on the numbers above the door.

Venice's heart dropped. She felt the paramedic wasn't telling her the entire truth.

"The doctor will answer all the questions you have. We need

to go on the tenth floor where your grandson is."

Venice quietly sobbed into her hands, fearing the worse. First she lost Bruce, and now she was on the brink of losing Evan as well.

Once the bell rang for the first floor, the elevator doors opened. They both hopped on and the elevator doors slid closed. A couple of seconds later, the elevator stopped on the tenth floor.

Ding. The doors parted and the paramedic led Venice down the bright white hallway to the room where Evan was placed in. It was too quiet on the tenth floor. It almost seemed like no one was here.

As they reached Evan's room, Venice peered through the window. A doctor hovered over Evan as women and men in white scrubs followed orders. The looks on their faces said it all.

"The doctor will come soon," he said, turning around and walking back, leaving Venice alone.

A dark-skinned young woman, hair tied in a ponytail, headed toward Venice from the front desk. She smiled as Venice gave her a once-over.

"Why don't you have a seat?" she said as she motioned to the chairs lined against the wall a few feet away from where she was standing.

Venice wiped her eyes and responded, "No, I'm fine. I want to know what's going on in there."

The young woman softly placed her hand on Venice's shoulder and insisted Venice to sit down. After coaxing Venice for a little bit, she gave in. She subtly rocked herself back and forth, taking deep breaths.

"Ma'am, can I get you anything to drink? Water or something?"

"I want to know what's going on in there!" she yelled and pointed in the room Evan was in.

"Ma'am," she expressed, "the doctor will let you know what's going on as soon as he can."

Venice looked up at her for a moment and then nodded.

"Okay," she whispered. "I'll be right over there if you need anything," she said, pointing to the desk.

Venice nodded, just wanting to be left alone. She knew she had to call Denise so she could come down to the hospital immediately, but the longer Venice sat there, the harder it became to reach into her pocket and pull out her cell phone. She didn't want to have a conversation about Evan. She didn't want to have to explain what she was witnessing right now.

Everything she'd feared was unfolding right before her eyes.

CHAPTER 25

Twenty-four hours later.

Bruce sat in the chamber in front of the panel where the board of directors would shortly arrive. He was agitated and frustrated. It had been a long forty-eight hours. To his left, just a little over teen feet away, was another desk positioned beside him. Moments later, Marvin was escorted into the room by an agent. Marvin took his seat as the agent left to the back of the room, taking his position.

Marvin snickered as he faced forward. "I heard about Evan. How's he doing?"

Bruce brought his hands together, tightly folding them in front of him, ignoring Marvin.

"Have you gone to see him yet or are you too coward to?" He chuckled. "It's a shame he survived if you ask me." He waited for a response, a reaction, anything he could get his hands on, but little did he know Bruce had other plans in place.

Marvin craned his neck sideways and stared at Bruce, who kept his focus on the panel even though he was raging inside. But Bruce knew better to give Marvin something to feed on. This time, he was going to let Marvin take the steering wheel as he worked from the back. He wanted Marvin to *feel* as if he was in control, that he was the "big dog." In time, however, Marvin would realize who was really in control.

Bruce grinned as he turned his face to look Marvin in the eyes. "You're wasting your breath trying to get under my skin because it's not going to work."

"As long as I keep pressing your pressure point, eventually you will explode."

"Okay."

When the door opened to the chambers, one by one the board of directors walked in, filling each seat on the panel. The brunette sat in the end, followed by the men in suits. The man who sat in the middle pointed at Bruce.

"Please state your name and your ID," said the agent.

Bruce cleared his throat. "Bruce Storm, 513-510-231-958."

"Thank you," he said as he looked down at his file. He looked up and looked at Marvin. "Please state your name and ID."

"Marvin Stone, 212-412-061-980."

The agent replied, "Thank you." Then he proceeded to look through the file that was sitting in front of him.

The room was dead silent.

After a few minutes, the agent looked up, first at Bruce, giving him a hard look, and then at Marvin.

"Mr. Storm and Mr. Stone," he began, "do you know why you have been summoned today into the chambers?"

"No, sir," they both replied simultaneously.

"The brawl outside of the agency was brought to our attention when one of our agents reviewed the security footage. This behavior is unacceptable here at the agency. For the sake of the agency, we have decided to deactivate both of you for three months, starting today."

Marvin jolted out of his chair. "That's a load of bullshit!"

Bruce could see the rage in Marvin's eyes. He lowered his head as he fixed his suit before facing up again.

The speaker of the panel raised his voice. "Your actions have led you here, Mr. Stone. Do not raise your voice at the panel. If you didn't want to be deactivated, you should have thought a better way of handling your personal business. I'll be more than happy to deactivate you for a year if you want. I have no problem with that."

Bruce could hear Marvin's heavy breathing from where he was sitting.

The rage in Marvin's eyes reached its peak. Marvin glared at the speaker before sitting back down.

"Sir?" Bruce chimed in.

"Yes?" the speaker responded.

Bruce pulled out a folded envelope from the inside pocket of his blazer. "It has been a pleasure working for you, and for this agency, but my stay here has been long overdue." He raised the envelope in front of him before putting it on the desk. "I am officially resigning from my position as Agent 513."

The speaker looked to his right and then to his left before he met Bruce's eyes. "I'm sorry to hear that, Bruce. We all wish you the best here. As for retirement proceedings, the head of your department will explain everything to you. You'll still be in our system until you're cleared. Do you have any questions?"

"No, sir," Bruce responded. He rose from his seat and thanked each one of the agents.

All the agents rose from their chairs. "It was a pleasure having you work for the agency," said the speaker.

Bruce nodded, quickly glancing from one agent to the other. He exited the room, feeling content. He walked down the hallway approaching the elevator. *This is just the beginning*, he thought, smirking to himself.

CHAPTER 26

The night turned in and unlike any other day in Lake View, the winds had picked up their speed. The howling noises could be heard through the homes, begging to enter. Leaves rustled across the concrete and roads. Children enjoyed hot chocolate in their pajamas as their parents sat in the living room drinking coffee.

Mr. Brar, on the other hand, poured himself and Bruce iced water. The bottle made a loud *clank* as he set it in the center of the table. He looked at Bruce as he lowered into his chair.

Bruce filled in Mr. Brar of everything that happened from the moment the SEA came and dragged Bruce out of his home.

"I'm going to kill that bastard," Mr. Brar exclaimed. "I'm going to kill him. I haven't had blood on my hands for over a decade, but I'm willing to kill him, Bruce. I am." His pupils dilated as the words spilled out of his mouth.

Bruce ran his fingers through his hair, letting out an exhausted sigh.

"Evan would have died if it hadn't been for you," Bruce said. He propped his elbow on the table, resting his head on his hand. "It's all bullshit, Mr. Brar." Bruce looked up, pinching the corners of his eyes. He scanned the room before meeting Mr. Brar's eyes. "I gave my letter of resignation today."

Mr. Brar was taken aback. "I thought you wanted a seat on the panel?"

"I did before, but that's not what I want anymore," Bruce said, as he picked up his glass, "I'm going to shut down the agency."

Mr. Brar's face shattered into different expressions.

Bruce took a sip. "The agency is not what used to be. It's supposed to protect the public but it's only created power hungry monsters. Now it's all about getting the job done and moving up," he said, pausing for a moment. "Marvin was engaged to Roy's daughter at one point. Roy announced he was going to step down in the near future months and I think Marvin wants to run the agency so desperately that he's trying to win back Shadow, get married, so he can take over."

Mr. Brar shook his head, feeling as if it was the most ridiculous thing he'd ever heard. "That sounds absurd, Bruce. People only get married when they're in love. If she doesn't love him, she won't marry him. It's simple. No one can force someone to get married."

Bruce cleared his throat, flicking his eyes from Mr. Brar to his glass and then back at Mr. Brar. "We're talking about The Secret Eye Agency here. We—sorry, I mean *they* are capable of doing anything. Mr. Brar," he emphasized, "I entered the agency with a clean slate. How did they know I had a family? How did they know about Geneva?" he asked. "They have their ways. If Marvin wants to get married to the girl he wants, he'll find a way, even if he has to drag her to the alter, unless she kills herself first."

"Evan told me the girl knows about the agency. Do you think she knows about who her father is?"

Bruce shrugged. "All I know is that I don't trust anyone who is linked to the agency," he said as he ran his index finger around the rim of the glass. He pushed the glass forward. "All right, I should go," he said, getting up, "I'll give you a call once I get to the hospital and let you know how Evan's doing."

Mr. Brar nodded.

"Thanks for the drink."

"You know I don't drink alcohol."

Bruce patted Mr. Brar's back as he left the kitchen, heading to the front door.

"You're not doing this without me." Mr. Brar shouted from the kitchen as he heard the doorknob turn.

Bruce halted. "I wouldn't have it any other way."

"It was nice seeing you after twenty-something years."

Bruce smiled as he closed the door behind him.

Mr. Brar remained sitting in his chair, pouring himself another glass of cold water. "To family," he said under his breath before chugging it down.

CHAPTER 27

Evan's eyes snapped open. The room was white and silent. *Am I dead?* When he tried to move his head, he felt incredible pain. He was very well alive. When he tried to move his arm, he grunted in agony. It was sore and on fire. He took a deep sigh, not knowing where he was or who had brought him here, but the one person he didn't want to see was Marvin. For all Evan knew, this was all part of Marvin's ultimate plan—to make him suffer even more just as Evan thought it was all over.

He closed his eyes. It was quiet and peaceful. Evan thought about what Marvin had told him, about his father being alive and his mother. It was something that Evan couldn't begin to grasp. Twenty-seven years of being under the assumption his father was dead, then learning he had never died in the first place put Evan through quite a shock.

Evan heard the sound of a door opening. Terrified of who it might be, his eyes remained shut. When the door closed, there was silence.

The sound of a chair being dragged across the room rang in his ears. Then, a heavy sigh. Evan could hear the person shuffling in the chair, trying to get comfortable. As much as Evan wanted to open his eyes, to see who was sitting beside him, he knew it was safer just to keep them closed.

Then the door opened again. One of the nurses working on the floor walked in wheeling a cart with medical supplies she needed to use on Evan to treat the burns. She wore plum-colored scrubs, her hair tied in a bun.

She gave a soft smile. "Hi, Mr. Storm," said the nurse in a soft voice. "I'm going to change his bandages."

Evan felt the hair on his neck rise up. In that instant, he knew who that was. Evan would recognize his father's voice out of thousands of people speaking. His breath caught in his throat.

"I would say about two weeks until he gets discharged. However, he'll still be in the process of recovering. He's got first degree burns on his face. You see all that swelling and redness? So, it'll be a few months before he'll be able to do diurnal activities. He's been in and out of sleep..." she said as she uncovered his legs. "His feet and legs really took a hit, though. Luckily someone called the ambulance when they did. Things could've been much worse."

"Yeah," Bruce said. He stood up from his chair, walking closer to get a better look at Evan's legs. "How many cases do you get like this?"

The room fell in silence for a moment. "Not a lot," she said. "They're usually left to die. He got lucky, *really* lucky."

"He did," he said as he pondered how Mr. Brar had put his life on the line to save Evan. The prayer he'd said when he was held in confinement. "Is there any more paperwork I need to fill out?"

"No," said the nurse, slowly peeling off the bandage from his right foot. "Just the discharge papers. That's all."

"Okay." He watched as the nurse did her job. She removed

the bandages, applied ointment on the burns, then put on fresh bandages. Ten minutes later, Bruce thanked the nurse for her service as she pushed out the cart, again leaving Bruce alone with Evan.

Evan's eyes flickered open. He saw his father standing there with his back toward him.

"Dad?" Evan said, trying to hold back all the emotions.

Bruce's head jolted toward Evan's voice. He'd been waiting for Evan to wake up. Words seemed to slip away from him.

Tears shimmered in Bruce's eyes. He felt an emotion he had buried long ago come up to surface.

"God," Bruce managed to say, then breaking into a cry, said, "You're awake."

Bruce bit his lower lip to stop it from quivering. Bruce knew how slim his chances were to see Evan...alive. Now, the moment he'd been waiting for was finally here. He looked up for a split second, thanking God for this miracle.

"Yup. And you're alive." Evan smirked. He winced, feeling the pain afterward.

Bruce swayed into his chair, scooting it closer to Evan's bedside. He reached and placed his hand over Evan's.

"I have," he said, trying to take a breath, "*a lot* of explaining to do..."

"You do," Evan responded, feeling a bit tired and drowsy. "What happened to Mom?

"We can talk about everything when you're better. You need to get your rest."

Evan nodded, trying to remain conscious.

"Denise and Ryan stopped by to see you but you were asleep."

"Oh...really?"

Evan looked at his father, wanting to say more but he struggled to keep his eyes open. With each blink, Bruce became increasingly blurry. Evan slowly drifted away, falling asleep.

Bruce buried his face in Evan's shoulder, feeling over-whelmed. He'd been given a second chance, and all he could do was hope and pray he didn't screw this up.

He eased back into his chair, and watched as Evan slept, reminding him of the day when he and Geneva brought Evan home from the hospital after his birth. All Bruce could do was watch Evan as he slept, feeling like it was the most incredible thing in the world.

He wiped away the tears with his thumb and let out a deep sigh of relief.

The door opened. Bruce looked over and saw the receptionist's head peek through the cracked space. She motioned Bruce to step outside.

"What is it?" Bruce asked, slowly closing the door behind him.

"There's a woman here to see Evan."

"Is she on the list?"

"No, sir."

"Then send her home."

"Okay, sir."

Bruce quietly walked back into the room. He moseyed his way back to his chair, keeping a close eye on Evan. Before he could sit down, the receptionist once again called Bruce out of the room.

"Sir, she's saying she's Evan's next-door neighbor. I told her the protocol but she insisted on speaking to someone."

Bruce shoved his hand into his pockets. He clenched his jaw and asked, "Where is she?"

"She's in the waiting room."

"All right," he responded and strolled in the direction of the waiting room.

When Bruce approached, Shadow looked up from her lap, shaken up to see Bruce standing in the doorway. She recognized him from the pictures Evan showed her. According to Evan, Bruce had died.

Bruce steadily walked over to the row of chairs facing Shadow, sitting across from her. He propped up his elbow on the armrest, resting his chin on his fist. His eyes focused on Shadow, not knowing what to think of her.

"You're Shadow, I'm guessing," he finally said.

She nodded. "Evan said you died in a car accident, but judging by where we are," she said, looking around, and then fixing her eyes on Bruce, "there was never an accident."

Bruce nodded. "Why are you here?"

"I wanted to see Evan."

"He's sleeping right now. I think it's best for you to go."

Her eyes filled with tears. It made her uncomfortable being emotional in front of someone she barely knew. She looked up at the ceiling, not really seeing it, trying to let the tears flow back.

Bruce got up and walked over to the end of the row, picking up a Kleenex box from the end table and handing it to Shadow.

"As long as he's out there, he's going to keep hurting people. He won't stop until he gets what he wants." She looked at Bruce helplessly. "I don't want to run anymore."

"How did you meet Marvin?"

She looked up at Bruce in confusion. "My dad introduced me to him. Why?"

Bruce began to pace back and forth with his arms crossed at his chest. He stopped in his tracks in front of Shadow. "And where did your dad meet Marvin?"

"At a coffee shop…why does this matter?"

"Everything matters. I don't know you. You're an outsider and I don't trust anyone on the outside, especially when it comes to family." He stood in silence for a moment and then asked, "What did Marvin tell your father what he did for a living? What does your father do for a living?"

"He told my dad that he was a criminal lawyer. My dad is a biological scientist—"

"Do you know what the agents are capable of?"

"Yes, a little bit."

"Okay." He moved onto the next part of the interrogation like a detective. "Did he threaten you after you moved here?"

She nodded.

"Did he come to your home and make threats?"

She nodded.

"It's safe to assume you feared for your life, correct?"

She nodded.

"Did he give you an ultimatum?"

"Yes." She quietly sobbed. "Why are you asking me these questions?"

Bruce rested his hands at his waist ignoring her question. "Then why is it that you continued to see Evan knowing you were being watched? Why didn't you tell Evan to stay away?"

"I did," she whispered and wiped her nose as she answered, "I told Evan how dangerous Marvin was. I told him it was better if we didn't see each other, for his sake, but…"

Bruce clenched his jaw.

Shadow saw the look in his eyes change from steady to fury.

"You didn't make it clear enough then!" he shouted. "You put *my* son in danger. He could have died because of you!"

Shadow felt her heart sink and her nerves turn into a knot in the pit of her stomach. She blamed herself too.

"I know. I'm sorry. It's all my fault."

Bruce paced with his hands on his hips. It took time for it to sink in before Bruce realized how he was treating Shadow. Bruce stepped back, ashamed of himself for talking to Shadow the way he did. He peered at her as she buried her face into her hands. He sighed, and then took a seat in front of Shadow.

"I'm sorry," he confessed. "I'm angry at myself, not you."
Shadow didn't say anything. They sat in silence. After
Shadow gathered her composure, and wiped away the tears,
she looked at him, seeing a spitting image of Evan.

She looked down at her wrist and then back at Bruce. She
fought back the tears, feeling already drained from the tears
she shed.

"Evan," she said, breaking the silence, "saved me. I *can't* lose
someone who risked their life for me. I'll spend the rest of my
life trying to make up for what he did for me. I get why you're
protective. I know how it feels not to be able to trust anyone,"
she said as she rose. "Please let him know that I was here."

Bruce nodded.

Shadow picked up her purse and left Bruce sitting in the
waiting room. The florescent lights that she walked under
and white tile underscored the sterility of the hospital. It was
quiet. The environment up here was different. There weren't
doctors making rounds or nurses coming in and out of rooms.
It wasn't hectic like it was on the lower floors. It was safe to
say anything that had to do with the SEA was different to the
norm.

She stood in front of the elevator, waiting to get on. The
sound of footsteps caught Shadow's attention. When she
turned to look, Bruce was standing in the middle of the
hallway looking defeated.

Bruce had come to the realization that if he didn't let
Shadow see Evan, then he didn't deserve the forgiveness he
hoped for from his children.

He gave her a pained smile. "When you love someone so
much, you stop thinking about yourself. You can't blame
yourself for something someone else was willing to do. All
he wanted to do was to protect you. You protect those you
love. He risked his life for you and he wouldn't have done that

if you didn't mean the world to him." He walked forward. "C'mon, let me show you to his room."

Bruce led the way, with Shadow walking not too far behind him. As they approached Evan's room, Bruce opened the door for Shadow. She smiled and thanked him. He watched through the window as Shadow cautiously walked over to Evan's bedside, placing her purse on the floor and unbuttoning her coat. Bruce noticed that Shadow's focus remained on Evan the entire time. Once she got closer, she kissed him on the cheek, making sure not to press too hard. She pulled the chair closer to his bedside and held his hand gently.

Evan's eyes fluttered open from Shadow's soft touch. "Hey," he said, his voice hoarse.

She kissed his hand and met his gaze. "How are you feeling?"

"I've seen better days," he replied with a chuckle. His face cringed with pain.

Shadow's faint smile appeared and disappeared with a blink of an eye. "In my past life, you were the love of my life."

"Shadow," Evan slowly managed to say.

"What's wrong?"

"We don't have to do this right now."

"I know, but I need to get it off my chest."

"Fine. But if I don't remember any of this when I wake up, you're gonna have to repeat yourself." He saw a faint smile appear across her face.

It took her a moment before she responded. "Everything's foggy to me but what I remember is that I lied. I cheated. I broke your heart. I stole from you. I did a lot of things that someone who wasn't in their right mind would do. You were always there for me...I never understood why you stuck around."

Evan cleared his voice. "I wondered the same thing about you."

"What if we hurt each other again this time around? I can't—"

"Shadow, listen to me," he said, locking eyes with Shadow. He began to feel drowsy again. "We have another chance to be together. I'm not going to hurt you. I'm not going to leave you. All I want to do is love you and be your support system. Does that sound good to you?"

His eyes fluttered. Evan tried his best to stay awake but he drifted in and out of consciousness.

"Yes. I love you too, Evan," she said and softly kissed his hand.

"Huh...?"

Shadow smiled and watched as Evan fell deep into sleep.

Bruce fidgeted in his chair outside of Evan's room. He thought about Shadow and felt sympathetic for what she'd been through. After bombarding her with questions, Bruce realized Shadow had no idea what her father did for a living or the fact that it seemed Marvin was intentionally put into her life—but for what reason? That's what stumped Bruce. What reason did Roy have to recruit an agent to seduce his own daughter and stand by as she feared for her life? For the life of him, he couldn't figure it out but knew that whatever Roy was hiding was bound to come to light.

Bruce got up from his seat and walked toward the door. He peered through the window before he quietly entered the room. Bruce could see her puffy pink eyes and nose as she looked at him.

They maintained eye contact as Bruce made his way over.

"I'm so scared of losing him," she whispered as a tear streamed down her cheek.

"You're not going to lose him." He said walking closer.

"How are you so sure? As long as he's out there—"

"We're going to put an end to all of this."

Shadow leaned back in her seat, feeling the world around her quietly and suddenly changing. "I want to help."

Bruce shook his head. "I can't let you do that. *Evan* won't let you do that. You two need to live your lives. Let us take care of this."

She let Bruce's words digest in her mind. She looked back at Evan who was sound asleep. A sense of relief overcame her. She was finally going to be able to live in peace and have a future.

* * *

And like every ending, there was always a new beginning. For Evan, Shadow, Denise, Ryan, and Bruce, this was their new beginning.

Evan's eyes fluttered open to the light dim in his room. He lay on his back, looking up at the ceiling. It took him a couple of seconds to figure out where he was and then everything began to register. In the corner of his eye, he saw someone in a dark gray pantsuit standing beside his bed. He didn't feel the presence so it took Evan by surprise. He slowly shifted his head in the direction of the person only to look up to see Adrian peering down at him.

"It's not over yet, brother," he whispered.

Startled, Evan blinked to see if what he was seeing was correct and just like that, Adrian disappeared into thin air. *What wasn't over?* Evan frantically looked around for a clock and when he spotted one on the opposite side of the wall, it was 3:30 in the morning.

Evan sighed, terrified about what was going to unravel next.

EPILOGUE

It was September 16, 1933. Stephan Hex and Mary ogled the sleeping newborn as if they had never seen something so delicate and innocent.

"The midwife said the mother had not named the little one."

"It is a pity, isn't it? For the mother to die after childbirth breaks my heart." He paused for a moment as he observed the baby. "Mary, I cannot imagine the pain her husband must be going through."

"It is very unfortunate," she replied, unable to take her eyes off of the newborn. "Very." She peered into the cradle with a smile. "I want to name him Dean."

Stephan let the name sink in. He met her eyes and slowly a grin crept across his face. "My darling, that is a lovely name."

She looked at Dean and then back at Stephan.

"Stephan…"

"Yes, my darling."

"I want Dean to carry on my family name."

"You do?"

"Yes."

Stephan pondered on the thought for a moment. He knew it

was not traditional for children to take on the mother's maiden name, but he loved Mary more than anything and wanted to see her happy. The last few months after their miscarriage had been hard on Mary. The doctors informed them that Mary would be able to bear a child, but the chances were low due to complications after having a miscarriage. Adoption was their next option.

From a previous marriage Stephan had a son, Ben, who was nine months old now. Bringing another baby into the family only would expand and bring more joy to their family. This was something Mary was yearning for.

He took her hand and softly laid a peck on it. "Of course my darling."

She gazed at the bundle of joy. "Our little Dean Storm," she whispered with delight.

*＊＊

Samantha sat on her bed, as the sun shone through the drapes in her bedroom. The world continued to go round and round. No one out there knew the pain she was feeling. The moment where she held her newborn for the first time replayed in her mind like a broken record. She held on to that moment knowing it would never come again. She'd shed every last tear there was. She forced herself to eat, but after taking a bite, she no longer had the appetite.

Derek hadn't asked how she was doing. They hadn't talked after that night. He would come home after he'd had dinner with the men from the office. He would play golf on the weekends and attend company events without Samantha. "She's under the weather," he would tell anyone who questioned her absence.

Adrian, on the other hand, would stop by during the weekends when he knew Derek wasn't going to be home.

During the weekdays, he tried his best to come and comfort Samantha. Although neither of them said much to each other, it felt better to sulk together than alone.

Samantha looked down at her lap. The revolver sat in her hands. For the past thirty minutes, she stared at the gun and came to the realization that she would no longer endure any more pain. Derek would no longer be able to hurt her, control her. She would be set free by the weapon. The answer was right there in her hands.

This was it.

She slipped her finger into the trigger and as she did, her heart began to pound louder and louder. She brought her hand up to the side of her head as she looked out the window. It was a beautiful day and she knew if she pressed the trigger, she'd finally be at peace. The torture would end, and somewhere in the unknown, a new beginning was waiting for her.

She squeezed her eyes shut.

And then…

***

Evan woke up, gasping for air.

It had been nine months since Marvin set the kitchen on fire, leaving him to die. That night changed everything and days moving forward; life itself felt overwhelming. He feared for his life each day knowing it wasn't over yet. He wondered whether he would find Marvin waiting for him in his bedroom after work, with Shadow nowhere to be found. At times, he felt a panic attack about to arise. Months of sleepless and restless nights continued with different nightmares now. But he tried his best to hide his fears from Shadow as much as possible. The one thing he hid from Shadow was what happened in the hospital the night he'd seen her.

"What did you do this time?" Shadow asked.

Evan turned to look over at her. She was sitting up, her back resting against the headboard. She was smiling.

Evan rubbed his eyes and looked at her stomach. As the due date neared, oddly, Shadow's body craved less sleep. Some nights, she would get three to four hours, and then start the day, feeling completely rested. Granted she'd take a nap in the middle of the day or after work, to wind down. Evan didn't know how she managed to do it. And Shadow insisted on working until the last two weeks before her delivery, which Evan wasn't on board with. He had to convince Denise to put Shadow on maternity leave because Denise just so happened to side with Shadow. It didn't surprise Evan since Denise heavily believed women were capable of doing anything they wanted, pregnant or not. Denise and Shadow supported each other like sisters from birth. Overall, Shadow's pregnancy had gone smoothly, which both of them were thankful for.

"Is it the same one? The one of me holding the gun?"

Evan nodded.

They sat in silence for a while.

The memories raised questions that neither of them could get answers for. What was the memory hinting? Evan woke up right before he was able to see what happened next. That irritated him. And it made Shadow question herself. Was this memory hinting she was going to repeat the same cycle? She hadn't remembered anything from her past life after she'd become pregnant with Bright. Both of them would spend afternoons entertaining the answers to their question but neither of them found the one that made any clear sense. They'd forget about it for a couple of days until Evan woke up from another memory.

Evan placed his hand over her stomach and rubbed it in a circular motion. "What's baby Bright doing?"

She laid her hand on top of his. "He's sleeping. He's a good little boy."

"I hope he takes after his mom or otherwise we're gonna be in big trouble."

Shadow giggled.

"You know, I don't think everyone's going to be happy that we already named the baby without even asking for their input."

When Evan and Shadow found out they were having a boy, it took them a week to finalize a name they both liked: Bright Storm.

"You're probably right." He leaned closer to her stomach and whispered, "Your mommy is sneaky. She's going to try to feed you mashed cauliflower and tell you that it's mashed potatoes."

She playfully shoved his face away from her stomach. "Oh, stop it."

"Let's be serious for a minute. They tasted nothing like mashed potatoes!"

She laughed as the image of Evan's face the night he tried her new dish a week ago came into her mind's eye. It was priceless.

"We need to be more health conscious. I don't want to feed our child processed foods. Have you seen the videos online? It's disgusting what goes into the food we buy from the grocery store."

"And what you eat is so good? Yeah, that's right, I know what you bring home in those grocery bags, Mrs. Storm," he teased.

"I'm a pregnant woman," she said. She grabbed his pillow from behind him and smacked him across the chest. "What am I supposed to do? Starve?"

"And you've become so violent in the past few months, too,"

he giggled, taking the pillow from her hands.

She leaned closer and gave him the glare that he never took seriously. "And again, I'm pregnant."

Evan mustered a laugh, placing the pillow behind his back. He gazed at her. "I love you so much." He kissed her on the forehead and wrapped his arm around her, pulling her in closer and leaving enough room for Shadow to switch positions whenever she felt the need to.

She laid her head on his chest, enjoying the peaceful night with her husband. "I love you too."

It was nights like these that made Evan feel like the luckiest guy alive. Soon, he was going to become a father. His heart filled with joy knowing they were having a baby together and he would be born into a family that would shower him with love and protection.

And then he was reminded of what he'd done to Samantha. How he'd given her and Adrian's baby away. It pierced his heart thinking about how Samantha must have felt that night when he'd instructed the midwife to give the baby to what he thought was a more deserving family. Evan played the devil's advocate at times to make himself feel less like crap. Maybe giving the baby away was actually a good thing. The baby probably would have had a better life in a different home, he'd tell himself. Still, he couldn't justify what he'd done. The life he once lived was still unclear to him.

He ran his fingers through Shadow's hair. "Are you hungry? Are you craving anything?"

Shadow didn't respond. He craned his neck sideways to find her fast asleep.

ABOUT THE AUTHOR

Born and raised in California, Gurpreet Kaur Sidhu always felt different from the other kids. With an insatiable appetite for reading and writing, Gurpreet would often find herself at the receiving end of a cold stare from one of her teachers – reprimanding her for working on literary ventures when she should have been paying attention.

All those secretive moments spent scribbling paid off, however, and now Gurpreet is launching her debut novel "STORM".

In addition to being a highly accomplished writer, Gurpreet is a passionate businesswoman, holding a bachelor's degree in Business Management while running a women's clothing company with her younger sister.

Aside from fervently writing and managing a burgeoning business empire, Gurpreet can be found savoring the scents of her most recent kitchen-made delicacy or pumping away stress at the gym.

Follow Gurpreet on Instagram @gurpreetksidhu316 to get the latest updates from her developments.